PRAISE FO

"*Havoc* demonstrates the healing and redemptive nature of the human-canine bond. A bond of such incredible strength it transcends war, distance, and time. Written like an adventure, with heart-pounding combat sequences, high tension, and suspense as well as moments of deep emotion, connection, and bonding. *Havoc* is a must read for anyone who appreciates heroes of both the two-legged and four- legged kind. The ending will have you believing any broken heart can find true love."

AIR FORCE MASTER SERGEANT SAMANTHA MAGHAMEZ, DEPARTMENT OF DEFENSE MWD HANDLER, TRAINER, AND EVALUATOR

"I love me a Ronie Kendig novel! *Havoc* is high octane, high stakes, and higher tension. Chemistry, action, emotion, and canine heroes—this story has it all. Just don't start reading before bedtime unless you're willing to stay up all night."

TOSCA LEE, NYT BESTSELLING AUTHOR

"*Havoc* was a fast-paced, action-packed read. Ronie Kendig nailed the goofy yet intense character of a loyal MWD Malinois. Her strong heroine and heroes—one-, two-, and four-legged—will have you falling in love and cheering them on the whole way!"

LORA HARRIST, MWD BREEDING PROGRAM FOSTER

"I've been a huge Ronie Kendig fan for a long time, and this one was no exception. Kendig brings her expert knowledge of military working dogs, the life and struggles of veterans and combines it with broken characters who will lay down their lives for those they love. Tenacity and strength undercut this story of two broken hearts finding each other—and the love of a good God."

USA Today Bestselling author Lisa Phillips

"Wow wow wow!!! I couldn't put this down. I've devoured quite a few of Ronie Kendig's books, and this one is up there in competition for a new favourite! The banter, the romance, the action-packed pacing—I'm obsessed with every second of it."

Jane Maree, Goodreads

"Ronie Kendig's characters don't merely walk onto the page they stride in and in two seconds flat they own the room. I was captivated by page one and devoured it as fast as I could."

Nicole, The Unending TBR

"5 stars for Kendig and *Havoc*! *Havoc* is fast-paced, nonstop action, and pure greatness . . . we are taken on a ride of thrills, danger, romance, and faith. Ronie Kendig is a master at combining all of these pieces to make an epic story."

Chelsea, Goodreads

HAVOC

A BREED APART: LEGACY || BOOK 1

RONIE KENDIG

sunrise
PUBLISHING

"Cry *'Havoc!'* and let slip the dogs of war."
-William Shakespeare

DEDICATION

To all the military working dog handlers and four-legged heroes, as well as the amazing team at Lackland Air Force Base responsible for carefully selecting and breeding these incredible working dogs, as well as the caretakers and trainers who tend to the daily needs of over 800 dogs in the kennels. Bravo to the Adoptions team who evaluate dogs for disposition and place them where it's best for the dog.

My personal thanks to all of the above for my MWD washout puppy, AAndromeda, part of the AA8 litter born February 7, 2022 and adopted February 2023.

ACKNOWLEDGMENT

Thank you, Marine Sgt Gabriel Martinez, Purple Heart Recipient, husband, father, and hero! It is an honor to call you friend. Thank you for talking so openly and directly with me about your experiences wearing prostheses.

PROLOGUE
TWO YEARS AGO

OUTSIDE THE WIRE, BAGRAM, AFGHANISTAN

THE SLEEK, SEXY BODY SAILED THROUGH THE AIR, EFFORTLESS IN ITS raw intensity to catapult itself across the sun-heated desert at the fleeing form. Muscles defined and rippling spoke of the relentless training and pace kept to maintain readiness. With a thud that knocked the breath from her intended target, Marvel DOO2 sank her teeth into the arm of her target. That thousand pounds of pressure locked in place, she landed. Skidded around without breaking her hold and snapped that powerful neck in a jerk that pitched the target down.

Sergeant Crew Gatlin sprinted toward the seventy-five-pound Belgian Malinois, noting Marine Corporal Ehretz, weapon tucked to his shoulder and sights trained on the target, skirting up around the front. They'd been on routine patrol when the unfriendlies started firing on them.

Crew reached Marvel, caught her collar and held firmly—though did not instruct her to release.

"Drop the weapon," Ehretz demanded of the combatant as Mouse and Taco flanked him, weapons trained on the local

1

fighter who'd tried to take potshots at the team that'd been patrolling the area.

Boots dug in, Crew clipped the lead on as he held onto Marvel's collar, proud the military working dog had done her job with fervor. The target tried to hit Marvel with a rifle, but the Malinois snapped her head, side to side. Dug her paws against the arm, trying to extract a chunk of flesh as punishment.

The man howled and went to his knees. Adrenaline and pain were likely interfering with his ability to make smart choices, but Crew willed him to let go of the weapon.

Blood slid along her jowls and down that powerful corded neck.

Finally, the rifle clattered to the hardpacked earth.

"Marvel, out!" In tandem with the command, Crew drew Marvel's collar straight up, a move that encouraged her to release the arm by restricting her airflow, a measure that invariably forced her to unlock her jaws.

The man broke free with a yelp and scrambled away, shielding his arm, and trying to put as much distance between himself and the fur-missile.

Crew drew Marvel away, though she resisted, eager for another chance to eliminate a threat. The girl was as hard-hitting as many of the elite operators they'd worked with.

Crack!

Thwat-thwat-thwat!

Pivoting, Crew was about to release Marvel when he registered the scene before him—the target was now deceased. Taco was cursing up a storm as he held his arm. The local must've had another weapon, and rather than die of humiliation in an American holding cell, he chose death by operator. A request granted by Taco and a short burst from his M4.

With no apparent threat present, Crew deployed the tethered KONG and let Marvel snag it from him. He gave a couple of good tugs to let her know she'd done a good job, then produced her black KONG. When he showed it to her, she immediately released the roped one, and he flicked the rubber chew toy into the air. Effortlessly, she launched upward, her muscular, well-toned body violence in motion, and snagged it from the air. She landed, chomped it twice, then trotted to the side and dropped to the ground where she crossed her forelegs, and squeaked her reward. Crew let her, knowing the team would need to call this in.

Ehretz muttered an oath. "Let's load up and head out."

Crew frowned. "You mean, let's call this in—"

"Hassle, man," Ehretz grumbled. "I just—"

Gaze locked with the corporal, Crew keyed his mic. "Base, this is Charlie Four on patrol with your recon team alpha. Situation now secure, but we came under fire. One enemy target neutralized. We'll need clean up. Sending location now."

"Good copy, Charlie Four," came the reply through comms.

"What was that?" Ehretz demanded, stalking toward Crew. "I said—"

Marvel swiveled into position, head down, lip curled around the snarl that told the Marine to back off.

Hand up in surrender, Ehretz shifted backward with a nervous grunt. "I said we'd leave it—"

"I'm not letting some Marine grunts derail my career because they don't want to be hassled with protocol." Crew felt the same curl to his lip that Marvel still held. No wonder the guy was still a corporal ponying his rank around newbs on their first deployment.

"You need to remember you're assigned to this team. You follow—"

"Don't." Crew flatlined his expression. "Don't go there, or you'll be eating your stripes for dinner."

The ruddy-faced kid faltered. Couldn't be more than twenty-five. Maybe a hundred pounds dripping wet, trying to engage in a manhood battle with an operator who had ten years, multiple deployments, and more kills than he wanted to admit. No way he was going to let a punk like this tank his career because he was too freakin' lazy to follow protocol.

"Whatever, man," Ehretz growled. "Load up. We're checking out the field two klicks north."

Two klicks . . . Crew glanced in that direction. A hill blocked his view. "That area's off limits." He started back to the mine-resistant ambush protected vehicle to let Marvel enjoy the A/C.

Ehretz rolled his eyes and stomped back to the MRAP with the others.

"Hey," Taco said as he hung back. "Don't let him get under your tac vest. He's just jealous—dude wanted to be a handler like you. Couldn't get in."

Jealousy? Seriously? What was this, middle school?

Minutes later, they were packed like sardines in the MRAP and he sat with his legs V'd and Marvel between them. Her fur radiated the heat of the Afghan summer as she panted heavily. He'd need to water her and make sure she got some A/C time. Maybe do that while Ehretz and the team broke protocol yet again by scouting the off-limits area.

What am I doing here, man?

He'd transitioned to handling a K-9 within Special Forces teams, but he'd been pulled in for yearly qualifications again. To keep Marvel fresh and vary her experience, he'd requested a couple of routine patrol opportunities. But it sucked being stuck with a corporal who had a thirst for power. He missed the teams, his buddies.

Missed Havoc. He grinned, patting Marvel. While the dog at his feet was pure violence and raw power, she'd been bred for that. Malinois were little more than psycho and all business. But Havoc on the other hand . . .

Years ago, rumor told of a stray hanging around the base that had been mated by an MWD. Breedings weren't allowed outside the strict military confines of the DOD breeding program, but the SEALs handling the sire thought it funny. Made lewd comments. The dam delivered six pups . . . Havoc being one of them.

At least, that was the story. Crew met the thick-chested, goober of a dog when the Malinois was about two years old. Assigned to Bagram, he saw the dog all the time. Even off base. Knew better than to befriend a stray, but the dog wouldn't leave him alone.

One day, Crew noticed possible blood and realized the dog had been shot. He'd put his field vet training to work and operated on the eighty-something pound dog. Took care of him. Fattened him up—well, really, just got him less-scrawny. And that dog turned into one of the most beautiful working dogs he'd ever encountered. On medical hold with a torn meniscus, Crew spent his downtime with Havoc. Fed him. Trained him. The dog was lethal-loyal. Military refused to let Crew run him through certifications though. Told him to focus on the dog assigned to him—Marvel. Sexy girl that she was.

Crew smoothed a hand over her sleek skull, and she lifted her jaw straight up, to look at him . . . upside down. "Psycho."

At the affectionate misnomer, she thudded her tail hard against the steel deck.

The MRAP lumbered offroad and angled down. Through the narrow slats-for-windows, the terrain made itself known. Hard to tell for sure in an armored personnel carrier, but it seemed this was a bowl, a valley. The thought made his gut churn. Not a great position for them since they were apparently on the floor of said valley.

Crew had a bad feeling about this. "Ehretz," he shouted toward the front where the leader sat right, front. "I need to get Marvel back. She's overheating." It was a partial truth. She was hot—most MWDs were in the Afghan heat.

"After this," Ehretz barked back. "Everyone out."

This guy was looking to get killed. "This isn't smart—"

"What's not smart is disobeying my orders."

"Despite your ego, Ehretz, I do not answer to you. I'm tasked to this patrol, but I will not do anything that puts my super"—he nodded to Marvel, who was one rank higher than him as rules stipulated—"in danger."

"Then stay here, you whining pansy."

Don't. Don't do it. Killing a corporal wasn't a good way to end your career.

Maybe, but it'd feel good.

"Do you need some crayons to find your way back?" Crew regretted saying it as soon as the words escaped his lips. He wouldn't get in trouble—much—but it wouldn't help the situation here.

In response, Ehretz cut the engine on the MRAP. Which meant Crew had to bail with Marvel or they'd get baked alive waiting for the team to return. "Your funeral," Crew muttered. "Marvel outranks everyone here, and you'll get dereliction of duty for letting a superior die when you could've prevented it."

"If you're so worried about how your career ends, then I suggest *you* not be found guilty."

I'm going to kill him.

Instead, Crew took a moment to let Marvel get some water, rustled the thick fur along her neck, and sighed. "You can rip out his throat any time you want. Okay, girl?"

Marvel stood, tail wagging her whole back end. If Havoc were here, he'd have gone for the kill.

"Guess you hate him as much as I do." He caught her ear, gave a firm squeeze, and drew his hand up, rubbing it in the way that nearly drew a groan from her that he took as her agreement. "Knew you were a clever girl."

They climbed out and he slung his weapon to the front, holding firmly to Marvel's lead. Climbing out the back, he found the team standing at the edge of a flattened area. Hills rose on three sides, and to his two o'clock a crevasse cut through the hillside, winding hard to the right and disappearing. But between here and there? Flat open 'kill me' space.

"Look." Taco pointed across toward the crevasse. "It's one of ours."

Frowning, Crew couldn't see what the guy referenced. He angled aside and that's when he saw the tail end of a military Jeep. What in the world was it doing out here?

Mouse drew out his nocs and peered across the distance. Cursed. "I think there's someone in it—I see blood. I think."

What? How did that . . .? There weren't any reports of missing vehicles or men.

Guess they could've come out here after Crew and the Marines left base. But wouldn't they see tire tracks out to the truck?

Something wasn't right.

Only then did Crew realize Marvel was shifting, sniffing—in that deep-throated way of hers when she was really hauling in scents—and turning. Had she caught wind of something?

She made several circles, then lowered her back end and piled a deposit in the dirt.

Right behind—

"Okay, fan out," Ehretz said, sounding tough and official. "Eyes out. Gatlin, you're with me."

"Neg—"

Ehretz stepped back. Right into the smelly brown excrement. Cursed. Slipped.

Boom!

Boom!

Even as he secured Marvel and struggled to understand where the threat was coming from, Crew felt the soft thud of dirt and rocks hitting his shoulders. Dust and screams filled the air. That hadn't been weapons' fire but explosions. Was someone launching RPGs at them? Grenades?

Weapon up, Crew scanned the chaos. "Marvel, heel. On me." He patted his leg. Saw a plume of dust that slowly settled into a mound of dirt. Then his mind began to assemble what he was really seeing. It wasn't rocks . . . it was chunks . . . arms . . . fingers.

Son of a . . .

7

Mouse. Mouse was gone.

Howling came from Crew's four—Taco was there, his face shredded and bloodied.

Crew took a step forward, and somehow, amid the tight panting of Marvel, the shouts of Ehretz demanding to know where the shooting was coming from—panicked idiot—heard the all-too-quiet *click* of a pressure plate. Freezing in place, he cursed.

Marvel started forward.

"Stay!" he shouted, which he knew better than to do. *Emotion travels down-lead.* "Marvel, stay. Down." He lifted his gaze to the others. "Nobody move—it's a minefield." His thoughts were catching up, racing his heartbeat. "This whole thing is a trap."

A private lay curled on the ground, holding his arm that was now handless. To Crew's five, Ehretz was whimpering as he held his gut where a large piece of shrapnel stuck out. His face was peppered with small holes. Likely nails. It was a crude, cruel method that was all the same effective.

"Base, this is Charlie Four. We are in need of medevac and ordnance retrieval. Team is trapped in a minefield and have one fatality and multiple injuries." Crew swallowed and forced himself to think quick around the adrenaline. "I'm on a pressure plate." He flicked his gaze to Marvel. Had she taken any shrapnel? She'd been close to Ehretz. Even as he wondered, he saw the blood glistening on her coat. And neck. No! "MWD has taken shrapnel as well."

"Charlie Four, this is Command. Situation understood. We are deploying QRF and medevac. ETA in twenty mikes."

Twenty minutes? Were they freakin' kidding?

He eyed his girl. Recalled how she'd been acting weird, going in circles. She'd smelled the ordnance. All around her. No doubt it'd confused her.

She slumped onto the ground, her pink tongue dangling far out as she panted rapidly, making him worry that she had more wounds he couldn't see. Internal wounds.

"Guess now you don't have to worry about your career ending . . ." Ehretz's lame attempt at a joke was sick.

His life ending wasn't in his plans for the day. "Not what I meant."

Ehretz shifted. "I'm . . . I think I'm clear. Going to get the medkit."

"No!"

The corporal took a step.

Boom!

The blast was close—too close.

Crew had a second to brace. To tell himself to keep his leg in place. Even as the concussive wave punched his chest. He felt himself falling back. Angled. Contorted to keep his boot on the plate.

He landed hard. Teeth jarring. Dirt and dust rained down as he waited for the blast that would take him off the map. It didn't come—instead, he felt blood trickling down his temple and neck. His gaze landed on—Oh no. The gruesome sight made his gut roil. Half a leg and boot lay nearby, severed from a body.

Who lost their leg?

Only then did he feel it—the heaviness that said something was terribly wrong. That the boot was his boot. He was now a solid ten feet from the pressure plate—the one that had blown. Separated from his boot and the lower half of his leg. Holy . . .! Dropping back into the dirt, hearing hollowing out, Crew knew the countdown to Death's arrival had begun. Scrambling, he snatched the Combat Application Tourniquet from his tac vest. Struggled to slip it below his knee where blood gushed. Fingers slick, he pulled the band over and secured it. Twisted the rod—it slipped, but he caught it. Groaned and tightened it.

He growled, gritting his teeth. Feeling his gut heave.

Tighter. Tighter. Tighter.

It hurt like a mother, but if he didn't cut off the blood flow . . .

His vision blurred.

Strength fled his body.

Garbled noises reached him. He opened eyes he hadn't realized he'd closed. Saw a haze . . . blurs . . . a small black form blurring toward him. He cringed. When a slobbery tongue swiped his face, Crew tried to laugh. "Hav . . ." He felt violent, jerking tugs . . . backward . . . back . . . and surrendered himself to Death's embrace.

1

TWO YEARS LATER

TEXAS HILL COUNTRY

Smelly, tender liver extended to the snarling dog, Crew shifted on his legs, feeling the pinch of his prosthesis as he crouched before the wiry-haired mutt. Though mostly gray and appropriately named "Phantom" by the shelter staff, the dog stared at Crew as if he'd just made the biggest mistake of his life. Of Crew's life.

But Crew had met Death. And told him where he could stuff it. So he wasn't afraid of a smelly, ill-tempered mutt. "We have a lot in common," Crew said, tossing one of the treats halfway between him and the newest pick-up. "So you can trust me."

Phantom fastened his brown eyes on Crew and inched forward. Lowered his head to the treat, eyes doing a quick once-over of the smelly morsel. He hesitated, then swooped the thing up with his speckled tongue and swirled back to the corner, where he planted his rear and refused to look at the human invading his space.

Crew straightened to his full height. Maybe this one wasn't right. Slightly food motivated, and while he wasn't showing *fear* of humans, he really wasn't fond of them either. *I can relate.* "Bet you put your life in someone's hands and they let you down, huh?"

Phantom lowered himself to the concrete and rested his snout on his outstretched paws.

Bored, huh? Crew pocketed the smelly treats that normally worked and pulled out a bright green tennis ball.

The mutt lifted his snout. Did a full-on head tilt.

"That's more like it." Crew bounced the ball so hard it smacked the concrete loudly.

Ears perked, Phantom came to attention.

"Now that I have your interest . . ." Crew bounced the ball to the mutt, who snagged it before it could hit twice and vanished out the small door to his exterior run.

Crew smirked. "Now we're talking."

Within an hour, Crew had Phantom doing a recall and release with the ball. He had some bad manners—snatched the ball as Crew reached for it a couple of times—but that was on Crew. By reaching for the ball, he placed a high value on it. Which Phantom challenged him for.

"What do you think?" asked Kera, the shelter manager, as she found them in the open yard.

Crew nodded. "Has potential, but I'm not convinced he's working-dog material." He ordered Phantom to sit, and the dog complied, so he rewarded him with a treat. Then down. And he did. But heel . . . yeah, the mutt wasn't quite so eager.

"At least he knows some basic obedience now," Kera said. "That'll help him get adopted."

Yeah, but sure doesn't help me. "Think this guy will go fast." Ghost expected him to procure dogs, and while they did purchase from breeders both stateside and abroad, Crew still came to the shelter once a week. Looking for *the* dog.

He returned Phantom to the kennel. "Good luck, buddy. Don't blame you for taking the couch life over operations. That's more we have in common." He rustled the dog's head, trying not to think how much this boy reminded him of another . . . "Find a hot girl and settle down, 'kay?"

Since being separated from his leg and the military, Crew had gotten back in shape, more for his mental state than for any other reason. He sure wasn't one of those guys who fought to get back out there so they could blow off the other leg. He liked being attached to his limbs. Had no idea what to do with his life, but then Ghost offered him a job procuring dogs for the ranch. Kept him busy, his mind off the pile of dung life had handed him.

He headed up the hall to the front lobby and aimed for the door. Considered heading over to the private shelter. His heart just wasn't in it, though.

"Want to get some dinner tonight?" Kera's voice held nerves and a coy flirtation.

He chuckled. "Same answer as always." She was cute, but she was also at least ten years his junior. He might feel desperate for company these days, but he wasn't a cradle robber. "Have a good one."

She shrugged and winked. "Can't blame a girl for trying. Maybe someday you'll say yes."

Unlikely. "Next time," he said, lifting a hand as he pushed open the door.

Smacked by the unseasonably humid weather this year, he sucked in a breath. It so easily pitched him back to that minefield. The grit and smoke. The acrid taste of explosives. The smell of his own blood pouring into the dirt. In his Raptor, he cranked the engine, A/C, and radio. Sat there, gripping the wheel tight. Gritting his teeth. Remembering Marvel's pained whimper . . . that arrogant Ehretz getting nearly everyone killed. The cocky, son of a gun might not have killed the entire team but had ruined every life to a one.

Crew pounded his fist on the console. Now, he couldn't find the right dog for the ranch. He huffed. Knew sitting in the heat of his own putrid mood would only make things worse, so he buckled up and headed down the road. Not ready to face Ghost with his failure again, he whipped into his favorite coffee joint. Parked, bypassing the drive-thru. His sister had been a barista and always ranted about the drive-thru and the toll it took on the store. So, in he went.

Two people were in line ahead of him. He tugged out his phone and saw a text from Ghost, who said they needed to talk. That's one thing he appreciated about the legendary handler— he didn't hassle people. Simply made sure they knew what he wanted and left it up to them to get it done.

Which is exactly what I'm failing to do. There had to be a dog out there . . .

"Can I help you?" Brown eyes glittered over a rosy blush as the barista smiled at him. Her name tag read JENN and was decorated with stickers of animals and fat little smiley faces. "What's your flavor?"

"Large half-caff, please." He tugged out his wallet even as he adjusted his ballcap lower. "With room, two packets of raw sugar, and light cream."

"You got it." She rang it up and lifted a cup, marker poised in her other hand. "Name for the order?"

"Crew."

"That's original." She smiled, her stark-white teeth on display. "Are you a veteran?"

He tightened his jaw. "I am."

"Thank you for your service."

Though he wanted to say he'd offer thanks for hers *if* she'd actually serve him the coffee so he could leave, he instead played nice. "Thanks. What do I owe you?"

"It's on the house."

He faltered. Felt the eyes of the other customers on him. Knew his pants covered the prosthetic leg, but somehow felt they could see through the black material. "That's not necessary."

"It's no problem." That smile of hers was bright enough to land a 747.

"Uh, thanks." He moved to the pick-up area, tugged his cap lower, and glanced at his phone. Pretended he was doing something important. Anything to avoid—

"Amy?" Jenn called from this end of the counter, now delivering coffees. "So, are you from around here?"

Don't look. Don't answer. Ignorance is—

"I just moved back after finishing my degree."

Not the kind to be rude, Crew nodded. "Congrats."

She picked up a cup filled with pink liquid. "Sue?" After handing the drink to a woman, Jenn settled her hip against the counter and smiled at him as if she weren't having a one-sided conversation. "Congrats will be if I can land a job. Daddy's still all over me about it, wanting me to help pay off the loans."

He wanted to groan—Daddy. Meant the girl still lived at home. What was she? Eighteen? Another barista set his coffee on the counter.

"So many of my friends are in the same boat—a degree but no job."

"Huh."

"What about you? Where do you work?"

Nope. Not happening. He pointed to the coffee. "Can I get that?"

She looked surprised it was there, lifted it, grabbed a marker, wrote on it again, then handed it off with a giggle.

"Thanks." Crew stalked out of the café, cursing himself for not using the drive-thru. He stomped down the steps and headed to his truck. Stopped short at the SUV parked next to it and the guy standing between the two vehicles, grinning way too big.

Jibril Khouri laughed. "Get her number?"

Crew lifted his coffee cup and rotated it to Khouri, revealing the number written in black marker.

"Why don't they ever give me their numbers?"

"Ain't like I'm advertising *all this* is available . . ."

Jibril laughed and thumped his shoulder as he trailed Crew

to his truck, the limp almost unnoticeable these days. Gave Crew hope that his own less-than-normal gait would improve.

Crew sipped the hot brew, then squinted at ABA's founder and CEO. "What're you doing here?"

"I was coming back from picking up supplies and talking with Ghost when I saw your truck. He needs you back at the ranch."

Right. The earlier text had said they needed to talk. "Good copy." But for Ghost to send someone after him . . . That didn't sound good.

"Guess the shelter didn't have anything again?"

"Oh, they've got something," Crew said, angling toward his truck. "Mostly animals traumatized by irresponsible owners or dogs too feral to know treats are a good thing. Found one I thought might work, but . . ."

"He wasn't Havoc?"

Something spasmed in Crew's chest. "See you back at the ranch." He climbed in his truck without another word. Hated that Khouri had brought up Havoc. There would never be another dog like him.

Marvel had been a fantastic Malinois, but Havoc was next level. He'd saved Crew's life. When the Army flew Crew to Landstuhl to be stabilized after the landmine chewed off his leg, Havoc had been lost in the shuffle. By the time Crew was stateside at Walter Reed to begin a lengthy, excruciating path of healing and physical torture—aka *therapy*—he'd inquired after his four-legged partner, but nobody could find the dog.

Once through the wrought-iron gate with the A Breed Apart logo in it, Crew eased up the mile-long drive to the ranch's main parking lot. Took a moment to appreciate the work happening here. Two-dozen handlers working roughly fifty dogs. Khouri had started the ranch to meet a need after an accident left him minus a femur, much like Crew. He'd then recruited the original handlers: Heath "Ghost" Daniels—who recently bought out half the company—Aspen Courtland, and Timbrel Hogan. As a contract security company with working dogs, they had a name and reputation to protect, and everyone who stood on this Texas Hill Country property felt it in their bones. Here, they were part of something fierce. Only those who'd handled dogs in a working environment understood the depth of the bond between MWDs or CWDs and their handlers. The dogs weren't *pets*. They were tactical partners.

Skirting the vet clinic and the green that separated the side lot from the kennels, he parked in front of the admin building. Headed up the sidewalk, nursing his coffee and his gut tightening with each step. Many handlers had trod these halls. Had they felt the same gnawing fear when Ghost asked for face time?

Stacking explanations and excuses a mile high in his head, he banked right and strode down the hall to Ghost's office. Door open, laughter wafting out seemed a good sign. Crew did a quick look-see.

Perched against the front of his desk, Ghost held his wife in front of him.

Whoa. Privacy invaded.

Crew pivoted and took a step in the other direction.

"Gatlin."

Crew cringed. Stepped back toward the office, but kept his gaze trained down the hall as he heard whispered byes and a kiss . . . then Darci brushed past him. She gave him a look that held equal parts anticipation and fear.

What the . . . ?

"Hey." Ghost grabbed his attention and motioned him into one of the chairs. "Have a seat."

"Am I getting detention?"

Ghost sniffed. "Nah, but maybe a few demerits for interrupting my time with Darc."

Crew gave a nervous chuckle. "Fair." He lowered himself into the padded chair, wondering what was up. Still kinda hard to believe he was sitting here with Heath Daniels, working for the legend himself at this ranch. His reputation across the spec-ops community was larger than life. They'd done a few missions together before he'd been hired by Khouri, then bought out half the ranch. It'd never be old to operate under the man's leadership.

"Shelter have any good candidates?"

There it was—direct as always. "One had potential but . . . he belongs on a couch with a hottie."

Ghost nodded, eyes assessing.

"Sorry, I know I'm letting you down—"

"Negative." Tall and athletic, Ghost adjusted his tan ball cap with the ABA logo emblazoned across it that shielded his brown eyes. "After what you did with Havoc in A-stan?" He sniffed. "You have those instincts, not me. So if you say it's a no-go, then that's what it is."

Crew expelled a breath he hadn't realized he'd been holding. But . . . that still left him short on his procurement quota.

Ghost grunted, his gaze raking over Crew.

Man, he hated when the guy did that. Braced for the incoming friendly fire.

Squinting against the afternoon sun that sliced through the window, Ghost considered him. "How's your heart?"

Now Crew scowled. "The minefield didn't affect my heart."

"Not much does, from what I hear." Ghost leaned back in his chair and tucked his hands under his armpits. "Except Havoc."

"That's low, even for you."

A smile almost made it to Ghost's eyes. Then vanished. Along with any semblance of amusement. He straightened and leaned forward, resting his arms on his desk. "I found him, Crew."

Why couldn't he breathe? "Not funny."

"I'm serious."

"You know—" He swallowed hard. "He's dead. They said—"

"He's *here*." Ghost's expression was steady, confident. "Took longer than I wanted and ate up more than a little goodwill capital, but he's here." He angled his head to Crew's six. "Khat's examining him."

Crew lifted his ballcap. Adjusted it. Tugged it back on. Ignored the place his prosthesis pinched. Flared his nostrils. "If you're jerking my chain . . ." But his friend held his gaze, unflinching. "If he's here . . . if you really did this . . ." Dangerous hope squirreled through his chest. "If this is legit, I'll marry you."

Ghost laughed. "Thanks, but I like who already shares my bed. Less hairy." He was on his feet. "C'mon."

Crew followed, but as they left the admin building and crossed to the clinic, despite his close friendship with Ghost, he felt like this was an ambush. Felt like he was walking onto that minefield in Afghanistan again. Only, this time, he was sure he'd lose more than a leg.

2

LOS ANGELES, CALIFORNIA

Anonymity had its benefits. A plethora of them, in fact. She'd take that every day in every way if it kept the sharks at bay.

The fist punched hard from her right.

Warehouse behind her, Vienna Foxcroft eased her spine backward and with her left hand, blocked the blow. Threw a right cross. Nailed the guy in the jaw. He spun away as she stepped back, angled her body so it was parallel to the ground, and nailed the guy in the head with her boot. She landed, hurled herself into an aerial, again using her leg to connect with the second assailant's head. V touched down and drove upward, drawing her legs up into hooks as she snapped out her right, heel thudding center mass.

Adrenaline drove her, but she remembered her position. Aware of her body in relation to the others coming at her. To the others fighting to stop the attack. The car revving behind them. Drug dealers trying to blow the sting.

"This way!" the sandy-haired hunk shouted, motioning her to him.

Lifting her chin, she started that way. Palmed the waist-high wall. Launched upward. Hiked her legs and vaulted into the air. Arms tucked to her chest, she rotated midair. Drew out the weapons holstered at her thighs. Landed, boots sliding on the oil-slickened concrete. Fired at the assailants converging on her.

Calves burning, she strained to maintain focus. Take down the bad guys. Do her job. Get paid. Lie low.

Vienna knew finding traction to stop in the oil slick on the road would be tricky, so she held her weapons sans triggers and side-spiraled out of the oil. Heard the crack of their weapons. She pitched herself forward into a roll. Over a barrel and the oncoming 70s model Pontiac Trans Am. Slid across the hood, over it, to the other side. She dove for cover behind a stack of crates.

Hands hit her back. She heard the click of the carabiner. Drew in a breath even as she saw the muscle-bound oaf scale the crates. Launch at her. He swung a bat at her. *Crack!*

Her head snapped back. She stumbled backward. Growled. Then shoved upward. Felt the crane haul her straight into the air as she aimed at him and the other two men. The first went down. She shifted her gaze to the leaking oil barrels. Smirked with an elaborate pause, being sure to keep her angle correct. She fired. The men went down. An explosion flipped the Trans Am twice.

She dropped, and angled herself sideways, spiraling toward the ground. Shoved out her boots. Nailed the landing with a partial squat. Touched the ground. Took in a breath. Kept her face down, hair spilling forward and concealing her features. Then slowly rose . . . up . . . up . . .

"*And cut!*" Director Kerr Macleod pronounced.

"Yeah!!" Five-eight Baako al Masry clapped, then turned and high-fived her, his shaved head catching the studio lights that had turned night to day for the filming. "You nailed it."

Vienna sagged in relief. "Finally. Only needed six takes."

Patting her shoulder, Baako grinned. "You've been under a lot of stress."

She managed a smile as Frode Haugen, the other stunt double strode toward her. "Good work," she said, acknowledging how well he'd pulled off the fight they'd choreographed. "Loved the way you—"

"Okay, listen up, everyone," Macleod called. "We've got the clearance to work outside Istanbul, so be ready to travel." He peered over horn-rimmed glasses. "That's it. Clear the set for the next scene. Felicity, Mark, you're up!"

Sweaty and out of breath, Vienna let the production crew remove the harness from her and secure it. A production assistant handed her a bottled water. "Thanks, Iris."

The girl started, surprised to be acknowledged. "Of course."

"Irrreeeeene," Felicity called the wrong name in a shrill voice from near Macleod. "Where's my Perrier?"

The PA cringed, nodded her excuse to leave, and hurried toward the star of the TV show "Cleared and Hot."

Shaking her head at the ridiculousness that was Felicity Vale, Vienna removed the leather jacket and began untaping her wrists. She started for her trailer, cutting across the parking lot-turned-RV-residences for the cast.

A man climbed out of a Porsche. Tadeo Torres, Felicity's heartthrob boyfriend from Spain, had quickly risen to fame and fortune, had the requisite olive skin and black hair, but those eyes of his were as green as her own. It was a striking combination, unlike his cocky attitude. Not only was the man a tall drink of water, he knew it.

But he'd always been nice to her. Not that it had anything to do with how much she resembled Felicity. Right, nothing at all. She smiled a greeting, not wanting Felicity to again accuse her of trying to steal him. As if Tadeo would stoop to her level.

"Heeeey!" He swaggered up to her with no shame or hesitation and wrapped an arm around her waist. "Miss me?" His lips were aiming for hers.

She planted a hand on his chest. "Vienna."

His eyes widened at her declaration. That million-dollar

smile faltered, then went full force. "You think I don't know my own girlfriend from her stunt double?" He released her. Huffed a laugh as he backstepped. "Just testing you, Vienna."

Like the last time when he *did* kiss her before she'd realized what was happening? "Felicity's on set now." She nodded toward the filming area and started for her RV.

Some people might think it sucked that Felicity had the fame, fortune, and fiancé when Vienna got all the danger, risk, and anonymity as a body/stunt double. But that enabled her to have all the thrill and excitement of being part of drama without the complication of the paparazzi chasing her around town, or the pressure to keep her face perfect. She'd lived with that her entire childhood, thanks to her mom's career.

After showering and changing, she donned yoga pants and a black tank. She ignored the script—she'd review it, and get ready for her stunts, later. They'd practiced for weeks and had it down pat, but another review never hurt. Right now, though, she needed a mental break. Space to breathe. Maybe she'd head over to the food trucks and grab something to eat. She pinched her waistline.

Hm, maybe just stay in and eat celery. Couldn't afford to eat the two-hand burrito she really wanted.

Her phone rang. Recognizing the ringtone, she grabbed it off the table and answered it. "Dad." His responsibilities made calls from him few and far between, so she savored every one.

"How's my Stardust?"

Vienna sniffed a laugh and moved outside onto her small fenced-in patio with canopy, table, and chairs. The nickname had come about when she'd gotten her first stunt gig a few years ago and he proclaimed her a star like her mom. She balked, stating that all her roles were behind the scenes, so she was more like star dust. "Busy, but good. You?"

"Wonderful. I am well," he said, his voice gregarious and a deep baritone. "There is a big vote coming up."

"Ah." Vienna chewed the inside of her lip. "So, is this your way of saying you won't be in touch for a while."

"Afraid so, but also for you to be careful."

And not tell him they were going to Turkey, because he would go ballistic. "Nobody even knows who I am, Dad." She'd made sure of that, taking her gran's maiden name. But he wouldn't let up unless she vowed to live like a hermit. "And we're locked down filming for the next few weeks."

"Good, good." Relief really seemed thick in his voice this time. Like way more than normal.

"Everything okay?"

"Yes, yes. You know me." Did his laugh sound hollow now, too? "I like you aware rather than . . ." Nerves weighted the pause. "But"—he chuckled—"you have no boyfriends, right?"

Nice deflection. "You're the only guy in my life." Sadly. Came with the territory. Most men found her pretty until they realized she held black belts in Krav, Jiu jitsu, and Kali. That and most guys were looking to milk her connections to her powerful jet-setting parents.

"Have you heard from your mother?"

"Her production schedule was pretty packed," Vienna said, having no idea if her mother even had a gig at the moment. Mom had been furious when V chose MMA and being a body double over becoming a pampered, catered-to, botoxed fake. Like Amelie Wolffe, legendary actress often referred to as a brunette Grace Kelly. Everyone loved her mom. Admired her. Wanted to be her.

Except Vienna.

"She doesn't hate you, ya know."

Vienna went inside and snagged her trail mix, side-eyed the powdered donuts . . . then decided mom-guilt wasn't worth losing her job or killing herself. "When's the vote?" *Now who's deflecting?* Always easier to talk politics than family.

"Two weeks."

She nodded. "Okay, cool. You warn Carl and Melie?" Both

her siblings had families of their own, but her brother was rarely far removed from Dad's work.

"Yes, but I wanted to check on my Vienna."

"You've done your duty," she said quietly, grateful he at least attempted to show he cared. "I'm all good, warned, and looking forward to your call afterward."

"We're throwing a big Christmas gala. Melie will send you the details."

"I can't promise—"

"It is Christmas, Vienna. You will be there."

No point in arguing. "Of course." She'd just have a last-minute complication. This was how the Wolffe game was played—act like you cared. Keep up appearances. With two parents so wholly in the limelight, facades were key. "You should come visit *me*."

"Someday, my stardust. But I must go. They're calling me in."

Disappointment pinched at the back of her neck. "Okay. Love you."

"All my love. Shine bright."

BLANCO COUNTY, TEXAS HILL COUNTRY

With two deep breaths for courage, Crew faltered at the door to the exam room. Couldn't take those last couple of steps to cross that threshold. Heard Ghost mutter a hello, then came the happy response of Khat Khouri.

"How's—" Ghost went silent.

Crew swallowed. Couldn't do this. Havoc . . . alive. But here at the ranch. Meant he'd be working. Crew couldn't . . .

Ghost reappeared. "You okay?"

"I . . ." He swallowed. "Why's he here?"

"For you," Ghost said, looked at him as if he'd lost his marbles.

"Bull."

Ghost's jaw muscle worked. "He's here for. You." He nodded slowly, acquiescing, indicating there *was* more. "I think he's perfect for a job—"

"No." Crew felt his cookies climbing his throat, ready to be tossed. "I told you—I'll scout dogs, procure them, but no missions."

"If you'd let me finish . . ."

Crew ground his molars. Waited.

"I've been working on locating Havoc since you were at Walter Reed. When I finally found him, it took almost a year to secure Havoc." He angled his head toward the door. "A SEAL I know does side gigs as a movie consultant. He's tied up but said there's a TV drama that needs an MWD team for a couple of episodes. I committed to send a team." He nodded to Crew. "Timing is pure coincidence, but I think it's a good fit for you."

"I . . . Filming? *What?*" Crew tried to chew the facts. Mostly the one that Havoc was here. Back from the dead. On the other side of the door.

"I blindsided you—sorry." Ghost gave him a cockeyed nod. "There are no ulterior motives. If he hadn't guided us across the minefield, we'd never have reached you in time to stop you from bleeding out. What you put into him paid off. Just seemed right to reunite y'all."

Blindsided was a good term for it. But . . . he had to admit, Ghost had never done him wrong. And . . . Havoc. Here. Wow.

Barking erupted from the exam room. Incessant. Insistent. The big lug demanding he show himself.

Ghost smirked. "Think your guardian angel knows you're here."

"'Course he does," Crew said as he forced himself to cross the threshold. Braced—as a tan-and-black missile launched at him. Caught the beast of a dog. He barely kept his feet, feeling Havoc's sharp nails digging into his arms and thigh. The move was like old times. Pitched him right back to Afghanistan, to the mutt hanging around the chow hall, begging scraps from the hooches set up by SEALs and other Green Berets.

A warm, slobbery tongue slid up the side of his face. Frantic-licked his nose, ear, jaw, beard—

"Okay, okay," Crew said, shifting to relieve the pinch and letting Havoc down, hand instinctively sliding to his collar. His vision was a bit blurry. He swiped the wet drop escaping and ducked. Ran his hand down his boy's sides. Emotions rushed over him—relief, giddiness, gratefulness. Throat raw. "Good boy . . ." Then saw his quirky left ear—and hauled in a breath. He held Havoc's head, stared at his face, then Ghost. "He's numbered."

Ghost nodded. "Guys and I made sure that happened. After saving your life and his heroic efforts, higher-ups agreed."

Crew's laugh came out more a breath. His thoughts freefalling back to that minefield, the jerking tugs Havoc used to drag him to safety. Buried his face against the powerful neck capable of snapping bones. Then when Havoc again demanded kisses, he earned a powerful headbutt that nearly gave him a bloody nose. Went up on his hind legs.

Crew straightened and braced, all too familiar with the chest and neck strength of the Malinois.

"I hear you're going to be in a movie," Khat said.

"Television drama," Ghost corrected.

"Why do they want *him*?" Jibril balked as he wandered in. "I'm prettier!"

"Yeah, exactly," Crew taunted back, hooking Havoc's lead onto his collar. "They had enough actresses and needed a man."

"You asked for that one, brother," Khat said, folding her arms. She gave Havoc an appreciative smile as he insisted on more petting. "He is all cleared. Everything sounds and looks good."

Crew grinned at the mutt he'd trained from the ground up, who sat, attention focused solely on him. "What do you think? Ready to be famous?" When his Malinois barked, he offered him a KONG. Tossed in the air. Havoc snatched it and went to town, teeth squeaking over the toy.

"Come on back to the office. I'll get you all the details. They need you in L.A. tomorrow." They returned to the admin building, where Ghost gave him a pack of information, flight details, contacts, a promise that he and Havoc would have an RV to bunk in while out there.

"How long?" He smoothed his hand over Havoc's head, still disbelieving he was here, they were together again.

"My contact said about six weeks."

Not like he had more pressing engagements. "I'll need a crate for Havoc. And food—for me, too. Unless you feel I need a diet."

"Maybe for your ego, but yeah—all sorted." He pointed to the packet. "You'll find a list of supplies that should be waiting for you onsite. If anything's missing, there's a credit card. But maybe don't suddenly find a girl you can stand and treat her to a weekend on the town."

"No promises," Crew joked. "Everyone knows I can't resist shelter eyes—you know the way their eyes get all melty—"

"I meant the *two-legged* variety."

"If she doesn't have *four* legs, not interested."

Ghost tossed a KONG at him—but Havoc leapt up, snagging it from the air. They both laughed, amazed at the lightning-fast reflexes. "Yeah, but the thing with you is that the ladies are always interested."

"Not my problem." He tapped his thumb against his prosthesis, then went back to stroking Havoc's sides, noting he was a bit on the thin side. "Where'd you find him?"

"After you got shipped out to Landstuhl, the handlers—across branches—went to bat for him. Got him tatted. That earned him a free pass to the States." He let out a heavy breath. "But then he went MIA. Got a call last week about him, and best we can figure—he has two microchips, and one got him transferred to Fort Leonard Wood."

"How'd he get two? I gave him one shortly before . . ."

"Guess some idiot didn't scan him right when we got him qualified. Probably figured with his history, he didn't have one, so he got another." Ghost shrugged. "They were giving him a check-up when the second—the original one—was discovered. It had our team number. I got the call."

"And they said you'd never amount to anything."

"Y'know," Ghost said, "that day when you sacrificed your leg for the ID-10-T error, I'd gotten wind of your situation just as I saw Havoc trotting outside the wire like he was on a mission. When he banked north, I followed because I knew . . . knew you had seen something in him that nobody else did. Trusted him— and it saved your life."

The pain . . . the constant pain . . . numerous surgeries . . . Crew focused on his four-legged hero. Remembered burying his face in his neck after the explosion. The guys working double time to save him. Havoc nearly rabid when they separated them. "Do, uh, the TV people"—he tapped his prosthesis— "know?"

Ghost leaned back and considered, brow rippling. "Do they need to?" He asked it as if something had changed, something in Crew.

"Negative."

"You sure—"

"Forget I asked."

"Okay, get out of here. You have to pack, and your flight is at zero-seven-hundred. We booked a seat for Havoc, too. He's listed as a service dog."

Crew snorted. "Yeah, military service."

"Hooah."

On his feet, Crew started for the door. He hesitated and turned back. "Hey." He glanced at Havoc, then the boss. "This means . . . a lot." He would not cry. Not after just telling Jibril the producers needed a man. "The world. Thanks."

"Don't get too sappy. You know I never do anything that doesn't benefit the ranch." Ghost slapped his shoulder. "And remember, you're his handler, so just like in the military, he outranks you. Anything happens to him, you'll answer to me."

"Thought you brought him back for me?"

Steel resonated in Ghost's eyes. "I did."

And right there, Crew realized it wasn't just a feel-good measure. "You wanted me off the couch."

That steel-like expression didn't falter. He adjusted his ballcap. "Stay frosty."

3

LOS ANGELES, CALIFORNIA

Old insecurities came to the fore as he walked up the umbilical into the airport, Havoc trotting ahead, zigzagging the scent cone as trained. Crew wasn't worried about the Malinois getting a hit, but he was worried about being a one-legged grunt on a set where perfection was . . . perfected. Enhanced.

"Beautiful," a woman said with an appreciative glance at Havoc. "Thank you both for your service."

"Our honor, ma'am." Crew didn't pause as he made his way down the concourse to baggage claim. Focused on figuring out life with Havoc. At Bagram, the dog had shared his hooch in an unofficial capacity. Despite the numerous times the team had gone out, every time Crew was back in the hooch, Havoc manifested. His hand automatically reached for the velvety ears.

A guy stepped closer.

Havoc snarled at the man, who stumbled away, apologizing.

Ya know . . . this might not be so bad. Crew wasn't into entertaining people and their questions, and Havoc seemed to be of the same mind. "Rock-solid team, dude."

At carousel four, he grabbed his ruck and pivoted.

31

"Sergeant Gatlin?" A thirty-something balding man stood there, shooting nervous glances at a muzzled Havoc. "Drew Crist, sir."

"Don't call me sir. I work for a living." Reassurance was the eighty-pound Malinois pressing a shoulder into Crew's calf to remind him he was there.

Confusion flickered across the very clean-shaven face. "Okay, sure. Um . . ." He pointed back in the direction he'd come. "I'm here to take you to the set. Do you have everything?"

"Except my leg."

More confusion.

His joke, which was designed to put civvies at ease, did the opposite with this stiff-shirt. "All good. Lead on, Drew."

The guy headed out to a blue van with a studio logo emblazoned on the side. After slinging his ruck onto the floorboard at the back, he took up the entire middle row with Havoc splayed across two of the seats, belly up. Only time this hard-hitting Malinois bared the jewels was for Crew. The submission posture was an ultimate sign of trust. That and letting Crew pick up his KONG. The entire forty-minute trip—which was only a few miles but traffic more than tripled the time—Drew rambled on about the city, movie stars, and his own connections. Guy knew how to talk the talk.

"What I can't figure," Crew said, more to himself than looking for a reasonable answer, "is why this director wanted a Crew out of Texas." Another lame joke that cleared the guy's head like a stealth bomber. Though, he was pretty sure most of what Crew said would do the same.

"Oh, it wasn't Kerr," the guy said with a snivelly laugh. "That order came from our security advisor."

No idea who that was or how he knew about Crew or A Breed Apart, but it was a gig that kept him from focusing on failing the procurement requisition. Then again, they did have Havoc now . . . so he was one dog up, right?

Finally, they pulled through the security gate, where Crew

was given a 24-hour pass. He eyed the plastic card, wondering at the short timeframe. Hadn't Ghost said six weeks? Would he get a more permanent one later? "Hey—"

"Here we are." Drew lurched the van into a spot and nailed the brake. "This is you."

Havoc's nails slid on the leather seat nearly gouging his autograph into them as he'd done to Crew's thigh more than once.

Crew glanced at the mid-sized RV, then climbed out and followed the guy inside. It was roomy as far as coaches went, but anemic compared to his house back in Texas. Yet . . . it'd do.

He spotted a large feeder on a mat in the kitchen area. Was relieved when he realized the food bowl wasn't filled. Havoc rushed to it and inhaled the water. It pitched him back to Bagram, to the time Havoc had the bloat and ended up needing a life-saving surgery. Most MWDs were pexied as soon as they were qualified and before they got deployed, but since Havoc wasn't an official MWD—well, not before the explosion—it'd cost Crew months of extra duties and all his spare cash to save the Malinois from bloat. Peace of mind went a long way.

Crew eyeballed the bed in the closet-sized bedroom. Wasn't even sure he could stretch out all the way. At least it wasn't a bedroll or cot.

"It has satellite and the fridge is stocked. Everything requested is either in the pantry or the back closet," Drew said as a tweetle sounded. He read a message on his phone. "They're ready for you."

"I'll let him take care of business, and we're all yours."

He let Havoc relieve himself, cleaned up the mound, then piled back in the van. There, he secured a muzzle over his snout and anchored it to his collar. Havoc huffed his objection. Tried to lick Crew. Ten minutes later, he stood on the edge of an outdoor set where filming was already under way. A long track had a camera crew pacing the action and a handful of actors through a scene.

Crew glanced around the area behind the cameras and directors. Looked at Drew. "Where's his kennel?"

"What?"

"The kennel—he needs to be crated when he's not—"

Boom! Crack-crack!

Havoc's head swiveled toward the action. He came up onto all fours, wholly focused on the action. So was Crew. A fight sequence with weapons—and just like Ghost warned—was unrealistic.

But the hand-to-hand . . . maneuvers, the rapid-fire strikes of—

A ponytail.

Hold up. Attention wholly snagged at the auburn hair flitting across well-tanned, well-toned shoulders had him negotiating a better position to watch the fight. A woman in a black-leather jacket and tactical pants fought two much larger men. And this wasn't wholly fake fighting. She had *skills*. Knew how to throw a punch, take a punch. Her responses were . . . "Flawless."

Havoc let out a whine of anticipation as he inched forward, tugging at the lead that Crew held in a firm grip. Another whine as if to say, "I want to play."

"Me, too, boy," Crew muttered.

The woman beautifully executed a spinning hook kick to the head of her opponent. Another actor attacked from behind, but she ducked. Fingers touched the ground as she extended her right leg out and swung around, swiping the man's feet out from under him.

Granted, it was all choreographed. Crew knew that. Told himself that. Yet he couldn't stop from admiring the beauty, the poetry in motion. It was one thing to rehearse martial arts or act them out. Whole 'nother ballgame to move with the experience and relaxed confidence of an expert. "Smoke my brisket and butter my biscuit . . ."

"I'm sorry, what?" Crist frowned at him.

"Is that the actress . . ." What was her name? Last night, he'd looked up the stars attached to this show. "Fe . . . licia?"

"*Felicity*?" Eyes wide, Drew shook his head and scoffed. "Goodnight, no. Felicity Vale is over there under the canopy with costar Mark Harrison."

Crew didn't bother looking. Nothing could compare to the firestorm on the set. "And *her*?" He watched the woman do an aerial. Fire a weapon. And while it might not be realistic, it sure was *hot*.

As part of the act, two oversized oafs surged at her again.

Havoc lunged, barking around the muzzle, straining to protect the woman.

The unexpected reaction yanked Crew's arm hard, but he held on tight. "Havoc, heel."

"Cut, cut," came a disgusted command from one of the producers or directors.

Eyes turned to Crew, who now had a very compliant Havoc at his side. As if he hadn't just interrupted a perfectly good sequence. "Sorry."

"Oh, look at the cute dog!"

"S-sorry, Mr. Macleod," Drew said, hurrying forward, shoulders hunched as he groveled. "You—I was told you were ready for them."

The lanky man with thinning hair, skinny jeans, and a black T-shirt angled away from the monitors where he'd been watching the filming. He came out of his chair and stood, glancing at Havoc, then finally focusing on Crew. "Take it you're Badem's team?"

"Badem?"

"The Turk—the man giving us orders regarding security?"

Had to grant it was not a common nickname, but since they were in L.A. and The Turk that Crew was aware of didn't even live in country—had to be a different guy. "I was sent from A Breed Apart. In Texas . . .?"

"Yeah, yeah. Right." Tucking glasses up onto his receding hairline, Macleod inspected Havoc with a nod. "Tough-looking."

"Saved my life, so yes. He is."

Crew slid his gaze past the man's shoulder, beyond the cameras to where Lara Croft's sexier cousin stood with her counterparts, talking and blocking out a sequence, slo-mo. The short athletic guy with her stuck out his jaw in Crew's direction and the woman glanced over her shoulder.

It was one of those Hollywood moments—*ironic, right?*—where the wind kicked up—or was that a fan on set?—and her thick auburn hair whipped in the air. A detonation happened somewhere in his gut because this woman had all the moves, the sultriness, and the tough-as-nails expertise that made him want to reconsider his vow to stay single.

Trying to haul himself back behind that self-imposed restraint, Crew registered someone in his periphery swarming in to pet Havoc. With a practiced move, he slid in between his dog and the woman with more batter on her face than mama's flapjacks. She was beautiful if you liked plastic, but not his speed. "Slow your roll, lady." He held up a hand. "He's not as friendly as I am."

She huffed, leaning away from him. "You call this friendly?"

"Not really, but I figure you wanted to keep that hand, not feed it to Havoc."

"*Havoc?*" she balked. "Why would you name a dog that?"

"Fluffy was taken."

Sniggers and gasps rattled around the gathered cast and crew, and that's when Crew realized by the looks everyone was shooting his way that he'd just deflected the star of the show, Fel-whatever. "No offense. He's just trained to respond without commands, and I don't want anyone getting hurt." He eyed Macleod. "I believe you were given a list of rules about *not* engaging Havoc."

"They all were," Macleod said with more than a little irritation. "Maybe Felicity didn't read her memo." With a whistle to silence the crew, he straightened and addressed everyone. "Okay, people. We sent out the heads-up about having a military working dog on set. As a refresher—don't approach the dog without permission, no sudden moves toward him or his handler, Sergeant Gatlin, and no food treats." He eyed Crew. "That cover it?"

"Mostly." Crew adjusted his ballcap and glanced around, thinking maybe he should play nice with the Hollywoodites. "I mean, I know everyone wants to hug him—he's got those soulful brown eyes." That earned a few laughs. "But this guy's trained to give some violent affection without a word from me. He reads body language better than I do and will respond if he perceives a threat. Don't be afraid of him—but respect the dog. Work is play to him, so he's eager to do it."

Murmurs and awe seemed to put everyone in their place.

"Okay, back to work, people." Macleod shook his hand. "Iris Greene is our PA and will take you to costume so they can measure you. Afterwards, they'll run you through the scenes where we need Havoc in play. Sound good?"

"Like a plan." He shook the director's hand. "Honored to be a part of this. Thank you."

Macleod nodded. "Iris will get you taken care of."

He followed the petite PA around the set, where he got another glimpse of Ms. Poetry-in-Motion, then headed inside. Even as the team measured him, he couldn't shake the feeling that this gig was going to change his life. And that flung his thoughts back to the last life-altering event that stole a token from him—his leg. Wasn't looking for a do-over.

"Ready?" Iris asked an hour later. "I'll take you to the stunt team now."

"Yep, give me five to let Havoc take care of business." Crew walked him outside, let him relieve himself, then gave him some water. Since Iris was talking to someone, he pitched the KONG for Havoc, then did some tug time. When he tossed it again, Crew caught sight of the stunt crew finishing a scene.

Poetry-in-Motion was at it again. Her mastery of Krav left him breathless and feeling like Havoc, itching to get in on the action. When the PA returned, he angled toward her and pointed to the stuntwoman. "She . . . that's more than just rehearsed. She has experience with Krav."

"That she does," Iris said. "She has multiple black belts— Krav Maga, Jiu Jitsu, and did MMA fighting for a while."

Crew let out a quiet whistle. "You got a preacher on set?"

Greene frowned. "I . . . I don't think so. Why?"

"Cuz I'm going to marry her."

The PA twitched. Scoffed. "Well, good luck. She hates men."

Undeterred, Crew smirked and indicated to Havoc. "Why do you think I brought him?"

"Did that work?" Frode asked as they regrouped in a huddle while Kerr reviewed what they'd just shot. The guy had a very native name but he'd grown up in California.

"Yeah, but maybe don't overcompensate on that last punch." Vienna rubbed her collarbone, then stretched her shoulder and neck.

"Didn't want you to make me look bad."

She laughed. "Not possible." Her attention swung to her friend, whom she'd done a half dozen films with and had developed a solid rhythm. "What'd you think? I might've been a fraction early on the reverse hook kick."

Baako touched the small scratch at his temple. "A little . . . but it happens. Nothing—"

"V, Baako, Frode?" Kerr strode across the set with the muscle-bound oaf and dog that'd interrupted filming earlier.

Inwardly, she groaned and fought the urge to cross her arms. The posture cost time if she had to defend herself. And even if she didn't need to, it made her look weak. Focusing on their director, she lifted her chin as the trio approached.

"Couple of small hiccups in that last take, Kerr, but I think it worked well."

"Looked good on our side, too." Kerr shifted toward the newcomer. "I think you heard me earlier, but this is Sergeant Crew Gatlin and MWD Havoc." He eyed the sergeant as he nodded to each of them. "That is Baako al Masry, Vienna Foxcroft, and Frode Haugen."

The man was a mountain of tatted muscles. Had to be six-two, six-three and built like a tank. No matter how cliché that sounded, the guy was anything but. The way he stood in a relaxed-but-ready stance with all the assuredness of a man who owned his existence. And the casual grip he had on the dog's leash. Was that enough to restrain the dog he himself said would instinctually respond to a threat? Shouldn't he hold it tighter? With the way he'd shut down Felicity—which had given Vienna no small amount of pleasure—from petting his dog, she wondered about him. Most men would be flirting with Felicity, tripping over themselves to get a date, even though the show's lead had a committed boyfriend. Her gaze shifted to the dog.

Mahogany eyes took in each one of them in meticulous assessment. Protruding around a black rubber toy, the dangling pink tongue suggested maybe Havoc wasn't going to rip them apart. Yet. The dog moved closer with raw intensity, making Vienna go still. Sniffing loudly around the toy, the dog trailed his snout up her pant leg, across, then down the other.

Soldier-boy jutted his jaw. "Just checking you out. It's okay."

Laughing as the Malinois pushed his shoulder into Vienna's thigh, she wondered if the sergeant meant him or his dog. "Gorgeous animal."

"He is that. Thanks."

"Get Gatlin up to speed so he's ready to start filming." Kerr nodded to them, then the handler. "Talk to Iris or Drew if you need anything."

"Thank you, sir."

When Kerr headed back to the camera line, Vienna shifted

away a step, letting the guys take the lead on this. Impressive canine but the handler seemed a bit on the juiced side. No interest in a guy who doped to bulk up.

Frode extended his long, hairy arm, and the guy accepted it. "Welcome to the craziness, Gatlin."

"Appreciate it."

"You have any acting experience?"

Not if that blank stare was any indication.

"No." The guy shifted, hands clasping before him as he widened his stance, lead still held firm. "But I'm a quick learner, and Havoc is even faster."

"What is he?" Baako asked. "German Shep—"

"Careful." The handler had a nice smile beneath the scruff and ratty hat. His neck—maybe even his head—seemed too big for the tactical shirt he wore . . . "Tends to get crotchety when people call him a German Shepherd."

"Him or you?" Vienna hadn't meant to ask that out loud, mostly because it was the lamest flirt line on the planet.

Gray-green eyes met hers, oozing confidence and some . . . *thing* that reached straight through the aerial harness she was still wearing and squeezed her lungs. A slow, slick smile— different from the forced one he'd flashed at Felicity—slid into his bearded face. "Both, I guess." He smoothed a hand so casually over the dog's ears. "Havoc's a Belgian Malinois. No matter what the military said."

"What's that mean?" Why was she still talking to the guy?

"A private security team left some dogs behind, in particular a gorgeous female Belgian Malinois. One of our MWDs made her a mama. Wasn't unusual for private security to abandon their dogs rather than incur the costs to ship them back, which makes zero sense to most of us, but it's real." He cocked his head to his partner. "Havoc was part of that litter."

"And the military took responsibility for the pups?"

"Not even," he said with a nice laugh.

"But he—"

"Let's get to work, people," Baako said, clapping and starting away from them.

Frustrating Vienna, who had a plethora of questions. But Baako was right—they needed to get the sergeant up to speed and she didn't want to be up all night helping a newb figure out how to act. First, they went over the basics of blocking a scene, making sure he didn't get in the way of camera angles, how to position himself and the dog for best lighting and angles.

"We're background," Baako said, "so stay out of Vienna's shots. Most scenes are blocked to make sure she can execute in a way that FX can later splice in Felicity."

"Seems kinda backward to me."

What did that mean? Vienna cast him a sidelong glance as they moved to the set where they'd work. She unrigged herself from the harness with help from Frode and let him pass it off to the team.

"In what way?" Baako asked.

"Why put pancake batter onscreen when you already have pure beauty happening there?"

Breath stolen, she opened a bottle of water, wanting to know if he'd meant what she thought he did. Then again, if he was flirting, then he was no different than any other man on set. After all, hadn't he been flirting with Iris as they headed to costuming? Even with Felicity?

Why do you care?

She didn't. It just helped her slot him in the right category.

Baako studied him hard and long. "Right. We might agree with you, but get it straight that V's off limits."

"So, Foxtrot's yours," Gatlin said.

"Fox*croft*," she bit out her correct name as she glowered, "and *she* is no one's." What was with this guy? "The stunt team is pretty close-knit, and we protect our own. Now, if this testosterone war is over, we need to walk you through the scenes." Moving to the ladder, she indicated to it. "Can Havoc scale these?"

"Easily, but how are we making sure he's not going for the kill? Because if I send him, that'll be his goal."

Well, that was blunt. And unsettling. Vienna palmed the metal frame. "We'll do scenes with just Havoc and me. Lowkey, no action, nothing to trigger him."

"Only things that will trigger Havoc are my commands and an attack on my person." The guy oozed fortitude the same way he oozed those operator good looks.

Huh. She'd never realized that before—there was a difference between rugged good looks and *operator* good looks, just like there was between clean-cut and bad-boy. Like Felicity's Tadeo and Baako. Neither had distracted nor induced her to dare dating again.

And speaking of good looks . . . she had a feeling when Soldier-boy here put on his tactical gear, he wore it with the blood, sweat, and death that came with it. Owned it. She looked forward to seeing that. And on that note, she realized she'd been staring.

And he'd returned that favor.

Remember, just like every other guy.

"Regardless," Baako cut in, clearly not liking the zipping whatever-it-was between her and the sergeant. "There are key shots we need with the dog, so you'll film those on various sets and locations. They want him coming off the ladder, like V said, and then sailing off the landing. We'll need bite sequences on arms, a leg . . ."

Gatlin nodded, his attention trained on the information and intensity ramping as Frode and Baako walked the scenes. She did it, too, watching the way the Malinois continuously looked to his handler for cues. Monitored Frode and Baako.

With the afternoon heating up, they took a water break. Beneath the canopy, he gave Havoc some water and let him cool down. A few feet away at the food table, she peeled an orange.

"So," he said as he turned to her, "Vienna. You named that because that's where your parents conceived you?"

Taken aback, she gaped at the indecency of that question. "Are you always this inappropriate?"

He looked chagrined—for two seconds before a grin split his fierce visage. "I excel at it, I'm told."

Disbelief snatched her breath, then a laugh escaped.

Frode joined them, talking to the sergeant about being a soldier. Fighting her amusement at Gatlin's audacity, she shook her head. Felt wet slobber between her fingers. Grimacing at the slick-as-snot feeling, she glanced down, surprised to find Havoc at her side. Was he trying to bite her?

Havoc shouldered into her leg again with an eager pant, then thrust his muzzled snout at her hip, demanding some love. It was hard not to be smitten with the working dog. She let her hand find his skull, amazed at how silky it felt. Loved the velvety ears. Wow, the fur around his neck and shoulders was thick and luxurious. Wouldn't have guessed that with the short coat he had.

"Hello, handsome." She felt more than saw Gatlin swing toward her as she rubbed those ears again and looked at him. Saw . . . shock. A near-frown. "Am I doing something wrong? Is he going to attack me?"

"With his tongue, maybe. The freakin' traitor." There was no condemnation in his tone. Only amusement. And a hefty dose of shock. "He usually just snarls at everyone."

"Finally," she said when the dog's demand for attention grew more incessant. "A guy's attention I don't mind."

4

LOS ANGELES, CALIFORNIA

"You failed me. Turned your back and betrayed me, right in front of the enemy. That's heinous, but what I can't"—he opened their RV door and stabbed a hand toward the interior—"Hup. Go on. In."

Havoc hopped inside and bolted to the water bowl.

Crew climbed up behind him. "After all we've been through, you turn on me? I trained you, and because of our history, they got you stateside. You'd still be eating dirt and rock if it weren't for me." He opened the kibble bag as Havoc licked the water bowl dry. "I mean, I know we're in a strange environment and some people here don't really look like *people*, but c'mon, man."

He dumped the kibble in the bowl, then leaned against the counter, taking some of the pressure off his prosthetic leg for a second. "Okay, obviously I dropped the ball—two days of training ago, when we first showed up, I should've stated that there are clear lines of demarcation: girls are the enemy. Plain & simple. They chew you up and spit you out. You know that we *don't* cooperate with the enemy."

Inhaling his kibble, Havoc didn't look up.

"You're a piece of work, you know that? Snarl at every Tom, Dick, and Baako, but Wonder Woman you cozy up to while my back is turned." He shook his head. Havoc's shouldering into the stuntwoman had been repeated every chance the maligator got to be around her.

The narrow head finally swiveled to him as Havoc licked his chops.

"But no, you had to get up in her face and lick her. Act like you aren't the killing machine I made you into." He snorted, still thinking about how she'd nailed the acting and stunts. So fluid and confident. "Flippin' traitor. But let's get this clear: I saw her first."

Light flickered and rocks crunched.

Crew pivoted to the door, and in a heartbeat, had his weapon aimed at the person there. Took a breath as the face registered.

Frozen holding the door open, Vienna Foxcroft lifted her eyebrows as she stared at the gun.

He cursed and lowered the weapon. "Sorry." Returned it its holster. "I . . ." Shoot, had she heard what he'd said to Havoc?

Hair down, face aglow, she was a whole lotta woman that stole his breath. "I think they gave you the wrong job. You should work security. Or bouncer."

"I'd be bored out of my skull. I know—I've done both before."

She indicated inside. "May I?"

How in the world was he supposed to get any O_2 with her coming closer? "Sure. Sure." He backed up. Whacked his head against a cabinet. Cursed again. Palmed the dinette table and the back of a captain's chair to his left to give her room.

She stepped up into the RV and was *right there*. In his space because this RV was not a mansion. And she capitalized on it, her shoulder bumping his chest as she gave him a bemused look. "I'll bring a bar of soap next time."

It had been a long day of work. Crew resisted the urge to sniff himself. "I . . . could use a shower . . ."

"I meant for your mouth."

Surprise cut through the tension that she'd called him on his language. Like Mom always had. "Fair." He nodded. "Old habits die hard." Nodded again, trying to think around her green eyes and the memory of those hook kicks. No way she could've showered after her stunt work, yet she smelled good. Real good.

"Mm." She shifted aside just in time for Havoc to go up on his hind legs and plant his paws on her chest. "Oh!" She laughed, hands smoothing down the Malinois' ribs, eliciting a squinty-eyed look of pleasure from Havoc who had his tongue dangling a mile-long.

Cheater. "Havoc, off."

"It's okay," Foxtrot said, petting Havoc's face and ears as his MWD leaned into the lovefest. "You're probably the only guy around I'd let do this. But you're a hero, aren't you? So you deserve it. Maybe I'll bring you a bully stick next time. Or does that violate your no-treats rule?"

There was a bit of a challenge in her question, but . . . he liked it.

No. *She's the enemy, remember?* "I'll make an exception, even though it's cheating. How d'you even know about pizzle?"

"My brother's Doberman loves them." She cringed when Havoc ran his tongue up her face before dropping to all fours.

Havoc then negotiated the RV, licked his water bowl, and finding it dry, gave a dissatisfied huff before he hopped up onto the bed in the back and slumped onto his side with a groan. After retrieving the bowl, Crew filled it with water and noticed Foxtrot moving to the door. "Love him and leave him, huh?"

"Just came to relay a message." She flicked her auburn hair from her face as the beam of a floodlight hit her. "They didn't have your cell number on the group text, so Kerr asked if I'd come and let you know the flight got moved up."

Slowing, confused, he set the bowl back on the floor. Flight? "Sorry, that must be for someone else. I'm just here for the dog scenes."

"Are you sure?" Frowning, she pushed open the door and gave him a look, then Havoc. "I mean, you do know that what we're filming here are just early scenes, right? The majority of the sequences are being filmed in Turkey."

"Tur—" Crew choked. Then laughed. "This your way of getting back at me because I said I was going to marry you?"

Her eyes widened. "Excuse me?"

Okay, so PA Iris hadn't told her. "Never mind. Look, there's a mix-up. I'm just supposed to be here—L.A. That's it. Help out, work the dog, head back to Texas." *Shut up, you sound like an idiot.* "Good luck, though."

She backed up, her expression saying he was wrong, that he'd missed a briefing.

"I'm not an actor, and I've done enough deployments to last a lifetime." He was getting ticked the more he talked, and the last thing he'd do was ship out with the enemy. "Y'all have fun cuz this boy is keeping his boots on this side of the pond."

"Well, you might want to talk to Kerr, because he said you're going. Mentioned a scene with Havoc and a palace."

"It's a mistake."

"Sure. I'll catch you later."

Please, God, don't let this be real. She was just pulling his chain, right? As the door closed behind her, he yanked out his phone, knowing one person could clear this up. Thumbed into his recent calls and selected one. Heard the connection click and then it rang. This . . . this couldn't be happening. Through the window, he watched Foxtrot stroll down the sidewalk and bank left.

"Get your star on the Walk of Fame yet?" Heath teased.

"You said L.A.," Crew growled. "You freakin' said I'd come out here, do this gig, and go home. Tell me I'm not shipping out to the other side of the world."

Silence met his barked words.

Which meant one thing. "You *knew* about this?"

"Got an itinerary update earlier," Heath said in resignation.

"Can't do anything, about it—the contract is signed. Till those episodes are done, you're theirs."

Son of a . . . "I told you"—Crew hooked his hand over his head—"*told you*, I wasn't deploying again." Through the window, he noticed some curious stares. They weren't close enough to hear his words, but he turned around. "It's why we agreed I'd procure. No missions."

"Crew."

"No, this is muffed. I said I wasn't going anywhere. Can't." Hadn't he risked enough already? He needed an inhaler to ease the pressure in his chest.

"It's a *film*, Gatlin. That's it. No contact. No combat."

"Yeah, and you said, 'just L.A.,' but look how that's rolling."

Heath's silence had the weight of an M1Abrams tank. "The only enemy you're facing right now is yourself. You're overreacting."

"Heck yeah, I am. I'm out. Missing a leg, remember? You know my time is limited in the leg. Here, I can hide it. On a plane for fourteen hours, I can't. What if I'm bunked with someone over there? And let's not mention that I've got a dog that isn't certified in anything but stealing the girl out from under me." His boot hit the bowl, sloshing water over the vinyl.

"What girl?"

"Stop changing the subject."

"You changed it, Gatlin," Heath laughed. "Listen, I made it very clear in the contract that you could only work Havoc for no more than eight hours at a time, and that you needed your own accommodations because of the dog. They're in breach of contract if they don't provide those things, just like we're in breach if you bail."

Grinding his teeth, he punched open the screen door. It struck the exterior and slapped back at him. He shoved it again and nearly broke the thing off its hinges. With an excited whimper, ready to work, Havoc bolted out. Crew followed him and paced the small enclosed patio. The Malinois sniffed and marked the entire fence line.

"This sucks, man. Can't believe . . ." He wouldn't bail because he'd never gone back on his word, and he'd let Heath down. "Swear it's nothing more."

"Think of it like a vacation."

He could hear something in Ghost's voice . . . "What aren't you saying?"

"Crew—"

"Give it to me."

Ghost expelled a thick breath. "ABA was recommended to Macleod by Majid Badem."

Crew faltered, his anger frozen by the name, the implication. "The Turk." *It* is *the same guy.*

"Said he wouldn't let the film crew in country without legitimate assets onsite, and when Macleod mentioned filming a dog team, Badem insisted on us."

Us. The ranch. Heath's livelihood. Growling, Crew held his head again.

God, what are you doing to me?

"There's no known threat. It's strictly preventative."

That'd mean it wouldn't be. Trouble always came when you didn't want it to.

"And I don't have to tell you what this could do to ABA if we bailed."

We bailed . . . More accurately, you bailed.

Crew muttered an oath and recalled the bar of soap Foxtrot promised for his language, a memory that plied at his foul mood.

"We clear?"

"Good copy," Crew muttered, irritation surging again. Going to freakin' Turkey when he'd swore he'd never do that again. Never leave U.S. soil. Keep his not-all-there self stateside.

"So . . ." Ghost's long pause seemed to hold a laugh. "Tell me: what girl?"

"Shut up, man." Crew ended the call and slammed a fist into the small table. Regretted it as soon as he heard a crack—the table, thankfully, not his knuckles. Ghost would be ticked at the bill. Served him right.

"Hey, Soldier-boy."

He pivoted, avoiding Havoc who was investigating his destruction, and found Foxtrot standing on the other side of the narrow road that separated the line of RVs. Felt stupid if she'd seen him punch a table.

Holding a water bottle, the enemy now wore workout clothes and runners. How had she changed so fast? "C'mon," she said, cocking her head down the road. "I'll show you a place to work off that anger."

The way he worked off anger wasn't acceptable in most circles. "Thanks, but—"

Havoc sailed over the fence.

Heart in his throat at seeing his dog bolt toward her, he called to her. "Stand still and don't run!" He bolted after his dog, his nub hating him for the action.

Havoc rushed her. Circled her. Came around and slammed his side into her. Again. As if he'd traded handlers. He went up on his hind legs to get more loving.

Pulse staggering as the adrenaline dumped, Crew huffed a laugh. "You piece of—" His gaze rammed into Foxtrot's as he clipped off the curse.

"The gym's this way," she said, pointing to her left. "You . . . need to change?" There was something amazing in those eyes, the way they challenged and invited, lured and repulsed. Called to him yet warned him.

Yeah, big-time warning. *Enemy at the gates, soldier.* He should go back to Texas. Figure out a way to pay Heath back when the film company sued them for breach of contract. Because if he stayed here . . . "Sure," he said, remembering she'd asked him a question. "Give me five."

Holy Moses, he was in trouble because he had a feeling he'd follow this woman anywhere. Even Turkey.

The man had a powerful presence . . . and a whopper of a temper that made her hesitate.

Yep, just like every other man, V. Just like every other man.

Yet it distracted and excited her that he'd followed her to the gym. Tying her hair back, she turned and crouched to the side. Tucked in her earbuds, cranked up the Skillet playlist, then stepped onto the treadmill and activated it. Hit her programmed workout. It inclined and she started running. Mirrored walls enabled her to keep a watch on the others.

Baako and Frode were spotting each other on the dead lifts.

Soldier-boy was working his deltoids. Back at his trailer, he'd been next-level lit when she'd told him about Turkey. She hadn't expected a guy that big and in possession of himself—tenacity, self-awareness, wit, killer smile—to show fear but it'd crawled all over him like maggots on bad meat. Fear was territory she knew really well, so to see it on this larger-than-life guy . . . and then watch him crack a table in half with one punch . . .

What's the story behind that? Behind him?

After a twenty-minute run, she moved to the incline bench, grabbed a thirty-pound weight, and worked her abs and obliques. Her trainer had increased her resistance just last week, so she was moving a little slower. Did fewer reps. Probably looked weak to the sergeant with his Malinois stretched out on the mat at his side.

Traitor. Cheater—that's what Gatlin called his dog when he'd interacted with her. Come to think of it, that dog—Havoc?—had not given anyone else a second glance. Even here, with Frode and Baako trying to bait him, Havoc gave them a "you're boring" look, completely unfazed by their enticements.

But she knew it was more. Havoc was loyal to his handler, to

Gatlin. They were a formidable pair. Even as Gatlin did bench presses, the dog had rolled to where he was closer to the sergeant.

Vienna returned the weights to the rack, then taped her knuckles and wrists.

"'Bout time," Baako said, clapping as he stalked over to the mat, grabbing his own handguards.

With a smirk, she couldn't help but notice Sergeant Gatlin slowing to watch them as he sat on a bench and switched to working his very nice biceps. While Vienna restricted her dating life to a very select group of men—and never one she worked with—she could appreciate a man who displayed clear discipline and took care of his body like Baako and Frode. Though both were good-looking men, Baako was short with incredible upper body strength whereas Frode was wicked fast in running and with his punches. Both had asked her out when they'd first started filming together, but she'd put an end to that fast. Defined her boundaries. Now, they had mutual respect and worked well together. For her, trusting they weren't going to make a move went a long way in her confidence each time she placed her life in their hands during scenes.

Moving around the mat over the next half hour, she practiced knife defense and hand-to-hand, first with Baako, then Frode. The pace increased in intensity, her throwing in some Thai kickboxing to set Frode straight when he got a bit aggressive a couple of times. She held her own, as always, taking a few strategic hits in order to get her own in, when she stepped back, leaned sideways, and lifted her leg. Felt a presence at her shoulder. Faltered but didn't fail. Knew it was Soldier-boy.

She bounced aside as Frode drove in. Vienna angled away, with her practice blade held along her wrist, she swiped. Dragged it over his wide-open abs.

He cursed and growled, coming around, defeated. "Every single time."

She patted the back of his sweaty, bald head. "You'd think

you'd learn."

"Do you always let her win?"

Vienna scoffed at the audacious accusation that rumbled from the sergeant. "They don't pull punches."

Hands on his waist, he nodded to Frode. "He just did."

She frowned. "No, he—" Hesitation made her look at Frode, gauge his reaction.

Brown eyes widened. "H-he's just messing with you, V. Trying to get in your head. Drive a wedge between us."

Seriously? The jealousy thing, that's the tack Frode wanted to use to defend himself? "Are you even serious?" He was pulling punches? How long? She scowled at the sergeant, wondering how he'd figured that out. What his point was. Was he saying she was weak and these guys just went along so she didn't feel bad?

"I have no skin in this game," Gatlin said. "Just observing."

"You think you could do better?" Frode challenged and pointed to the tape that marked the ring. "Step up and put your jewels where your mouth is."

The sergeant smirked as his gaze slid to hers.

Vienna wasn't sure she wanted this fight. But it kinda irked her that his words made her doubt Frode. That trust she'd just been bragging about floundered in the air with his accusation.

"What, you afraid she'll bruise that tatted ego?" Baako sniggered.

Soldier-boy slid his gray-green eyes over her, top to bottom. Weighing, assessing. Then stepped back. "Thanks for telling me about this place. It worked."

Now she felt challenged. "I promise not to hurt you . . . much."

He wheeled around with a broad smile. "Baby, I'd welcome any pain you'd bring."

Irritated with the way he'd so casually called her 'baby,' she cocked her head and eyebrow. Backstepped, motioning to the mat. Wondering at the rapid-fire pace of her heart. The giddy twist in her core when he handed Havoc's lead to Baako, instructed the dog to 'stay,' and crossed that line.

"Want to tape your hands?"

"Negative." He rotated his hand and wagged his fingers, inviting her to bring on the fight.

She wasn't sure if it impressed her that he wouldn't tape his hands, or if it ticked her off. Being careless with safety was a guaranteed way to get hurt. "You sure?"

"Stalling?"

Heat charged through at the accusation. Flew her into action. Leapt up, spun, hooked her heel at his head. He ducked, but even as he was recovering, she landed and drove her leg into his side.

"Oof!" He deflected her next punch. "So not Krav," he muttered as he deflected and snapped in, viperlike, tapping her side, his hand gliding over her hip as he pushed, driving her off-balance.

Shoot. Okay, no problem. Easy recovery. She pivoted and threw a right hook.

He blocked—the move so fast and firm she heard a smack against the tape. In a flash, he slid behind her. Felt his arm hook toward her neck.

Vienna thrust her arms back. Laced her hands behind his neck—the sweaty, very thick neck—and dropped her weight, bringing him down. It wasn't as easy as taking Frode or Baako down. The man was so ripped it wasn't unlike slamming into a wall, but he braced. Went to his knees. It seemed awkward. Almost pained.

She seized the chance, realizing this was one area in which he didn't excel. Felt something very hard crack against her shin. Augh! That hurt. *Don't focus on it.*

His arm circled her waist even as he rolled hard to the right.

Yanked her back. Onto the mat.

No! She would not get pinned or let him put her in a sleeper hold.

She locked her legs around his waist and thrust herself upward. It knocked him off-kilter, though those clamplike hands tried to dislodge her. She managed, somehow—unbelievably—to gain the mount position. Threw punches.

Skilled operator that he was, he held his fists at his temples, blocking his face. Making sure she didn't nail him as she unleashed a flurry of punches—right, left—and he took it.

Was he admitting defeat? Done. Ready to tap out?

Havoc barked. Loud. Repeatedly. But Frode held him back.

Vienna twitched, fearing the dog would join the fight. As soon as she hesitated, she realized her mistake. Realized the sergeant's skill.

Crew's right arm shot forward. Not to strike. It slid along her neck. Latched onto her nape. And he hauled her down and straight into his obliques.

And in rapid-fire succession, he tapped her side and head. Not hard. More like a slap on the face. Humiliating—he made his point: he'd won.

She growled, wilted against him as he ceased sparring. Bent over him, she lifted and slapped his chest—that very firm chest—and huffed at him. But then those gray-green eyes smiled at her. Up close and personal, this guy was drop-dead gorgeous. Strong nose that wasn't Hollywood perfect. Tight cheekbones. A dark blond beard trimmed close accented a rugged jaw. Sweaty, face colored by sparring, he wasn't smirking or smiling. Something serious slid into his expression.

It was then she felt the heat of his hands, resting on her thighs . . . that were still straddling him.

Get off him, V.

A big snout shoved in between them, sniffing up the side of her face, then licking her cheek.

With a laugh Vienna slid off him. "You cheated." She pushed to her haunches, felt something metal knock her ankle—and glanced down but saw only his pant leg—then stepped aside.

"Tell yourself that if it helps." He pulled himself into a seated position and hooked an arm over his leg as he took the dog's lead from Frode. "Thanks."

Self-conscious at the way she'd been considering the perfect stranger—and he was definitely *perfect*—and was drawn to him, she swallowed. Avoided looking at Baako and Frode. She diverted her attention to her wraps, to pulling them off. Unwinding the tape. Noticed her friends' feet still close. She shifted around and moved toward the bench.

A very broad, sweaty chest pushed into her shoulder, slowing her moves.

Soldier-boy reached to help remove the tape. "Good sparring. You held strong."

Vienna jerked her hands free of his and shoved him back. "I don't need you to tell me that." Even as their gazes collided, she saw Frode and Baako high-five and head toward the door. "Think just because you have that dog and tattoos, you need to teach us poor Hollywood actors a thing or two?"

Irritation twitched Soldier-boy's cheek. "Never said that. I only meant—"

"You good, V?" Baako said, hesitating at the door.

"Always," she snapped, locked in a visual duel with the overgrown Soldier-boy before her. At six-two or -three, he was easily two-fifty. All sliced and diced. And pressing into her space. Even now she still felt his hands on her thighs and swallowed. Pushed herself away. Grabbed her water bottle.

"Message received." He started across the gym.

Feeling bad for her kneejerk reaction to what flared between them, she didn't want things to be weird. They had to film together, right? "Hey."

He waved good-bye over his head to her, not turning back.

"I don't date guys I work with."

He kept moving. Never looked back. But as he stepped into the night, she noticed . . . his pant leg. It'd caught on something. A few inches revealed . . . not an ankle or socks, but . . .

A prosthesis.

5

LOS ANGELES, CALIFORNIA

Showered, he sat on the edge of the bed and slid the neoprene sleeve over the nub of what was left of his leg. He'd lost everything below the knee in the explosion, and there wasn't a minute that went by that didn't remind him of the life-altering incident.

Except two nights ago. With Foxtrot straddling him. The look in her eyes that was definitely not sparring fervor. Man, if those guys hadn't been there, where could that have led?

No place good, that's for sure. Well, it might be *good*, but he'd get tanked. Ghost would ghost him. And God . . . well, that was the biggest problem. He'd made a promise to the Maker to jerk the slack out of his roll and get it together. Live right, treat others right. He wasn't perfect—his cursing that Foxtrot took exception with—was proof enough.

Then there was the fact that once she knew he wasn't all there, she'd pass him over like stale chips. He'd wondered during their wrestling, if she had felt the titanium leg when it'd struck her shin. He knew it had to hurt, but there'd been a lot of adrenaline and a lot of *stuff* happening.

57

His mind winged back to the mat. Foxtrot had curves in all the right places and had been *fierce*. He hadn't been sure he could take her down.

From the kitchen area, his phone chirped. He glanced and spotted it on the counter next to the sink and pulled himself upright. Hopped to the sink, using the walls to swing himself there. Leaning against the counter, he eyed the phone. A text from Ghost updating him with the itinerary and promise of supplies for the trip to Turkey.

"You suck," he hissed at his buddy, though he knew Ghost couldn't hear him. He tossed down the phone. As he swiveled, movement out the windows of the RV caught his attention.

Dressed in hiking boots, black tac pants and tank, Foxtrot stalked his way.

"Enemy incoming," he muttered. His gaze hit his boxers, but more importantly—the nub. Oh man. He hadn't told anyone he wore a prosthesis and didn't want anyone knowing. Especially her. What would she think when she found out he was missing his leg? He shifted, glanced to his room. No way he could put the leg on, hike into his pants and shoes before—

"Hey." Her voice sailed through the screen door. "Got a minute?"

Crew tensed. "I . . ." He looked at the door. Stayed in place as he reached down, slid open the lower cabinet door, and positioned himself behind it. "Uh, not dressed."

"I promise you don't have anything I haven't seen before."

Wanna bet? "Wow."

Her eyes widened. "I—" She thumbed behind herself. "Acting . . . not because—" She slashed a hand through the air. "Never mind."

"Done." It was inevitable that she'd find out, but the way she'd stared at him on the mat, hovering over him, ponytail dangling, the curiosity and question of whether it was worth crossing that line . . . That'd been real interest. In *him*, not his disability. The attraction had been born of mutual attraction, not pity. Last thing he wanted from her was pity or sympathy.

Foxtrot wrinkled her nose and glanced back to the road that was filling with people heading to the set. "Fine." She folded her arms and stayed out there. "I just wanted to apologize about sparring."

Two days on set without a word and she wanted to apologize for the sparring now? "No need." He'd never forget looking into green eyes that were alive with passion. First from sparring, then morphing into a look—regardless of the way she'd shut things down between them—of longing and desire. One he really wanted to answer.

Enemy, remember?

"There is, actually. If we have tension between us, it shows onscreen."

"Only tension I have right now is standing here in my skivvies." On one leg.

She smirked, her gaze tauntingly sliding down his bare chest and lingering for a hot second. "You do it well."

"C'mon now, that's not fair after the 'I don't date guys I work with' thing."

She nodded and turned away, then back. "So, we're . . . good?"

"Sure."

"You just trying to get rid of me?"

"There's a draft."

Her lips flattened, and she started walking. "See you on set."

"Yup." A breath whooshed out of him as he watched her head away. He hurriedly pulled the door closed and locked it. Skated Havoc a look. "Couldn't have warned me?"

He hobbled back to the bedroom and dropped onto the edge of the bed. Snagged his leg. Strapped it on. Glanced at his watch. Seven hours and about forty minutes was all he had before he'd need to hoof it back here and get out of it. Thankfully, Havoc provided the perfect reason to excuse himself. If he didn't, he risked blisters or pain, and more long-term problems like infection, which could lead to more loss in the nub.

Dressed, he grabbed the gear and headed over to the set. PA Iris showed him the props—a bite sleeve and suit. She also pointed to a small canopied area. "That's for you and Havoc between takes."

Took them long enough. They'd had to get shade and air in the building yesterday. He nodded. "Water over there?"

"Yes, and some kibble."

"Havoc already ate," he said. "No food during operating hours or he'll get sick." Thankfully, he'd been pexied, so they didn't have to worry about the bloat. "So, who's his first target today? I'll need to review—"

"I am."

Son of a blistered hot dog. Why *her*? He turned toward the woman who was cutting him off at the knees. "The heroine of the show is getting taken down by a K-9?"

Amusement flickered in her eyes. "She is—except I'm taking the hit for her. Right, Felicity?"

Oh yeah. She wasn't the lead on the show, "just" the stunt double.

"Yes, indeed," came the voice with so much syrup he might hurl. "Ohhh, you know what? I should do a take with the dog and handler." She strode toward him, gaze locked on him, not on Havoc. Manicured nails that could likely be classified as lethal weapons dragged teasingly down his arm. "Ewww," she crooned, wrinkling her nose, "you'd look *so* good onscreen next to me."

Crew frowned. What did that mean?

Vale leaned into him, grinning. "Don't you agree, Vienna? The camera would love this face next to mine." She touched her forefinger and thumb, splaying her other fingers up. "Perfection!" Cold hands caught his jaw and turned his face to hers. "Mm, yes." She giggled. "Kerr!"

Crew started at her near-shriek of the director's name.

Huffed a disgusted breath as she turned toward the director, and appreciated more than he should when Havoc snarled low and mean at her. "Leave it." After all, he couldn't afford a lawsuit because he let the beast deal with the woman.

"Can we do this?" Vale asked. "The camera would love this guy and his dog."

"No," Crew said, irritated she just assumed he'd want to participate. "I'm not an actor. They asked for Havoc, that's it. I'm here to—"

"You don't have to talk." Her eyes glittered. "Just work"— palms out, fingers splayed, she made circles at him like she was massaging . . . something—"all this."

Were there puke buckets nearby? This woman seemed the kind used to getting her way, and he didn't want this problem. "I can do that." Be himself? He had that down pat. "I'm no actor. If you want the take ruined—"

"Iris, get him a different shirt," Kerr said.

The PA shuffled toward him and measured his shoulders. "Not sure we have anything this big."

"He's not much bigger than Baako, right?" Foxtrot's cold tone mirrored the ice daggers shooting from her eyes.

"Only by six inches and a solid fifty pounds," Crew groused.

She shrugged. "People don't bulk up to *hide* that, do they?"

Wait. What happened here? Why was she so cold toward him? Was she upset he hadn't pandered to her when she'd shown up at his trailer? How had that made him the enemy? Did she really think he stayed fit to show off his body? Well . . . okay, maybe he did—he'd worked hard to stay in shape after the explosion. Especially when it got appreciative looks like the ones she'd given him in the gym.

Whiplash had nothing on the way things went acceptable to nightmare—Crew found himself in a skin-tight shirt that forbade breathing let alone handling Havoc.

"Oh, darling." Vale sauntered on set with a come-hither look and laugh. "You look like a dork. Not a hunk."

"Come again?"

She hooked those dagger nails into the buttons of his shirt and snapped open four, revealing his chest.

Was there a noose for him to hang himself? "Hold up." He refastened two. "Thought this was PG-13."

"Oh, sergeant," she said demurely, "there is *nothing* PG-13 about you."

I'm going to kill Ghost. Slowly.

"Why don't you put the suit on, Felicity?" Foxtrot stood with her arms folded and her lips tight. "Since you want to be in the scene with him so bad."

"Wait," Crew said again, glancing between the two women. This woman could not handle an impact from Havoc, and as much as he'd love to see her taken down, he didn't want anyone hurt and Havoc ending up in the custody of Animal Control. "That—"

"Oh, yes! We must—Kerr! We have an idea."

Foxtrot seethed.

Command, this is Havoc One, I need an immediate exfil.

"No." Crew drew up straight, no idea what Foxtrot's problem was, but he wasn't going to let anyone put his career or Havoc's in jeopardy. "No, I need someone strong enough to take the impact of a fur-missile. This isn't something to mess around with."

Finally Felicity Vale faltered. Heat made the woman's face look like it was about to slide off. She scoffed. "Fine. But we need to be in the scene together before Vienna gets sweaty in that suit."

That's something Crew would pay to see.

"Okay," Kerr announced. "Sergeant, you okay with this?"

Do I have a choice? He'd already failed in procuring Heath another dog, if he failed a simple demonstration and lost this gig . . . Ghost would be lit. And his buddy had found Havoc, so Crew was chin-deep in debt to him and wasn't going to whine like a baby about anything. "What do I do?"

And that's how he ended up crating Havoc in an airconditioned transport and stepping into a scene, arm hooked around the neck of Felicity Vale, threatening her.

"This is stupid," he muttered as filming began.

"Quiet," she hissed, her thick perfume nearly choking him.

Could he just sleeper-hold her and get it over with? The whole scenario bugged him. "If I have a force multiplier, also known as a working dog, why am I in close contact and holding her hostage? It doesn't track. Easier to just have Havoc take her down."

"Cut!"

Crew clenched his jaw. Adjusted his hat as he put distance between him and the Botox bunny. "Sorry. I just—"

"No worries," Kerr said, looking chagrined and annoyed. "We got what we needed."

Translated: they didn't care about authenticity. Just wanted what looked good. And apparently, today, that was him. But hey, it was over, so that dog could hunt.

"You enjoyed that," Foxtrot said as she took the bite suit.

"Like an acid bath."

She considered him as she stomped into the bite suit, feet first.

Okay, hold up. How did this woman always yank the anger from his chest? Crew held the sides of the suit, hearing Havoc yipping and barking from the transport, demanding to be let in on the fun. He helped her thread her arms into the sleeves.

"Is this going to hurt?"

"Like a mother." He rolled his shoulder and drew up his sleeve, revealing the most recent bruises Havoc had bestowed on him. "No stunt double for me. You sure you—"

She angled aside and lifted up her shirt.

Smoke my brisket . . . Crew's breath caught in his throat as she bared her toned, tanned abs and waist. He'd been so distracted by the very trim, toned, tanned abs that he'd almost missed her point—the bruises. And there was a wicked one. He thumbed its trek in a swath down to her hip. "Ouch."

"*I am* the stunt double," she said, shoving down her shirt and swallowing.

Tucking aside the curiosity about where else she had bruises, he shook his head and zipped the suit. Took her hands and placed them together near her core. "Hands like this above your belly button"—he tipped her arms out slightly—"elbows out to make sure he targets your arm."

Her lips parted and she stilled.

Crew smirked, very familiar with that expression. "Reconsidering?"

A touch of fear hit her beautiful face but she jutted her chin, embracing the challenge. "No."

Holy fluff, he was in love.

No, no. *Enemy, numbskull.* "Run straight and fast." He forced his head back into the game. "When he hits you, don't fight it. The impact will likely spin you around and/or take you down. You can tug and fight him, but be warned—this is playtime for him, and he takes it very seriously. The more you resist, the harder he'll dig in."

After a brief, disconcerted look, she nodded.

"Don't worry. I'll be right there to call him off."

"I'll be fine."

"I know you will."

Questions bounced in those green eyes as she peered up at him.

Not sure what that was about, he gave her a pat, then retrieved Havoc from the trailer. "Okay, Dude. Look . . . yeah, enemy, right?" He had to concede . . . "Maybe we both like this one, so . . . don't kill her, okay?"

Ears straight up, Havoc homed in on Foxtrot. Despite the affinity the Malinois seemed to have for the woman, right now, he was all business. He'd hit several guys, but somehow it felt like a gamechanger that he was going after Foxtrot. Not because she was a woman, but because she was . . . Foxtrot.

"Sergeant," Kerr called, "we'll want some closeups of Havoc biting. A few times sailing through the air. Tackling her."

Which meant each time would feel like a sucker punch to her. More bruises. "Understood." As they lined up the scene, Crew patted Havoc's side. "Ready?" Trying to push his emotion down lead to get the MWD amped.

As soon as Foxtrot stepped onto the set, Havoc's body went taut, snout closed as he let out an eager whine, instinct and training locking him onto the suit.

Crew gave her a nod and she started running.

Havoc lunged, barking, snapping. Demanding to be released. When she created a gap of about fifty yards, he released the Malinois.

Havoc surged forward, his powerful chest base enabling him to dig in with his claws and haul himself forward. Average Malinois in a full-run could reach thirty miles an hour. He tore after his target with a vengeance, body rippling with unrestrained fervor.

Concerned for this impact and for Foxtrot's safety, Crew trailed his dog, reminding himself to stay out of the camera's way.

Havoc went airborne. Sailed into Foxtrot. The impact echoed across the set. Knocked the breath from her—and from Crew.

He held his breath until he saw her go down. Feared she'd land on her back and crack her skull, but the girl had a natural instinct and beauty to her moves. She rotated and angled her body. Thudded to the ground. Bounced.

Yanking her backward, Havoc did what he did best—he thrashed his head. A primal instinct to break the prey's neck. But with the training to grab an arm or leg, they ensured no lethal injuries. There were SOF and SEAL dogs out there with different training, but Crew hadn't been looking to hone a killer, just a protector.

The cameras zoomed in, one on a track flying in for a closeup.

Though Havoc saw the intrusion of the vehicle, he didn't break his hold. Wouldn't break it. Vienna managed to get to her knees. Whacked at Havoc—not any harder than Crew did in training—and let Havoc dig in.

Incredible. She was a warrior. Lethal. Vicious. Beautiful.

"Cut!"

Crew darted in, caught Havoc's collar. "Havoc, out!" When the dog gave another thrash but didn't let go—it was then Crew saw Vienna wince. He hauled the dog straight up, forcing him to release. Nothing hard or violent. Just a measure the dog invariably found non-negotiable because he wanted to breathe. The Malinois unhooked his canines from the padded suit.

As soon as Havoc unlocked his jaws, Crew released the upward pressure and looked to the stuntwoman. "You okay?"

Cringing, Foxtrot climbed to her feet. "Yeah . . ."

"You sure? You look—"

"Kerr, how was that?" She angled around him with a glower.

They both looked to where the director and the producer sat hovering over a screen. Then a thumb came up.

Foxtrot shoved Crew. "*Don't* baby me." She unzipped the suit and tugged it down to her waist, accepting a water bottle from the PA. Man, the woman had it going on a million ways from Sunday.

"I'd never dream of it." He knew she could take down the best of them—almost got the better of him on the mat, even with all his training—but she also had a lot of defensiveness happening there.

Her gaze skidded to his, then back to the work. "What's next?"

They did a take from the platform, then shots of Crew restraining a frenzied Havoc. Had Crew toss the KONG a few times to send Havoc after it.

Full workday in, Crew knew his leg couldn't take much

more. The sweat and strain were rubbing it raw. "Pardon," he said to the producers, "Havoc needs to call it a day. Getting hot and worn out."

Kerr glanced at a device, then nodded his approval.

"Hey, heard you were ticked about going to Turkey," Baako said as he trotted up to him.

Crew skated a glance to Foxtrot—she's the only one who could've mentioned that—then smoothed a hand over Havoc's skull. "Should've read the fine print on the contract." His fingers met someone else's—Foxtrot was stroking the velvety ears.

"Oh, you read, too?" she snipped.

Gaze connected with hers, Crew started at the venom in her tone. What on earth? He had no idea what burr had gotten under her saddle, but he was done. Besides, his straps were pinching and he felt the rub on his nub. Time to check out.

"I should get going," Crew said. "Havoc needs to eat and cool down."

"Yeah, like someone else," Foxtrot said, narrowing her eyes at her friend.

Should've stuck to his rule—only four-legged females. At least they were consistent. This was why he wasn't into dating. Too many hidden rules he couldn't figure out or that changed based on a situation.

"Hey," the lankier Frode said. "The cast and crew are going out to the clubs before flying out tomorrow. Interested?"

Not remotely. "Cool, thanks for the offer, but the beast needs to rest."

"You or Havoc?" Foxtrot challenged.

Seriously? Crew could not get a bead on the woman. Married one day, divorced the next. He tugged his ballcap. "See y'all in the morning."

Iris hurried to his side and extended a manila envelope. "Kerr said you could ride with the lead cast to be sure Havoc has what he needs. Details are in here. We'll have the crate and everything onboard for you."

He should be grateful, but this was a lot like getting spun up. "Thanks." It meant complications with his leg. Humiliation. Firming his grip on the lead, he headed back to his RV. So ready to get out of the prosthesis. Rest his nub.

Havoc let out a half-whimper and pressed his side to his leg.

Appreciating how Havoc was always attuned to him, Crew dragged his hand over the narrow, silky skull. *This!* This was why he'd take a four-legged girl over a two-legged on any day of the year. Dogs were simple, devoted to their handlers. Mals could be a bit psychotic about it, but he'd take that over the second-guessing his every move and action with Foxtrot. Or any woman. Just too much work.

6

THERE WAS SOMETHING TO BE SAID FOR RICH, POWERFUL FRIENDS. OR security advisors. The luxury jumbo jet they boarded for the flight to Turkey? Well, even Vienna's father couldn't afford this. Or wouldn't. There were eight cabin/bedrooms, and flanking each of the two main stairs connecting the upper and lower decks were smaller bunkrooms that slept two each, sturdy accordion curtains providing a semblance of privacy from the gangway. Between the cabins on the upper level was a long stretch of space that served as a lounge with six recliners in front of a massive flat screen, two tables fore and two tables aft, and in-between, couches and tables.

While most traveling on the jet had bedded down, Vienna eyed Frode, who had rigged his gaming device to the big screen and was playing some bloody game with a white-haired character.

She burrowed into a recliner and called her dad. When it went to voicemail, she left a message. "Hey, just me. Wanted to check in. Give me a call if you get a minute." She thought to ask how things were going, but he'd always admonished her not to

69

talk business on calls. And she wasn't ready to mention the trip to Turkey yet, though she was pretty sure his security team kept him updated on her every move. "Okay, then. Love you. Bye." What was this vote about anyway?

She pulled up her browser and did a search for UN Council votes and stilled at the results that populated. Whoa, this was serious. She hadn't expected much, but it seemed a significant effort to impose sanctions against Syria for some security and human rights violations was coming to a boil. Seemed the votes on the council were divided and threats had been lobbed. No wonder her dad had been so tightlipped and worried about her—he was treading dangerous soil.

Don't worry. He knows what he's doing. And he had a private security team.

Yeah, but what about all the other people? What if—

Something whizzed past her head. She yelped and flinched. A second later, a blur of fur flew after the object.

Vienna rotated and came up, peering over the lounge area as the Malinois sailed upward and snatched a black toy from the air. He rebounded off the lavatory door and pitched himself around. Skidded to a stop. And started back.

Vienna couldn't help but smile, looked to the right, where Sergeant Gatlin stood crowding the gangway, just outside the cabin he shared with the dog.

Gatlin met her gaze for a second, then diverted his attention to the dog and patted his leg. Cold and unresponsive.

I deserved that. Sinking onto the sofa across from the recliner, she felt bad about totally shutting him down, snipping at him. So petty. But watching him flirt with Felicity had just gotten under her skin. The actress was beautiful, and everyone acted like she could do no wrong. But she was fake as Frode's knockoff Italian loafers. Couldn't he see that? Surely he wasn't shallow like most of the guys in LA. Or . . . was he? With bodybuilding and tatts invariably came a certain . . . attitude. She might not have gotten inked, but even those in her profession had a particular kind of pride, arrogance.

Though Gatlin had muscles and tatts, he seemed different. Friendlier. Intense. But the way he'd distanced himself after her snippiness, been curt with her . . . Drastic difference from the guy she'd sparred with, wondered what it'd be like to kiss him. Saw as she straddled him that he'd been thinking the same . . .

Guess his interest wasn't real. Should she apologize? Wasn't giving up her cabin on the plane enough?

Havoc trotted up the plane, his paws thumping steadily as he closed the gap between him and his handler. As he swept into view, his beautiful brown eyes spotted her. He diverted toward her. Hopped up onto the couch and stuck his nose in her face.

Vienna dropped back against the couch with a laugh as the Malinois invaded her personal space and planted a paw on her chest, sniffing her mouth like a fiend, hauling in scents around his black rubber toy that made him sound like a K-9 version of Darth Vader. She breathed slowly, guessing this was his thing. He tracked scents, so maybe that's how he figured out life, too.

"Havoc, come. Heel." The firm command demanded obedience, and Havoc used her chest as a launching pad.

She gusted a breath as he leapt away.

"Sorry." Crew was already turning into the room. "He has no personal boundaries."

"Like most guys."

Without a word, he ordered his dog into the room and ducked through the door, his muscular frame oddly dwarfing it.

She'd really made a mess of their . . . What? What was it? Connection? Interest? Why did she care that he was so cold toward her now? It was better to keep the guy in his place, not get hurt . . . Not fall into the ruse of dating. Only way to be sure she didn't again end up trapped.

Yet somehow, she found herself standing outside the door to his cabin. A door that stood ajar. The mechanical *shink* and *clinks* of him cleaning a weapon. For a fraction of a second, she saw his leg . . . the dark gray and blue one. Made of some metal or plastic. So it *was* a prosthetic. She'd have never known if she hadn't seen it. But it stole her breath, made her wonder—

"You going to stand out there all day?"

Caught, she swallowed, nudged open the door as he shifted on the bed where he'd worked on the weapon. Adjusted his pant leg so the prosthesis wasn't showing. He stowed his cleaning gear.

Now that she was here, she had no idea what to say. What to talk about. "Why do you hide it?" *Anything but that, you idiot.*

"I don't hide it," he growled, shifting even more, until he was perched on the edge of the bed, the gun barrel resting on the thigh of his good leg, hand braced over the knee with the prosthesis. "Just don't advertise it."

Feeling self-conscious for him, she nudged the door to—not closed, but enough to afford him some privacy. "Can I ask what happened?"

"Can't really stop you, can I?"

Oy, she'd really angered him.

He eyed the chair she'd assumed, then looked down. "Minefield. Three surgeries. Eighteen months of physical therapy."

"Sounds painful."

He grunted and shook his head as he ran a rod through the barrel. "I'm alive, that's what matters." He shrugged and set it aside. "Or so they tell me."

She drew up her pant leg and revealed a bruise. "I'd wondered what gave me this."

His gaze skidded to her leg. "Sorry."

Vienna laughed. "Please. It was a fair match."

Slowly, he looked at her. Earnestness etched the weathered lines of his face. "It was. A good one." He reassembled the weapon and stowed it.

Last time he'd said that, she'd rebuffed him. Felt embarrassed at how much she was attracted to him, especially with Frode and

Baako watching. Then her snippiness after his shots with Felicity. "I . . . I wanted to apologize . . ."

"No need." From a sheath at his ankle, he drew out a dagger. Then he retrieved a stone from his pack and started sharpening the blade.

"There is," she insisted. "I feel like I should explain that when most people find out who I am, they suddenly want to be friends, just so they can get an introduction to my parents. Usually my dad."

Crew adjusted his ballcap and guzzled water from a protein shaker bottle. "Why?"

She eyed him, surprised. Did he seriously not know? Oh gosh. If he didn't . . . why would she tell him? Make things worse? "My mom is Amelie Wolffe."

His left eye narrowed then he returned to sliding the stone over the blade. "Should I know that name?"

She sniffed a laugh. "Only one of the most famous actresses of the eighties."

"Huh."

"You really don't know her?"

"Negative." He eyed her and shifted, lifting his leg onto the bed, leaning back against the wall opposite the door. Seemingly relaxed, he let out a stiff breath. Was his leg hurting? "And your dad?"

"What about him?" Why did she feel defensive now? Because she feared him saying he knew her dad. That his interest in her was like Steffan and Frank. Brant.

"You said people wanted an introduction to your parents . . . plural . . . so, Dad?"

She swallowed. Here goes nothing. "Horace Wolffe."

He held the stone and dagger in the same hand and faced her, with a thoughtful look. "Are we talking about the senator involved in the UN vote?"

Heart racing, she studied him. Wondered what he knew. *Why* he knew that.

"Isn't he a billionaire or something?"

Her stomach plummeted. Just like Brant—almost word for word. "I should go." She stood and went to the door.

"Foxtrot. Hey. Hold up."

She faltered, her stomach squirming at the way he called her that. Turned back, sad. Frustrated. Scared.

He seemed to be hiding a smile. "I only know because Baako told me when he accused me of stealing your cabin and you away from him."

"*Me?*" she balked. "I am not his! I'm not anyone's."

Crew's cheek twitched in a smile. "I know."

Expelling a breath, she shifted toward the bed. "I can't figure you out."

He narrowed his eyes. "Same. Can't get a bead on you. Nice and friendly one second, biting my head off the next."

She shoved her hair from her face, unwilling to admit to jealousy. But it'd make sense to keep her justification focused on abuse. "Look, I just . . . I'm used to people working me to get to my parents, so I . . . I was rough with you . . ."

"Rough? With me?" He leaned back against the hull of the plane and adjusted his cap. "I'd like to see that."

She rolled her eyes and slumped onto the edge of the mattress.

"And thank you"—he motioned the knife around the room—"for the cabin. I don't know why you did that, but it's appreciated."

Lie, she told herself. "I knew you'd need the space with Havoc . . ." She looked at where his hand massaged his thigh. "You keep rubbing your leg. Is it painful?"

He started to turn away.

Vienna touched his arm. "Sorry. I don't mean to make you uncomfortable."

"Less people know, the better they treat me."

"Is that why you didn't tell anyone on set?"

"I requalified for Special Forces after the explosion, so I don't need special favors or exemptions from people who don't know—"

"Soldier-boy."

He stilled. Met her gaze.

"I don't care about the leg or how it happened."

He pressed his lips and glanced at the stone and dagger in his hand. "If only that were true."

She frowned. "You calling me a liar?"

Squinting, he considered her. "Why'd you give me the cabin again?"

Busted. She could lie, but he deserved honesty. "You're right—I gave up the cabin because, besides needing room for Havoc, I sensed you'd probably want privacy. After we sparred, I noticed your pant leg was hiked up—saw your . . . prosthesis." She cocked her head. "You haven't told anyone about it, so I guessed that you didn't want anyone knowing. In order for that to happen, you needed your own space."

Had she been wrong to do it?

"That was . . . thoughtful." His head bobbed in a nod. Then he looked at her. "Thanks."

And something happened there that suddenly made things feel both intimate and awkward.

"How'd you get into the stunt business?"

The question came out of left field. "Teenage rebellion." She laughed. "I despised all the pretentiousness and ridiculousness of my mom's fame. People stopping her—us—on the street. In airports, restaurants. We couldn't go anywhere without the insanity invading our time and lives. Amusement parks were a nightmare. Last Christmas we were mobbed trying to get on the new Star Wars ride."

"Wait, so she's still acting?"

Vienna snickered. "Yes, but don't bring up the fact she's now playing the *mom* in movies rather than the heroine." She laughed and picked at the coverlet on the bed. "When I discovered I had a knack for acting, I was so angry. Last thing I wanted was to end up like her, do that to my family—if I ever had one. Had a boyfriend once and um, got into martial arts." No need to elaborate on Brant or the nightmare of dating him and why exactly she needed MMA. "My mom was so livid when I got my first stunt gig with a film. She called it uncouth, unrefined."

Crew angled to her with a furrowed brow. "Has she *seen* you in action? Your skill? It's poetry!"

Heart aflutter at his praise, she felt heat rising into her cheeks. Realized few people saw *her*. "No, she . . . she wouldn't dare acknowledge such a lowly profession. Or fuel my so-called rebellion."

He gave her that knowing look again. "What'd your dad say?"

She giggled—and hated herself for it. "He paid for my training," she said with a nod. "Hired this master right out of the Philippines to give me private lessons."

"I think I like your dad."

"He's a good man," she said with a sigh. "A bit archaic, and he's crazy about my mom, even though they live totally separate lives . . . but yeah. He's good. We're close."

Weapons laid out around him, he focused on cleaning, sharpening them.

"What about you?" She scooted back against the wall and sat catty-corner to him. "What's your story? Parents? Siblings?"

"Still alive," he said, repacking his gear bag while Havoc shifted in his crate. "One younger sister. We didn't have much. Dad bailed after mom's third affair. Mom dumped me at Aunt Susie's when I was twelve. I went into the Army at 23. Here I am."

Vienna laughed. "That's like the Cliff's Notes of the Cliff's Notes."

He shrugged. "My life doesn't have the glitter and glamour that yours did."

Just like every other guy, thinking her life had been one of ease and riches. "Maybe, but it doesn't mean mine has been easy."

"Never said that." He worked the dagger again, then skated her a look. "You don't have to be defensive with me. I know your skills, Foxtrot."

Her pulse misfired, realizing this guy—a near stranger—saw her more clearly than people who'd known her for years. "Do you know my name, though? You keep calling me that." She tilted her head. "Why?"

He shrugged again. "Just sits right."

What did that mean? She studied this muscular man and his raw intensity. Direct, rugged. "I like you—I mean, the way you cut it straight. Don't give me bull or flatter me. Or try to get in with me or my family."

Gatlin considered her, threading a fuzzy thing through a barrel. "First day at the studio lot, I saw you filming a scene." He drew up his pant leg, revealing the prosthesis. "You were . . . a beast." He undid a strap. Removed the leg. "Flattery is insincere and designed to further the interest of the person giving it. I have no need to do that. You have the skills."

Vienna swallowed, watching . . . listening. Aware of the incredible trust he was laying in her lap as he removed his prosthesis in front of her.

"Every time you were on set, you were a force to be reckoned with. Beautiful, strong. Could tell you knew Krav with an intimate familiarity. Weren't just acting. I told Iris I was going to marry you."

"What?" She wrinkled her nose and felt a rise of giddiness she'd never felt before.

He adjusted, his stump stretched between them. "I didn't know your name or your parents. Just knew you were fierce and beautiful."

In other words, he saw me. *Not my name. Not my family. Me.* It made her marvel, realizing she'd been seen. "Are you always this blunt?" Because she had a feeling he was testing her. There'd been a shift in his expression when she said she'd liked him.

"Nah." In his tone rang some sarcasm. "I'm holding back. Don't want to offend you, scare you off."

She laughed. Loved that he made her laugh. "I don't scare easily." She stifled a yawn, even as she relaxed on the mattress beside him. "Do you always wear the prosthesis?" Man, she had no filter tonight, did she?

His expression tightened. "Can't. Get about ten to twelve hours out of it before I just need to take it off."

"Because it's painful?"

"Sometimes. But more than that—it's not good for skin to be in constant contact with the sleeve. It needs to breathe, so there's risk of blisters, infection . . ." He nodded to his leg. "At home, I use a wheelchair to give it a rest. It's a trade-off."

"You seem the type of guy who would have a rocket-propelled wheelchair."

He snorted.

"Is it hard to wear it?"

He hadn't met her gaze, and she worried it was bugging him to answer questions. "It's . . . different. Each person has to establish a new center of balance with the prosthesis. And that depends on so many factors. A lot of people think it makes me run faster, but that's sadly not true."

"Does it offend you that I asked?"

"Wouldn't have survived Special Forces if I were easily offended." He shifted himself onto the bed and leaned against the wall beside her. Massaged his thigh, his arm flexing into hers each time.

"Special Forces . . . Did you deploy a lot?"

"As often as they'd let me. Didn't have anything at home worth being there for." His expression tightened. "When I enlisted and told my dad, he threatened to ground me." He chuckled. "I was twenty-three."

She laughed, but then recalled . . . "You said he'd bailed . . ."

"He did." A nod. "But we had an understanding. Stayed with him once I got into high school. We tolerated each other."

Without warning, Havoc sailed onto the bed and wedged between them, half stretched over Gatlin. Vienna laughed and scooted over to give him room.

"What're you doing, man?" Crew chuckled.

With a self-satisfied groan, the Malinois adjusted, forcing himself into a comfortable position. Didn't care that his nails were digging into her thigh as he stretched.

Laughing, Vienna gave him even more room. Then the beautiful working dog angled onto his side. Rotated until he was belly up, head and shoulders across her legs. He stretched his paws into her face, as if pointing to her. Her hesitation at petting him washed away, and with another laugh, she rubbed his belly.

"What is this?" Crew balked.

Vienna smoothed her hand down his ribs, feeling the muscles that were sculpted as much as his handlers. "I think it's sweet."

"No no. That has to stop." He scooted aside, pushing the dog. "I didn't train him on the sly for a year for him to get called 'sweet.'"

"Aww, leave him alone. He's happy." She leaned down—

"No." Crew's amusement vanished. "Sit up."

Startled at what she heard in his voice, Vienna complied.

"Don't crowd his face. He's sensitive to being cornered."

"Oh, sorry." But she couldn't help the smile as she considered his MWD. "He's so cute like this, it's hard to remember he's a trained killer."

"Havoc's pretty even-keeled but his one trigger is crowding, feeling cornered. Never put your face near his. He gave more than one SOG buddy a painful reminder, and gave me one, too." Indicated to a scar that cut across his beard in front of his ear. "Violent affection."

Her gaze traveled down his thick, vein-bulging neck to where a tattoo stretched over ridged flesh. A tattoo over a scar. The thought pushed her attention to the sleeve of tattoos.

Obvious military ones intertwined with some she couldn't quite discern. What looked like feathers peeked out from under his sleeves. "What's that one?"

He drew the sleeve up and let the eagle scream at her. "In its talons is a flag that drapes down my back."

"That's a lot of ink, a lot of story there."

He nodded, his pinky stroking Havoc's left hind leg that stretched toward him. "Do you have any tatts?"

"No, I decided it was just easier not to have to cover them up for filming."

"But you don't mind bruises."

She didn't miss that his gaze went to her waist. Recalled his reaction when she'd showed him the bruises from hitting a crate wrong. Showing her trophies to Baako and Frode was second nature, so she hadn't given it a second thought showing Gatlin until she saw that spark in his eyes. "Hazards of the trade."

He reached over and took her hand, rotated it, revealing her scar. "And this?"

Vienna swallowed at his touch, but more—she just didn't want to hatch that story. Not now. Not when things were going so well. "A hard lesson."

He gave her a sidelong glance.

"But I don't begrudge it," she said. "It's part of why I got into MMA . . . and how I got into film."

"The boyfriend from martial arts . . ." There was something dark, dangerous in his eyes now. "He a part of that story's why?"

How in the world had he connected those dots? Alarmed, she tugged her hand free. Did not need him reading her like that. It led to controlling . . . She petted Havoc, who stretched his legs *allll* the way into her face as he again groaned. And she felt his handler's eyes on her still. Knew he was the type to wait a decade to hear that story. "I . . . he . . ." Crud, she could *not* go there. Too soon. Too . . . awful. So many things in that part of her life that she wasn't proud of.

Crew folded her hand over his. Tugged it to his chest, a move that made her suck in a breath as his gray-green eyes locked on her. "I don't need to know the story to know I'd kill the guy if I met him." He nodded. "Whatever happened, you're better for it. This woman who grew out of that? I'd want her on my team any day of the year."

Startled, she peered up at him. Surprised. Stunned. Those words felt like something that should come out of a longer relationship, not one only a few working-days old. But then they'd somehow formed a comfortable, familiar friendship. It was . . . fun. He was fun. Two years with Brant and she'd never heard those words or felt so . . . at home.

She imagined Crew wanted a response, but what was she supposed to say to something like that? Could barely process his utter belief in her. Or was this simply slick talk to get in her good graces?

Just. Like. Brant. "I appreciate that."

Crew smirked. Gave a slight nod.

This was too familiar, too . . .

He's different. But was he? "I should go." No idea how to get the MWD off her, she angled her legs to the side, and he slid off with a morose groan. At the edge of the bed, she felt Crew catch her fingers. That's what Brant had done, too.

"Hey."

Vienna jerked back, noting Havoc rotating upright at the same time she stumbled back to Crew. Braced herself on his shoulder as she realized he was at the edge with her. He was so tall, that sitting down still gave him an advantage. Hating the way her heart raced, she stared at him, that ballcap shading his eyes. Somehow that panic, the fear, bottomed out as she fell into that steady gaze. Without thinking, she tugged up the bill of the cap so she could see him better.

"Thanks for the cabin." His gaze held hers then darted over her face. Took in her eyes, her hair, her lips . . . "It was generous of you."

His eyes were so beautiful, and there was an anticipation there. "Sure." She traced a couple of scars at his temple and cheek. Touched the one from Havoc at his jaw where his beard was kept trim—not thick or bushy. But clean. Soft against her fingertips.

She should leave. This couldn't end well. He was just here for filming. He'd be gone in a week. And she wasn't dating. Ever again.

His hands rested on her hips. Stole her breath as they slid up to her waist.

Her stomach swirled realizing his face was coming closer.

No . . . *hers* was lowering. To his. For a kiss. One she very much wanted.

Holy Moses, what're you doing?

Crew wanted to stand. Take her into his arms. Kiss her senseless. But he'd removed the prosthetic leg. Couldn't come upright without assistance, his balance and center too off. And he wasn't going to pull her onto the bed, no matter how much he was tempted. Her rosy smell washed over him, and he homed in for the kill.

Havoc let out a low growl, startling him out of his idiocy.

Foxtrot shifted back, sucking in a breath.

With the way the maligator rotated upright and trained on the door, hackles rising over his spine, Crew knew his partner had detected someone in the gangway. "I think we have a visitor."

She looked there even as she shifted in front of the bed, blocking him from the door. "Baako."

Correction: blocking someone's view of his amputated leg.

Appreciating her effort, Crew brought Havoc to heel, which deftly concealed his legs.

The door nudged open.

Reading Havoc's body language, Crew snagged the collar, halting the fur-missile's midair launch. Restrained his MWD snapping at the intruder. Had to admit he took a bit of guilty pleasure at the guy's reaction—the way he tripped over himself to back up. Hit the bulkhead. "I've got him," Crew said with more than a little amusement.

"You need to keep that dog under control," Baako blubbered.

"What part of 'I've got him' isn't under control?"

"Did you need something?" Foxtrot asked imperiously.

Baako curled a lip at him, then diverted his attention to Foxtrot. "You had said you wanted to go over the scenes."

"It's almost three in the morning," she balked. Then, with a look back to Crew, she softened her expression. "I didn't realize it was so late. I'll let you rest." She touched Havoc's head. "Both of you."

Should he be irked that she was bailing on him for the other guy? "Good plan. 'Night."

Foxtrot moved into the gangway, and Crew bit back a curse. Wanted to throw something at the door. At Baako's head. Havoc leapt onto the bed and slumped against Crew's leg with a disgruntled huff. "Me too, buddy. Should've let you take a piece out of that guy, huh?"

What is happening to me?

Mom, Rina . . . it'd never worked out. They just used or abused. And who needed the headache of trying to integrate a relationship into their life? He should know better and had no desire to be shackled again.

But man, he'd wanted that kiss. Wanted her.

How did the loser end up with the girl every time?

Annoyed, he resecured the prosthetic leg, headed down to the hold to let Havoc relieve himself, then returned. Free of the leg again, he grabbed some rack time. Or . . . tried to. Seeing her standing over him, coming in for the kiss, would not leave him alone. Not to mention the story about her daddy being with the U.N. security council.

Invariably, being the operator he was, trained to recon and gather intel, he scoured the web for her dad—Horace Wolffe. Dude had a prestigious heritage with purported connections to more than one line of royalty, several generations deep. Self-made billionaire in weapons and space technology, Wolffe got into politics in order to make key changes to legislation handcuffing said tech companies. Never having served in the military, he was buddy-buddy with key brass and more than a few joint chiefs. Strategically positioned, he was a shoo-in for the U.N. Security Council. Impressive and explained a lot of the chutzpah in the guy's daughter.

But what made Crew more than a little uncomfortable were the rumblings between the UNSC and a certain country known for snubbing its nose at other countries and the U.N., whose authority they rejected. Syria felt like a game-changer.

The violent assault of tires on tarmac yanked Crew from his sleep. No idea when he'd fallen asleep, but he came up and found Havoc watching from his crate. Flying and travel were old hat to the Belgian Malinois.

Shoot. Crew had meant to grab a shower before they'd hit ground. He sniffed his arms and decided he wouldn't scare off the natives, but he should keep his distance until he could shower at the hotel. He put his leg on, then packed his ruck. Did a press check on his Sig, then holstered it at his side and drew his shirt over it. Done with that, he let Havoc on the bed while he collapsed the crate, then muzzled the beast. Shouldering his ruck, he stepped out and let Havoc take the lead. The four-legged hero darted to the lounge, no doubt looking for his new crush—Foxtrot. There, they found the cast looking out the windows and groaning.

Crew lasered onto Foxtrot, who slumped into her seat and shook her head.

Iris strode toward him.

"What's going on?" He shifted the ruck to a better hold.

"Paparazzi on the landing strip. Somehow word of our

arrival got leaked." Her gaze glittered. "That extra *gift* in your gear—you have it?"

The Sig. He cocked his head. "I'm strapped."

With a nod that said she was glad but still nervous, Iris sighed. "I'm glad you're with us, Sergeant Gatlin." She indicated to the door. "Vehicles will take us to the hotel, but they're having trouble getting through."

"I could make a hole."

She smiled. "I'm afraid that might draw more attention than we'd want."

"Likely."

"Hey." Drew hustled up to her. "Badem's teams are en route. It'll be cleared up soon."

Iris wilted visibly. "Thank God."

Badem. The Turk.

Crew did not like this. It was starting to feel too much like an op. He preferred to stay under the radar and dogs invariably drew attention.

Ten minutes later, six black SUVs lurched into the airfield. The drivers barreled through the waiting masses, who yielded to the vehicles, not wanting to be roadkill. The Escalades lined up on the tarmac, forming a barrier between the paparazzi and the plane. Likely as good as they could manage.

Once the cabin doors opened, Crew hung back and let the others deplane.

As she came toward him, Foxtrot eyed him. "You know you can leave that duffle for the crew to bring to the hotel."

"Safer with me."

She considered him, as if she wanted to say something. Was she remembering the near-kiss?

Dude, step off. Remember? Enemy at the gates. Doesn't end well.

"V." It was Baako again. Demanding her attention. "Let's go."

Hating that the guy gave her commands the way he instructed Havoc, Crew tightened his jaw. But he kept his gaze on Foxtrot, who seemed to take in the situation in much the same manner. Why did she put up with him?

She swung that green-eyed gaze to Crew. "You coming?"

He checked his six and verified they were last aboard. "Right behind you."

"So you can admire the view?" Baako sneered as he deliberately planted himself between Foxtrot and Crew.

"So I can *protect* said view." If he ganked this guy, would anyone notice? Care?

Baako turned and got in his face. "Look, GI Joe, you're way out of your league."

Tell me about it. But not in the way the guy suggested. He could take this guy out and nobody would notice. He let his chest fill and pressed it into the guy's space. Started walking, forcing the guy to walk backward. Backward. Toward the door.

Baako stumbled. Then wheeled around, tripping in his haste to exit the plane. Hustled down the steps to the tarmac.

Tucking aside his smile at the way he'd made the guy run, Crew deplaned and swept the scene. A sea of photographers swelled beyond the line of SUVs along with film cameras, news vans . . . Too easy for an unfriendly to try something. "Havoc, ready?"

The Malinois' snout closed. Ears swiveled to *armed and ready* as his perceptive gaze scouted the area.

Keeping a safe distance, Crew patrolled the line of vehicles, then back. When familiar green eyes turned to him, he realized Foxtrot had been on his stealth radar. He hadn't intended to pause near her, but he had. And he liked the way she seemed to have a bead on him, moving closer. Staying there.

A man in a slick suit and sandy brown hair and beard approached him. Trailing a half dozen people, including four bodyguards, the man deferred to a stunning woman with golden hair and a shy smile that did nothing to hide her very perceptive gaze. It was really interesting to see the man everyone revered defer to the woman who looked like a supermodel. What was their story?

Havoc watched the man, but didn't break behavior, snarl, or cower. He seemed as confident as the man himself. Which was interesting as the Turk veered toward Crew with definitive intent that made everyone watch.

"You must be Ghost's man." The Turk stuck out a hand as the words and implication arose—this was the guy who'd recommended A Breed Apart to the producers.

When Havoc came to all fours, Crew gave him a silent signal and accepted the handshake. The guy hadn't offered his name, so he'd follow suit. "Reckon so."

He laughed. "So much the operator." He motioned to the woman. "I am Majid Badem. Welcome to my country!"

7

ÇIRAĞAN PALACE KEMPINKSI HOTEL, ISTANBUL, TURKEY

Sitting in a chair out beneath the glorious sun, feet on the edge of the seat, Vienna closed her eyes and soaked up the gorgeously warm rays. The scent of the Bosphorus Strait to her left made her muscles relax. Sun, water . . . a palace—what wasn't to love? They'd had two days of chilling before things were going to crank up.

"Did you see the way Badem was kissing up to GI Joe when we landed?" Baako's jealousy-filled words ruined the moment. "Acted like he was so special."

He is.

At the unbidden thought, Vienna straightened, lowered her legs, and returned her attention to the chicken salad. What was happening to her? Barely a week with that guy and she . . .

"I did not think that man would kiss up to anyone," Frode said as he bit into a sandwich. "Have you not heard of him before, the Turk? He is known. Though he holds no political office, he has powerful connections."

"Pretty obvious considering where we're staying this time."

Vienna indicated to the grounds around them, the swimming pool to the left, the entire two-level structure across from it that housed the bar, the incredible center gardens that divided the formal palace from the grounds. "Not many people can secure an entire hotel palace for a film crew."

Baako tapped her arm. "How was your suite? Mine was dope!"

"Over the top," she muttered, thinking of the marble floors, tub, jetted shower, canopied bed . . .

"But like home, right?" Baako grinned. "I mean, that's what your home is like."

"My dad's home," she corrected.

"Same thing."

No, her home was a condo not far from the studios. Vienna faltered, surprised at the way he dismissed her correction. She doubted the sergeant would've done that. Which was dumb to think she knew him that well.

"This woman . . . I'd want her on my team any day of the year."

Taking a bite of spinach and chicken, she recalled his words, his faith in her. That near kiss. The way being there, staring down into his face reminded her of falling off a stunt scaffold . . . right into a healing hot spring. His eyes had been so nice, his smile so inviting.

"Hey!" Baako smacked her arm.

Vienna jerked away, then returned the slap. "What's your problem?"

He scowled at her. "I asked if you'd heard about the party."

"What party?"

"The Turk is hosting a celebration for the cast and crew. There'll be VIPs and local actors from the area," Baako said in a way that warned he was repeating his words. "He wants to welcome us in style."

"He did that with setting us up in this palace."

Gorgeous and glittering beneath the sun, Çırağan Palace was glorious, its cream stone a perfect contrast to the blue-green waters of the strait. The 19th Century Ottoman imperial palace boasted 310 rooms and had been converted into a luxe 5-star hotel with views overlooking the Bosphorus Strait. Even now, despite the devastating earthquakes in 2023 that claimed forty-seven thousand lives, Turkey exerted her magnificence, her unrivaled will to survive.

"I bet this palace is stunning at night," Vienna said quietly, her heart still affected by such a terrible loss of life. "It'd be amazing if Kerr could integrate it into the scenes to honor those who died and the resilience of this country."

"Heard that's already happening." Frode chomped into his chips then gave a cheeky grin. "Hey. Saw Gatlin head into one of those big suites upstairs with Badem and his girlfriend."

Surprised at the redirection of the conversation, Vienna shifted her gaze to the second level before she realized it. Scanned the dozen or more windows. She hadn't seen him since they'd separated on the tarmac, when he left with Badem and she'd climbed aboard an SUV with Frode, Iris, and Baako. Why was he giving her the silent treatment all of a sudden? Regardless, they had work to do. Stunts to rehearse.

Two days later, after a series of lighting and dry-run scenes in which there'd been little time to chat, she was sitting at the same table with them again, this time, chomping into a lamb gyro. "Anyone know where Crew and Havoc have been?"

"They've been working them up in one of the rooms," Frode said.

They hadn't even been at dinner, which had made her sad. She'd thought they'd . . . connected. "I'm—"

Cheers and laughter erupted in the near distance. Several of the crew hurried through the arched gate and down onto the terraced steps in front of the hotel and next to water. A din rose from that direction.

"What's going on?"

"Dunno." Vienna abandoned her salad and followed the others to an area overlooking the lower section on the side of the palace. A crowd swelled in, forming an arc-like barrier that hemmed in—

"Crew."

He was working Havoc in demonstrations for The Turk and his entourage.

She negotiated her way closer, watching as the beautiful woman with The Turk hid something while Crew huddled to the side, distracting Havoc from the process. A second later, he straightened. "Havoc, seek-seek-seek!"

The Malinois zigzagged around the crowd, sniffing and tracking the scent. He pretty much beelined to the girlfriend, huffing breaths as he went up on his hind legs, searching for his KONG. She laughed but held out her hands, diverting him.

Havoc dropped back onto all fours, tracking . . . tracking . . . He sat in front of a crate, and Crew reached into it. Produced the KONG, which he flipped into the air. Havoc sailed upward and snagged it.

The crowd cheered and applauded.

Crew came around and his gaze rammed into hers. Was it her imagination or did he falter before that smirk slid into place?

The Turk wandered toward him, clapping. Indicated to the side where a man was dressed in a bite suit. Apparently, they were going all-out with the demonstration. They motioned the crowd back.

"Leave it," Crew instructed, and the Malinois dropped the KONG and stood, staring intently at his toy, snout not two inches away. Instead of retrieving the toy, Gatlin led the dog to the far side, but he was looking at someone and said something.

Iris. While Gatlin drew the MWD around and focused him on the guy in the bite suit, the PA calmly walked over and retrieved the KONG. She then walked behind the sergeant, depositing the KONG in the hand he held behind his back. He slid the KONG into his pocket, all while amping the dog.

He gave a sharp nod and the dog took off running.

Vienna couldn't help but smile, remembering what that had

felt like. The adrenaline rushing through her, the fear of the unknown. The solid punch in the back when he took her down. Flipped her around.

He did two more demonstrations, then walked to the Turk, and shook hands. As he did, a handful of men joined them. These weren't locals or VIPs. The newcomers looked like security. But not uniformed security. The way they moved, heads up, hands at their sides, as if daring someone to mess with them. At one point or another, each man scanned their surroundings. Definitely security.

Who were these men?

Crew grabbed one of the guy's hands. Pulled him into a shoulder hug, patting his back. *He knows him.*

Either way, she wasn't part of that set. He seemed very much in his element, and she didn't belong there. Different worlds. Her dad had said that more than once in her teen years when she wanted to date the bad-boys. He'd been right then, and he was right now.

She moved back up the steps toward the arch into the courtyard of the hotel, thoughts heavy with confusion and . . . hurt. Iris . . . he sure seemed comfortable with her, enough that he trusted her to help in the demo. She'd seen them talking on the plane, too. Was the mousey girl more his speed?

"Felicity!" a girl exclaimed.

Cringing—the woman she doubled for was the last person she wanted to encounter right now—Vienna glanced to the side. Just in time to see a pretty Indian girl hurrying toward her, dark eyes alive.

"I can't believe it's Felicity Vale!" She all but body-tackled Vienna and wrapped her in a hug.

"Uh—"

"I can't believe it's you! I love your shows."

"I—"

"You're *so* good," the girl crooned, stepping back and holding Vienna's shoulders. "I can't believe you're still with Tadeo."

"I'm not—"

"But I mean, who wouldn't be? He's so gorgeous!"

"I'm sorry but—"

"Mahmoud! Come on!" The girl waved a guy over. "Take our pictu—"

"Vienna!" Crew Gatlin's commanding voice punched into the horrible, humiliating incident, pulling her attention in his direction. "Vienna!"

She turned, felt the girl doing the same, and saw Crew charging toward her with Havoc.

"Whoaaa," the Indian girl breathed at the sight of him. "I would totally ditch Tadeo for that."

Vienna's brain wasn't working. Maybe it'd checked out of the hotel and headed back to the States.

"Hey, Baby. I didn't think you were going to wait up." He strode straight to her. No qualms, no hesitation. Hooked an arm around her waist, drawing her snug against his side and pivoted around, expertly forcing the girl to take a step back. His head dipped toward hers.

"Sorry." Before she realized it, Vienna angled upward. Her face closing in on his. For a kiss. As if that was normal, every-day for them. Shocked at her stupidity, she planted a hand on his chest to stop him. Herself. Had he noticed she'd nearly kissed him?

The spark in his eyes as he dragged his attention away from her to the girl warned—as usual—the guy hadn't missed a thing. "Who's this, V?"

Mind experiencing major whiplash, Vienna blankly looked at the girl. "I—"

"Omigosh." The girl covered her mouth, bowed away, her embarrassment acute. "I'm so sorry. I am. So. Sorry. I thought you were—" Mortified with her mistake, she scurried off.

Dizzy from the rapid turn of events—from the hilarity of the girl's reaction, from the fact Soldier-boy rescued her, to the now-awkward moment—she stared after the girl. Had no idea what to do or say. Did not want to look at Crew and see that mischievous know-it-all look.

"Does that happen a lot, them mistaking you for Felicia?"

She noticed his intentional mistake of the name. "More than I care to admit."

Crew nodded. "I'll make sure I'm around more."

Frowning, she glanced up at him. "Wha—" Wait. That mischief was there.

"In the off-chance you happen to *not* veer off the kiss that'd been incoming thirty seconds ago."

Shock and the whole surreal incident made her laugh. And it was good to laugh. Better than stand there feeling awkward.

"Maybe we should practice," he said with a wink. "You know, so it isn't forced or awkward next time."

"There won't be a next time."

"You sound so sure . . ."

Shaking her head and fighting off a smile, Vienna started toward the hotel, aware he was still with her. "There's a party coming up." Why did that come out of her mouth?

"Heard about that." He looked ready to hurl.

"Havoc might need a rest before you do more demonstrations. I'm sure Iris would be glad to help."

Confusion flickered through his thick brow, and he cocked his head. "Hold up. Is that jea—"

"Take a shower, Soldier-boy. You need one."

"Agreed—a cold one."

He'd never met The Turk before, but the name alone commanded respect. Maybe a little fear and a whole lot of fangirling, *if* one were prone to that. Three days in his company had grown a deep admiration for the man. Now Crew knew that every piece of intel about this man—notorious not only for how he protected his people and country but for his work in the field of intelligence and operatives—was real, right down to the tailored suit, killer sense of fashion, and his American girlfriend. The security detail might impress someone who'd never been with an ODA, but Crew knew the guards hovering near the power-hitter were tracking every move and breath around them. Simply put, don't underestimate Majid Badem.

The Turk ran a hand over the leathered back of the wheelchair. "I hope it does not offend."

Offend? "No . . ." Crew just couldn't believe someone had thought to do this.

"Good." The Turk inclined his head. "I appreciate the presence of you and your dog. Both of you came highly recommended from Ghost, though I was a bit annoyed that he would not bring his Trinity."

"He's committed to the ranch and growing it, his family." Crew nodded to the chair. "Thanks, again."

"You are welcome." The Turk let himself out and closed the door. Left Crew more than a little bewildered.

He eyeballed the wheelchair—which would definitely help— and thought about the man who had delivered it to his suite. How had he known? Why did he even care? Nobody in Crew's life had ever cared about his needs. Not even Mom. She'd taken care of her boyfriend's needs, then remembered him and dumped him with his dad's sister. Aunt Susie had taken him in, but he'd simply been an extra mouth to feed. The only time someone had thought about what he needed was the recruiter who'd signed him up.

And well, Foxtrot had . . . She'd sacrificed her privacy on the plane so he'd have the accommodations necessary, considering his prosthesis and Havoc. Couldn't figure out why, but that was as unsettling as the Brits calling cookies 'biscuits.'

There was an odd mix of irritation and relief chugging through his veins as he thought of using that during his downtime. Stay in his room and do recon, and nobody would be the wiser to him using a wheelchair.

Had to admit that Havoc's little on-the-spot demonstration for the Turk had his skin crawling. He'd felt like someone had been watching him the whole time. Then he'd seen that local dive bomb for photos with Foxtrot, thinking she was the BotoxBunny . . . Foxtrot had looked so flustered and frustrated, not able to get a word in edgewise, so he'd acted on his feet. And she'd almost kissed him.

That was twice now. He hated how much he'd wanted both kisses. Defied every self-imposed barrier to dating he'd erected. But she'd stopped. Looked like a scared rabbit when she realized what she'd nearly done.

Maybe third time would be the charm?

What happened to Enemy at the Gate?

He groaned.

So . . . yeah, what made Foxtrot stop? There was no denying the mutual attraction between them, and he knew his reasons for keeping it platonic, but what was her story? Had to do with that guy he'd vowed to kill if they ever met, right? It couldn't be good. And it'd ticked him off to see vulnerability on a face that exuded spirit 99% of the time. Whatever scumball had done that to her deserved a come-to-Jesus meeting with Crew's fists.

He'd always been a protector. Looked out for others. So that's what this was, right? His insatiable need to protect those he cared about. Do what nobody had done for him. Just SOP, right?

Nope. Couldn't lie to himself. This felt like . . . more. Which meant it required distance. That had always worked.

Then again, he'd never felt *this* about anyone. Not even Rina.

Okay, God, look . . . I swore off dating. It'd been best for everyone. *But now You plant this woman straight-up in the middle of my path outta here. You know how relationships work in my life—they don't. So, maybe help a guy out?*

Crew hauled himself into the shower and scrubbed down. When he emerged, he faltered at finding a suit hanging over the back of the door. Didn't appreciate the idea of someone else being in the room when he was in his birthday suit. He glanced at Havoc laid out on the bed. "Tell me you brought that in." Then he spotted the tux bowtie, apparently for his Malinois. He held it out to Havoc. "What do you think?"

Havoc trotted over, sniffed it, then snatched it out of his hand and shredded it.

"Never been so proud," he chuckled. "Can I do that to my monkey suit?" But the threads of this olive-gray suit warned it'd cost a pretty penny. Which likely meant it was from the Turk. And no way in tarnation he was angering that guy.

An hour later, showered, limb put on, and dressed, he and his four-legged hero headed down to the ballroom. Music pulsated through the air, mingling with the din of chatter and laughter. Glitter and pulsing music.

Not my rodeo. Crew growled. Maybe he'd bail. Call in sick. In fact, now that he thought of it, Havoc needed a bath.

As if in response, Havoc shifted forward—like he wanted to escape the thought itself. In truth, he'd spotted a legend.

"Gatlin." Tyson Chapel, founder of Damocles, a private contract firm, crossed the grand foyer in black slacks, an olive shirt, and a suit jacket ready to bust its seams. The Damocles team leader looked as buttoned-up in ridiculousness as he felt.

"See they dressed you up, too. Come to bail me out?"

The man—equal in height, stature, and skill—met him in a shoulder hug/back pat. "Already tried bailing, but the Turk promised to make the stay worth it."

In other words, the Turk wanted their presence and firepower known if he'd hired Damocles. Which he apparently had. His whole plan to just do the gig and get back to Texas was way off course. Had The Turk hired Crew as well? Man, he'd feel like a heel after all the guy had done for him. "So, what's going on?"

Chapel's dark beard twitched. "Repaying a favor."

"To?"

He arched an eyebrow.

The Turk. Of course. "Is anyone *not* beholden to him?"

"If they aren't, he changes that. Watch yourself." Chapel

nodded. "What about the hottie I saw you lip-locked with?"

"Nobody saw that because it didn't happen."

Chapel's brown eyes pinned him. "Because she stopped you. Still trying to figure that out—you eating someone's face and them *not* wanting it. Not exactly SOP for you, is it? I mean, it's like something out of the Twilight Zone."

Hating the rub, Crew gritted his teeth. Met the guy's discerning gaze with his own fierce one. Back on track. "Is the Turk expecting trouble?"

"You know the answer to that," Chapel said as they made their way into the grand ballroom where skin and money were on full display. "Expect trouble so when it comes, you're prepared."

"But Damocles . . ." Crew scanned the crowd. Only as disappointment trudged through his veins did he realize he'd been looking for Foxtrot. "The team here—that's a lot of preparedness."

Chapel considered him. "It is."

A swath of glittering black and silver hugging perfect curves swirled into view, smothering his brain, his ability to move or think. "Holy Moses . . ."

Auburn hair half up, half down, Foxtrot shut down every other woman in the place who tried to act like they were pretty. She wore one of those Indian dress things with a cropped tank, bare midriff, and wide skirt. "I am in trouble."

"You know what happened to the last guy who went after her, right?"

Crew frowned. "Do what?"

"It was all over the news—her dad."

"What was?" How had he missed that when doing discovery on the man?

"Some guy dating her disappeared," Chapel explained. "Month later, guy washes up in Miami. Without his hands."

"Give me a break."

Chapel shifted in front of him. "Do yourself a favor, keep a wide berth."

Was he kidding? He considered the Damocles team leader, his blue eyes, scar along his nose and jaw, compliments of an ambush that nearly took his life. Noticed the tight set to his lips. "You're serious."

"Horace Wolffe didn't get where he is because he's good people. He has money and power and throws them around to make things happen." Chapel arched an eyebrow to where Foxtrot stood with Baako. "Doubt the apple falls far from the tree."

"She's nothing like that."

"Maybe, but you're already sans a leg. Don't want other parts of you to go missing, too."

"Funny."

"I deal in truth and violence."

Over the guy's shoulder, Crew saw Foxtrot shooting him glances. Chapel wasn't mincemeat—if he said something, Crew should pay attention. Including figuring out why the Turk would want so much firepower here. "What're you doing here? What's going on?"

"That attachment you've already formed—"

"What attachment?"

"The one that has you angry right now." Two more operators manifested around Chapel. "Shelve it, Crew. I don't want to bring a body back to Ghost."

"Considering that'd be my body you're referencing—same." Crew shouldered around the guy, annoyed and feeling . . . off. What was going on? "Later." He stepped to the side.

"You okay?"

Smoke my brisket. How'd she come up on his six without him sensing it or Havoc alerting him? "Yeah." He kept moving, looking for something to drink. Something not alcohol. He just didn't want that headache tonight. But he also wanted distance. From her. From Chapel and his warnings.

Foxtrot caught his arm and swung in front of him. "What's

going on?" Her makeup was soft yet accented the beauty she possessed in spades.

"Nothing." He'd half expected Havoc to respond, but the lug simply pressed his shoulder into her leg again, looking for affection.

"Hey." Her tone was sharp, hurt, snagging his gaze on hers.

And he lost himself again. Wispy strands of hair framed a face made for the silver screen, not behind-the-scenes stunt doubles. Add the glittering jewels adorning the very modest neckline of the cropped tank that danced with sequins—

"You look like the sunrise."

Concern smoothed from her face, replaced by a smile. "I wondered if you'd noticed."

"I'd never miss anything about you." Except the whole murdering-daddy-thing, apparently. That coldcocked his attraction. Dropped it to the floor. Well, maybe to his knees, because this woman was a whole lot of amazing.

"But you're upset."

He huffed. "It's nothing." Where could he get a—

Her hand slipped into his. "C'mon. Let's dance."

Stunned, he balked. "No. I don't dance." Why hadn't Havoc interfered at her yanking him in the other direction? In the ballroom, she swirled to face him. Lifted her arms and started dancing a jig, that midriff taunting him, reminding him of his thumb trekking over the bruise there that had faded.

I am dead.

He swiped a hand over his mouth. "I . . . I can't—"

Her arms encircled his neck.

Crew groaned. "This is so not fair."

She palmed his face, redirecting his eyes to hers.

Holy smokes, she was beautiful. And perfect. He let his hands settle on her waist—and tensed, too aware of her warm, silky-soft skin.

"Who is that man you were with?"

Bleeding me for information? That was a reality check. "A

buddy." Warnings rang in his head—giving her Chapel's name could get back to her Dad. Was that really even a thing, her dad killing people? Why did Crew feel like he was holding a pressure plate instead of her waist?

"What's going on?"

"Nothing."

"Three strikes, you're out."

He frowned. "What?"

"You've said 'nothing' three times." She arched an eyebrow. "I didn't believe you the first, second, or third time." Pink lips, green eyes, gorgeous olive skin . . . How could she be the daughter of a kingpin? He should just ask her, but how did you ask a girl if her dad killed her boyfriends who got too frisky?

At his side, Havoc whimpered.

It gave Crew the out he needed. "I should take him outside. Time for a break."

"You or him?"

He released her and stepped back. "Yeah." *Just stick to the gig, Gatlin. Get the job done, go home.* He didn't need a headache. Hadn't he already warned himself this wouldn't turn out well?

With a double click of his tongue to command Havoc, he stalked out of the room, his center of gravity wildly off. Not from the prosthesis either. Why? The one girl in a million he'd wanted to entertain . . . and her dad was the Godfather.

He walked Havoc up the green that stretched between the pool and the bar. Let him relieve himself, then angled around the pool to the far side, taking in the water. Leaned on the wall that divided the strait from the hotel grounds, noting she stood a half-dozen paces to his five.

"*What* is going on?"

At her sultry voice, Crew let out a moan of frustration and lowered his gaze to the wall, tightening his grip on the lead.

"And if you say 'nothing' again," Foxtrot warned, "I will kick you in the head."

"Promise?" He huffed, cursing himself for so easily falling

into flirting with her again. He'd been able to walk away from every long-lashed offer thrown his way. Except hers. Which told him he wasn't strong in this area—fending off the girl of his dreams. And holy cow, that's what she was, wasn't she?

Run, Forrest. Run.

"Talk to me. Please."

Had to get rid of her. Send her back inside to her BFFs Baako and Frode. "What do you care, Foxtrot? You told me in L.A. you don't date guys you work with."

She strolled toward him and leaned her hip against the wall lining the bay. "And that did absolutely nothing to deter you from pursuing me." She squinted at him. "Yet *that* man says something to you and—"

"You know." He turned to her. "Don't pretend you're clueless."

She started . . . stilled. Went quiet.

"You wouldn't be so up in my face if you didn't know, so don't put this on me as if I've changed or something."

"But you have changed." She shivered and jutted her jaw. "It's about my dad, isn't it?"

That simple acknowledgement was a loaded one—evidence that Chapel wasn't wrong. That some poor sap had swam the gulf without his hands. That this woman before him was a ticking bomb.

Never thought anything could be worse than Rina . . . Or mom choosing Walter over him.

"And you just took what he said and accepted it as fact?" She folded her arms. "Without talking to me, without asking. Decided to toss me aside?"

"Toss you—" He scoffed. "Unbelievable. According to you, I never had you to toss you aside. You've shut me down every time I've tried to get close." He held his hands out to the side. "Which way do you want it, Foxtrot, because I'm getting whiplash. You know what? Let's just call this what it is—a bad idea—and move on."

"Right." She shifted away. "Okay." She sounded off . . . her words piqued. Hurt.

Something in his periphery snagged his attention at the same time the lead snapped taut. Shadows shifted and moved, morphed from the darkness, and spirited across the courtyard as a low growl filled the air. Lights winked out.

"Fine. I'll leave—"

"No." Crew hauled her back.

"Get off—"

Clamped a hand over her mouth, feeling her squirm in his hold. "Quiet." Then she stiffened, and he guessed she'd sensed the trouble, too. Scanning the area, he urged her behind him and drew Havoc to heel. Drew his weapon even as he freed Havoc of the muzzle and lead, counting at least a dozen unfriendlies silently crawling over the wall from the water and into the crowds.

With a savage snarl, Havoc lunged to his right. Dug into an unfriendly who'd come up behind them.

Crew pivoted and fired rounds even as he heard chaos erupting behind him. Screams. Shots. Saw three black-clad men wearing balaclavas rush them. He double-tapped the nearest two and felt more than saw another collide with Vienna. His gut clenched, realizing she'd frozen. The guy took her to the ground. Aimed but knew the risk of hitting her was too high. Why wasn't she fighting him? The girl had killer skills.

Fur-missile flew. Impacted the attacker's spine, knocking him off Foxtrot, who scrambled to her feet. Her expression was blank, terrified.

Crew slid toward her. Caught her shoulder. "Hey." He waited till her eyes came to his. "You got this."

"Wh-what is happening?"

"Trouble." He nodded. "Do what you know. Don't think— just do it." He crouched and disarmed the man, stocking up on weapons to defend them.

Her lips parted, still lost in the shock and moral dilemma, but then her brow knotted. Determination came into sharp focus. She nodded, then her eyes widened. "Behind you!"

Crew whipped around, protecting her, and sighting the body flying at him. Eased the trigger back once. Twice. Behind him, he heard meaty thuds and cracks. Scanning the dark for more combatants and not seeing any, he swiveled to Foxtrot.

A flurry of soft gray billowed in the air as she nailed the guy in the head with that wicked spinning hook kick. As the guy went down, Crew sighted him, fired, and advanced. Fired again. Again.

Havoc was at his side again even as a shot whizzed past.

They needed cover and fast. "There," he said, pointing to the side of the building that housed the bar. "Go!"

In a crouch, she scurried to the side. He moved backward, protecting their six. He backed up until he felt her hands on his spine. Peered around the corner and took down another fighter. What the heck was going on? Why were there so many? What were they doing, targeting a film crew?

"Who are they?" Foxtrot asked around a rustling noise.

"No idea." He reached back. Caught her hand, set it on his belt. Curled her fingers there. "Stay on me."

"Crew, there!" With her free hand, she pointed to his left, where another four fighters were spilling over the wall. He fired. *Pop! Pop! Click!*

The three fighters diverted toward them.

Crew pivoted. "Go! Run!"

Face alive from the fight, she faltered. "But we can fight."

"Too many. Go, go." He felt his limb rubbing in the sleeve but gritted past it. Moved backward off property, invariably trusting Foxtrot to guide him across the street and up into an alley where darkness would shield them. Weapon trained on the route from the palace, ready to deliver unfriendlies into the afterlife, he saw a small mound of something where they'd been standing. What was that? No time to figure it out.

Relief chugged through him when nobody gave chase, and

walked, head on a swivel. They banked north onto a street. Spotted three men standing near a truck.

Vienna sucked in a hard breath and stopped short.

In the time it took Crew to assess—the men were smoking but the bulges and glint of barrels told them they were armed; so not innocent bystanders—Havoc lunged into action. Sprinting across the dark street at the men who came off the truck. His four-legged partner targeted one unfriendly. The other two drew weapons and fired at them.

Crew took cover behind a car, glancing back to confirm Foxtrot doing the same. "Stay down," he threw over his shoulder, then rose and fired at the incoming attackers.

The nearest guy fired—but the second time the gun jammed.

Crew dove at the man. Grabbed him around the waist and knocked him onto the street. Drove his fist into the man's face. Felt fire singe across his abs—a blade! He hissed. Hooked the guy's neck and locked his hands. Squeezed hard.

Grunts and wheezing hissed along his face. Howling emanated from the target Havoc was wrangling. Shots fired. Havoc yelped, and Crew wanted to check on his partner but couldn't release the guy yet. Felt the man's strength fading . . . fading.

Crack. Thump.

Grunts and strangled cries came from Foxtrot.

Crew nearly let his target go. Couldn't. Finally, the guy surrendered the fight. Went limp. Crew rolled, snagging the man's weapon. Pumped two rounds in his chest, ending him. Swung his aim at the fight Foxtrot was engaged in. Saw her doing her thing, knife in hand.

Where had she gotten that? And when had she changed into yoga pants? Guess she had both under the skirt—that must've been the mound he'd spotted back at the side building. A stream of moves and strikes. The guy punched her back. She stumbled backward. Her head cracked on the wall behind her. She groaned and her eyes seemed unfocused.

"Foxtrot!"

She blinked in the split-second the guy launched at her. Muscle memory likely told her to drop, and he crashed into the wall. With her preternatural skill, she whipped around and caught him. Arms around his neck. One hand gripped his right shoulder. The other his chin. She yanked in opposite directions, killing the attacker.

As the guy crumpled to her feet, she huffed a breath. A smile wavered there. Then . . . realization. Mortification over what she'd just done.

Crew rolled and saw Havoc still engaged in a battle, bleeding. He fired once, twice, three times at the attacker, who finally fell limp. Using a nearby car, Crew stood. Had to work to regain his center of balance. He eyed Havoc, the sound of that yelp still ringing in his ears, and assessed his wound. Messy, bloody, but thank God—only a graze. Crew then focused on Foxtrot, who stood staring at the guy she'd neutralized. He took her hand. Pulled her on. "We need to move."

It was better to keep moving, to get away from the bodies. Get to safe ground. He took them up a couple more streets, then banked right. Put at least two klicks between them and the men. Found a spot in an alley where they could wait out the trouble. He positioned Foxtrot behind him, Havoc at a heel, and peered between a van and a closed shop down the incline to the Çırağan Hotel. Watched emergency vehicle lights blur toward the hotel. The telltale sound of gunfire died out.

At his back, Foxtrot's breathing shuddered. He felt her hands on his back. Then her nose to his spine. Then a chill as her touch vanished. He heard her thump softly against the wall. Fabric dragged. A quick check showed her sliding down to a crouch. Her sobs deepened.

Weapon ready but aimed down, gaze on the chaos at the Çırağan, he let her cry. Let her process and grieve the life she'd taken. Ached for her, knowing what that first kill was like. Grieving was good. She needed to work through it. And though he'd do anything to undo what had happened, to remove from her the burden of having taken a life, he knew she didn't need him up in her business, babying her. She just needed room to grieve.

About the time things quieted at the Çırağan, he heard Foxtrot sniffle. Shudder out a long sigh. He heard her breath closer to his ear and glanced over his shoulder. Found her standing close, wiping her face. "Ready?"

She nodded.

"Let's move." They erased half the distance, moving quietly and quickly. They were about three hundred yards out when he shifted them beneath a tree, wanting to watch the happenings at the Çırağan for a while to insure they weren't walking into trouble.

"Something wrong?"

"Better to take it slow than make a mistake and pay for it."

In the twenty mikes they stood there watching, more emergency vehicles cleared out, leaving only a handful. That probably wouldn't change much with all the chaos and bodies.

"Crew."

He angled his head in her direction while he eyed the six or seven men now on active guard with assault rifles. Had to be Damocles, right? Had they lost any men? Who'd been the target of the attack?

"*Crew.*"

He started, realizing he hadn't responded the first time. "Yeah?" Nothing seemed like trouble down there, so they'd make an approach slowly. He stepped aside. "Okay, let's—"

She touched his shoulder, pulling his attention to her.

Was something wr—

Foxtrot pushed into his arms.

Surprise lit through him, but he let her in, coiled his arms around her. Cradled her head against his chest.

She curled into his hold and shuddered a few times.

"It's okay," he murmured, hoping he was right but knowing

she needed to hear it. "You did good." He cringed—remembered the last time he'd said that to her. Simple fact was she'd trained in street fighting for years, but training and real-world experience were two very different things. "I'm sorry you had to do that."

Her cries were soft at first, then deep again. "I killed someone."

After holstering his weapon, Crew smoothed her hair. "This may not help, but you had to. It was you or him."

"I don't—" She trembled. "I don't know how you do it . . ."

"Each one takes a piece of your soul."

Hands tucked beneath her chin, she looked at him, green eyes taking him in. One hand edged up and traced his beard. "Thank you for being there, for not . . . babying me."

"You're too tough—"

Her lips were on his.

His heart jacked into his throat, mind ricocheting. *Step off, step off . . . Godfather's daughter, remember?* "Hey," he managed around a kiss. "This . . . It's adrenaline . . ."

Easing back, she met his gaze. Then tiptoed up. Hooked her arms around his neck. Kissed him. Solid. Urgently. No propriety between them.

Strategically, this was not good. In every other way, it was perfection. But he didn't want her getting shot, so he rotated around and pressed her against the wall near the tree. Told himself to get moving. And . . . deepened the kiss and hauled her closer. Cupped her face and helped her funnel that adrenaline into something very passionate.

Havoc let out a groaned objection at being left out.

Laughing, Foxtrot broke the kiss but tightened her arm around his neck. Left only a breath between them. Visually traced his face. Kissed him once. Twice.

"So, this is what you were doing while our lives were on the line!"

8

ÇIRAĞAN PALACE KEMPINKSI HOTEL, ISTANBUL, TURKEY

Flanked by four armed soldiers, Vienna skipped a step to stay in stride with Crew, who held her hand as they returned to the hotel. Havoc trotted ahead, and crazy how she found comfort in the dog's presence now more than ever. He'd been so hard-hitting, no hesitation each time gunmen confronted them. Who had been everywhere. In the hotel, along the water, and in the streets. What had it been about? Why?

And the fallout . . . falling apart. She didn't want to think about it. So she focused on the chaos around them. The way the guards, weapons up, gazes ever scanning, stalked forward. She also didn't miss the smirks and fist-bumps the guys had given Crew at first. Clearly about her. About them kissing.

It wasn't one of her finer moments. First, she'd sobbed like a baby in front of him—well, technically *behind* him—then kissed him. She'd only intended it to be a quick "thank you," but being that close, the electricity that zapped her at being in his arms, the way his gaze hooded . . . it'd sucked her right in. Desire erupted—not so much sexual as a . . . fulfillment. A deepening.

109

It sounded better, but was that her reaching, trying to justify her actions? After Brant . . .

No, she'd never felt this way with Brant. And Crew Gatlin had ingratiated himself into her life so well that she felt as if she'd always known him.

Cliché much, V?

When they reached the side entrance of the Çırağan, the doors swung open under the power of local fighters—the Turk's men, she guessed. Moving swiftly, they banked left and came around the side corridor that led around another turn and dumped them into the grand foyer before the ballrooms.

The man who'd said something to Gatlin that made him withdraw from her strode toward them with his beard and hair dark against an olive complexion. He gave her a stiff look, then focused on the sergeant. "Shoulder?"

"Graze," Crew said with a shake of his head, never releasing her hand, but also not really acknowledging her . . . even when they diverted to a set of closed doors guarded by more men.

The man eyed her. Noted her yoga pants. She would not cringe or explain—she'd had them under her skirt because she'd felt naked in the formal attire. And thank God because wearing a billowing skirt while fighting gunmen had nearly gotten her killed.

He grunted as he talked with Crew. "What d'you see?"

"Three locals held position half klick north in a blue Toyota pickup."

"Exfil?"

"That's my guess. Any idea what this is about, Chapel?"

"Negative."

"We"—Crew's gaze swung to hers, filled with a ferocity but also . . . pride . . . concern—"neutralized them and hoofed it around to where your man intercepted us."

"Yeah." Chapel—an interesting name—stroked his beard, an apparent move to hide a smile. "Bennion almost missed y'all. Thought you were locals getting hot and heavy in the alley."

Crew tightened his jaw. "Inappropriate."

"You're right. It was—you were being shot at. But since you've never looked twice at a woman since I've known you, I won't remind you of the idiocy of your actions."

Now, Crew seemed ready to hurt someone. His shoulders squared.

Vienna felt her stomach clench and shifted.

"Chapel—"

With a sniff, she fought her irritation toward the man. "Is that why you tried to get him to ghost me over my dad?"

Chapel's expression darkened. "No, that'd be because operators need all the facts before engaging the enemy."

"*Enemy?*" she balked.

"He's baiting you." Tone quiet and low, Crew angled his gaze toward her, but he stopped short of looking at her. "Enough, Chapel."

She sniffed. "Anything but."

Was that true? The comment about Crew not showing interest in a woman before? Should she be disappointed that he kept company with men like this grouch? How could she when her own father had a notorious reputation, even if it was built on shadows and mirrors.

A side door opened, pushing a din of chatter into the area where they stood. She saw several people she recognized. Was the entire cast and crew in there?

"Vienna!" Baako's voice reached her before she saw him—he rushed through a cluster of people. His gaze struck Crew, then their conjoined hands.

Why that made her self-conscious, she could not say. Yet she slipped her hand free of Crew's, earning a stern look from him.

"What're you doing, you muscle-bound murderer?" Baako demanded.

Crew stepped into his path and nearly collided with him. "Hey." He held her friend's shoulder. "Dial it down."

With a feral scowl, Baako shoved the hand off. "I don't answer to you."

Crew stared the guy down, his chest pushing into her friend's space without even trying.

Several of Chapel's operators moved in around Crew and Vienna. Havoc let out a low growl.

"What is your problem? Just because you're G.I. Joe with muscles and tattoos, doesn't mean everyone else is!" Baako snapped. "You put Vienna in danger. Look at her! She's injured and you don't give a—"

"Hey."

"Back off. Clearly you don't care about her. You think you're all tough and bad with that dog—"

"What is *your* problem, Baako?" Vienna snapped. "Crew did the only thing I needed him to do—fight with me. Keep me safe."

"Yeah," said one of Chapel's guys who had a red beard. "Didn't see you running toward the bullets, Shorty. In fact, pretty sure I saw your sorry—"

"Get off me," Baako barked, then faltered as three more operators circled him. Herded him to the side.

It was a relief, yet she felt bad for him. Then again relieved. She knew her friend just wanted to be sure she was okay—they'd always looked out for each other—but his attitude was possessive and uncalled for. Familiar. Like Brant. Nausea swirled.

"Foxtrot?" That low rumble of his would get her every time. He was motioning someone toward them.

A woman.

Why did Vienna's spine stiffen?

"This is Glace, the medic for Damocles."

"Nora Glace." The pretty woman had a friendly smile beneath black bangs and bright eyes. "Let's go back here where there's privacy."

Medic? "For what?"

The woman gave Crew a look.

"Routine exam following an engagement," he said.

"*You* were the one who was shot." Vienna indicated to his arm.

Crew's thumb swept her cheek—and it stung for some reason. "You took a few blows, and I saw your head bounce off a wall." He gave a slow nod. "I'd feel better if you got it checked."

"I . . . shouldn't have . . ." She should tell him she was out of line with the kiss. It seemed so silly now. Illogical. "That . . . our k—"

"Adrenaline jacks things."

She nodded mutely, remembering him saying that—right before they'd made out again. And he was right—she'd felt the shakes of the adrenaline crash, but . . . wasn't it more? She did recall her head bouncing. Feeling fire in her face. "I'm fi—" She touched the spot and again pain pinched it.

Crew gave her a long, steady look.

The man had a powerful way of convincing her without a word. It was wild how the entire world seemed to vanish as he stood toe to toe with her, voice low, expression soft.

"D'you hear her?" Baako snipped. "She said she's fine—"

"Stand down, pretty boy," one of Chapel's guys said, shouldering in, using a lone finger against Baako's chest to urge him backward. "Accept defeat. She chose the better man."

"Shut up." Baako pushed forward.

"Just a quick check." Their gazes met and in Crew's, there was concern and . . . protectiveness. Hands still at his side, he lowkey laced his fingers with hers again, which felt like an anchor grounding her. Helping her find purchase on the shaky ground of tonight's events. Of life. "I don't want it on my head if you have a concussion and we don't address it."

"Okay." Yet Vienna experienced a strange flash of panic at the thought of being separated from him. Even as the dark-haired woman drew her to the side and Baako hovered, Vienna told herself not to look back at Gatlin. That was stuff for romcoms, not a stunt double. Yet her gaze found him on its own.

Sadly, his back was to her. With a click of his tongue, he drew Havoc alongside. Then Chapel led Gatlin, the dog, and the rest of the team into another room that buzzed with chatter and computers. "The attackers—any idea who they were?"

Why did it hurt that he never looked back?

"Now, then. First, we'll check your blood pressure, light response, pulse. Are you having pain anywhere?" Glace led her around an accordion-style divider where an exam table and medical equipment waited.

"What happened, V?" Baako asked, following them. "Why'd you go off with *him*?"

"Excuse me," Glace said, stepping to the juncture and blocking him. "You're not allowed back here right now."

Vienna watched her friend, felt bad for him. They'd always been close, and the team guys had been borderline rude to him. "It's okay, Baako. Will you be in the room with the others?"

His dark gaze hit hers. "Yeah. Kerr is trying to get us flights back home."

Home? They were leaving? She nodded. "I'll find you when I'm done here."

Although he bobbed his head, there was a twitch in his cheek that warned he wasn't happy. Yet he complied.

Glace gave her a bemused look. "Handsome but maybe overbearing . . .?"

"We've always looked out for each other."

"Ah," Glace said as she applied a cuff. "And now he feels replaced."

"What?"

"Gatlin," she said, gently lifting Vienna's eyelids to gauge pupil response. "Always wondered what it would take to pull that handsome lug off the market."

"Excuse me?"

Glace laughed. "Sorry. I've known him for a long time, so my curiosity—"

"The—" Vienna did not want to talk about a fledgling relationship, if that's what this was, right now. "The shooters . . . with all the gunfire, were many hurt?"

Bright-eyed Glace seemed to get the message and dipped her chin. "A few. I believe there were two fatalities and the EMTs took a handful to the local hospital. Team's intact. I patched up Tahj and will chew out Crew after the debrief."

"Debrief." She glanced over her shoulder, and while she couldn't see through the curtain, she imagined the doors behind which he'd vanished. "Should I . . ."

"In a moment. Just a few more things to be sure you aren't concussed."

"I was out there with Foxtrot—"

"Come again?"

"Foxcroft." Which now felt just plain weird on his tongue. "Foxtrot's just easier, more familiar." He shrugged. "We were out there with Havoc when the tangos came over that wall from the water with stealth and skill. Well-armed. Tried to get cover and advance to the hotel, but they were coming streetside, too."

"They surrounded the palace."

Crew nodded. "Then—as mentioned before—there were the three waiting in a vehicle a half klick out. We neutralized them and kept moving."

"Explain that 'we.'"

Crew met Chapel's steel gaze. "Foxtrot killed one—with her hands."

Rush Bennion whistled as he folded his arms. "Shooting someone is one thing, but killing hand-to-hand makes it raw, gritty. What is she—"

"An MMA fighter and stunt double." Irritation slammed up

against his protective streak that had been sealed into his heart by the way she'd kissed him. Nothing chaste about that. *Easy, easy . . . bring it down, Gatlin.* "She held her own, fought like a mother." The way she'd sobbed . . . "It rattled her, but she's tough."

"No wonder you were hot and heavy," Bennion chuckled. "I'd want to hit that, too."

Crew tensed. Jerked forward.

"Whoa, whoa," Chapel growled. "Rush, mouth." His gaze again hit Crew. "Back on track. Tell me what you're thinking about this hit?"

Roughing a hand over his face, Crew refocused. Didn't have to think long. "It was planned and professional. But not high-end."

"That's our thought, too. Probably not contract or private military."

"Unlikely. They hit the Çırağan, so that means the film personnel or the Turk. Right?"

"I will not take offense to that," came the voice of the Turk, who joined them. "While I have enemies around the world always looking for a chance to deal a blow to myself or my network—inevitable in my line of work—I do not believe this was about me."

"Why's that?" Crew wasn't sure what ticked him off this time.

"There are much easier ways to reach me," The Turk said plainly. "This location was specific to this film crew, so the reason lies therein."

"Agreed," Chapel said with a nod. "We've got some guys going over the feeds with hotel security. Haven't found anything yet."

"So, who were they, and who were they after?" Crew didn't like this because it alluded a still-present threat. Was Foxtrot yet in danger? "Foxcroft's dad is a member of the UN. There's a vote he's integral for."

"Noted," Chapel said, indicating to Tahj, who would work that angle. "With the celebrities here, there's a lot to consider. They hit hard and fast, but I daresay they weren't expecting the fight we gave them. There are a number of dead unfriendlies but nothing identifying. Weapons all over the place—AKs, M4s, Kalashnikovs . . . not especially helpful in determining allegiance except to rule out contract or private military."

"Cast and crew are stacked in the next room, and the local authorities are interviewing them, as are Nix and Cage," Bennion said. "With two fatalities and a half dozen at the hospital, we couldn't avoid local involvement."

"Fatalities?" Crew straightened. "Who?"

Chapel grabbed a device and thumbed around. "Charles Ellison and Frode Haugen—"

"Not good." He recalled that guy who matched him height and weight, but seemed much friendlier than his shorter, grumpier counterpart.

Chapel waited for him to elaborate.

"Haugen is one of Foxtrot's team. They're close." Which had no relevance on the situation, but it'd be another hard hit she'd have to work through. The guys would rib him again that he knew that about her. "But all that," he said, diverting their attention back to the mission, "and we don't know why these combatants struck."

"Maybe we should go room by room, look for stolen property or—"

"Hold up." Bennion indicated to a monitor that held security footage. His sudden interest drew the team closer. "Back that up."

The tech seated at the table worked quick to comply with the request.

Bennion bent closer, squinting. "What camera is this?"

"It, uh . . ." The tech glanced around the running feeds. "Northeast side of the building. An alley, really, where the garbage is picked up."

"Right there," Bennion barked.

They watched as tangos moved past the camera, firing, shooting. Then approximately seven seconds later, three more emerged carrying a long, narrow . . . carpet?

Crew's gut clenched. "They snatched someone."

The Turk slid his hands into his pockets. "All my men are accounted for, so this is a member of the L.A. crew."

"Time to talk to the celebs," Bennion said, clapping.

When Crew turned, he saw Havoc inhaling water from a bowl Glace had delivered. "Hey." He stepped closer to find out how Foxtrot was doing.

Glace handed him a wet towel.

"What's this?"

"Might want to clean up big-handsome before trotting him around some soft-hearted cast members in there."

Crew eyed the bloody fur around Havoc's jowls and neck. "Right. Thanks." He used a rag to clean up Havoc's face, glad his boy hadn't taken a bullet. The graze had seared off some fur, but nothing serious. He applied some salve and gauze but knew his partner would likely lick or chew it off before the night was over.

He blinked and recovered his original train of thought, eying Glace. "So, you checked out Foxtrot . . ."

"As did you," she teased.

Irritation tugged at him. "She okay?"

A smile danced in her knowing gaze. "Yes. Remarkably so for someone who did what you said yet is not a trained operator."

Pride replaced that irritation. "She's tough."

"And quite beautiful."

Crew ducked, eying the towel. "Yeah."

The five-five Glace touched his arm. "You found a good one there, Gatlin. Don't let her get away."

Wait. That sounded like a warning. "What do you—"

A whistle silenced his question, and he jerked to the door.

Chapel thumbed over his shoulder. "Need you and the sniffer."

"On our way." He shifted to the dark-haired medic. "Hey, um—"

Glace was already moving out with her kit and supplies.

Right. Frustrated, he drew Havoc to his side, then headed into the adjoining room. Even as he cleared the threshold, he searched the faces for Foxtrot. And almost immediately regretted it. She was there to the side with the director and producers, and in Baako's arms.

Son of a—

So much for choosing the better man.

"Okay, people," Chapel said, commanding the attention of the gathered.

Where had Crew gone wrong?

Breaking your own rules, that's where. Don't date. Four-legged females only. *This is why.* His foul mood pushed him to the far side of the room where he sat at a table, used the wet towel Glace had given him to wipe at Havoc's fur.

Her friend, died, idiot. Give her a break.

Yeah, but what excuse would it be next time? And there was always a next time. Rina had been proof of that.

"Sorry for the delay," Chapel continued, "a quick debrief, but first, we need you to look around and verify your friends are here with you. If anyone is missing—"

"Felicity." Kerr Macleod moved to the front from where he'd clustered with Foxtrot, who suddenly cared about who else might be in the room. "Felicity Vale, the star of the show, is missing."

Chapel gave Crew a nod, a silent order to take Havoc and search the hotel for Felicity. An order he was glad for—anything to get out of here and not watch Foxtrot cozy back up so fast to that punk. Tossing aside the stained towel, he moved toward the door with Havoc and Bennion on his heels.

"Dude, I'm sorry. I think that blow she took to her head was worse than Glace believed. No way she chooses him over you."

"Clearly." Crew redirected to the side where one of the Turk's guys stood. "Hey, I need to get into Felicity Vale's room to find something for Havoc to scent."

"Kerem." With a nod, he led him to the side and spoke to a man there, who gave him a key.

"Let's go." Quickening his pace, Crew strode out with Havoc and headed to the elevator.

"Crew." Her voice was a siren's call. One that slowed him. But man, he just did not have the energy for this right now. "Crew!"

He stepped in with Bennion and let the doors close.

"Cold, man. Cold."

Yeah, hadn't that been his mantra before he'd stepped foot on that set in LA? Keep his distance. Stay out of trouble. Keep his head clear.

Except . . . his head wasn't clear.

9

ÇIRAĞAN PALACE KEMPINKSI HOTEL, ISTANBUL, TURKEY

SHE COULD NOT CLEAR HER THOUGHTS OR PUT THEM IN ANY semblance of an order. Instead, they ricocheted all over the events of the last few hours. From being out beneath the stars with Crew, then the shooters . . . escaping with him . . . killing that man—again her stomach threatened to heave—to the way Crew then kept her focused until they made it to a safe spot, where she'd sobbed like a baby. Felt his protective stance, appreciated how those broad shoulders blocked any threat and gave her safe haven. Overwhelmed, smitten, she'd kissed him like there was no tomorrow.

And merciful heavens that man was a tower of passion! The way he'd pinned her between the plaster and his firm chest. His hands so strong and guiding. His kisses urgent yet so . . . gentle. As if he was holding back. It seemed so dichotomous. Yet was exactly Crew Gatlin.

But then . . . in here . . . she'd just found out Frode had been gunned down, Baako had hugged her, and that—*that*—was when Crew had to walk in. She saw the recognition hit his rugged features that she was in Baako's arms. The surprise, the anger, the resigned acceptance as he distanced himself.

"You holding up okay?"

Vienna glanced up at the pretty, dark-haired medic and struggled to sort her thoughts, so she simply shrugged. "Lost one of my closest friends, another friend is missing, and . . ." *Maybe lost the only man I've wanted to date in years.*

"It's a lot to deal with." Nora took up the seat near her. "You forgot what happened in the streets with Crew."

"No," she said with a hollow laugh. "I haven't forgotten that." Never would forget the feel in her hands as she'd killed the man. Yanking her arms in opposite directions. The sickening crack that signaled his death. A move she'd fake-practiced in training so many times but had been utterly unprepared for the visceral-ness of it all. "I don't know how he does it, how they do it—kill and move on."

"We know what has to be done, and we do it."

Vienna lifted her chin, surprise rippling. "Right. You're . . . you're an—"

"A combat medic. I've traveled with Chapel's teams for a few years." She shrugged and cocked her head side to side. "I figured it was more money, so why not? Thought it'd be less bloodshed, but that was naiveté."

"You were in the military?"

"Ten years."

"Did you work with Crew?"

The woman's expression seemed to tighten. "I did."

Oh wait . . . she . . . did Nora carry a torch for him? "You liked him."

"Liked?" She snickered. "There is a *lot* to like there, and it's not something I do or say lightly. But along with many other smitten casualties, he only saw us as compatriots. Nothing more." Curiosity glittered in her dark-brown eyes as she held Vienna's. "I see in your face the same questions ringing in my head."

"I . . ." Vienna shoved her hair from her face. "Sorry. I just wonder what it's like to work with him. To be around him *allll* day and not . . ."

"I confess, I tried. Tried my darndest to get him to notice me, date me. Never worked. I'm okay with that now. He's a good man."

This had fully stepped into awkward territory.

"I've known him for a decade and never once heard he'd dated anyone. Guys teased him that he leaned to the other side, but I knew better." She sighed and took a sip of water. "So, when I heard over the comms Crew was kissing someone . . ."

Vienna dropped her gaze to the table. "I . . . It was my fault."

Questions burned in Nora's eyes.

And even as she figured out where to start, Vienna couldn't help but realize the whole scenario had been adrenaline-jacked just like he'd said. "I was wrecked after . . . well, you know . . . I sobbed, and he just stood there, kept watch while I lost it in a major way. When I was done, he just looked back at me and asked if I was ready to move. As if it was another everyday thing for him."

"Which it was," Nora said.

"And I'd just intended to give him a quick kiss, say thank you, but then . . ." Heat scorched her cheeks and she again looked down.

"It wasn't a *quick* kiss."

"Not. At. All." Oh, man, remembering that moment made her want to be back there. Alone with him. Lost in that moment, in his arms. But even he said it'd been adrenaline.

"Clearly," Nora giggled. "I mean, he lost situational awareness, and that's never been something anyone could accuse Crew of."

"Well, I screwed it up."

"How?"

"I had just learned my friend was killed while I was gone, and my other friend hugged me. Crew saw it, misread it . . ."

"Uh oh."

"I tried to talk to him, but either he didn't hear me or he—"

"Hey, V." Baako slid into the chair next to her and perched on the edge. Draped his arm over the back of her chair and leaned in.

Frowning, she eased away. Surprised at her own reaction—they were good friends. They'd always hugged. But somehow, it felt different, wrong now . . . "Hey, I just . . . need to breathe."

"Sure, sure." Baako touched her shoulder. "Just wanted to see how you were holding up."

Vienna skated a look at Nora, who was watching with a critical eye, then back to Baako. "One of my closest friends just died. How do you think I'm doing?"

He finally seemed to check himself. "It's messed up, man. And with Felicity missing . . ." He shook his head. "Kerr is trying to contact Frode's family but hasn't been able to reach them." Somehow, his hand was on her knee. "Have you heard?"

Though his touch grated—he knew better—she shrugged it off. He was just concerned for her, right? Still, she crossed her legs in the other direction, forcing his hand away. "Heard what?"

"Macleod is hiring a private jet to get the cast and crew home."

"Yeah." Her heart jammed into her throat. "Wh-why?"

Eyes bulging, Baako scowled. "Girl, this must have rattled you more than I thought. We were shot at! It's not safe here. We need to get out of here ASAP."

But . . . what about Crew? That question would only anger Baako, but she did not want to leave without talking to Crew. Assuming he'd stay behind since operating was his territory. "What about Felicity?"

"They have people looking for her. We're not qualified to get involved."

"But we can't just leave . . ."

"Hey," Nora whispered and nodded to something behind her.

Vienna glanced over her shoulder, but didn't see what—

Crew moved into view with Havoc and Chapel's team.

She whipped out of her chair and hurried toward them. In motion, she wondered what she'd say. Saw the guy built like a linebacker tap Crew's shoulder and point at her.

Crew's gaze landed on her—and hardened.

Oh man. He really was ticked.

No time to chicken out. She quickened her pace. "Hey." What was she supposed to say or do?

"Gatlin. Chapel wants you."

After giving her a long look, he adjusted his ballcap. Turned away and started toward the others.

Vienna caught his arm. "Wait."

With a huff, he stalled. Wouldn't meet her gaze. Wouldn't turn back to her.

Apparently, he wanted her to work for this. Fine. She stepped around him and into his personal space. Set her hands on his abs and felt them contract, an involuntary reaction that yanked his beautiful eyes to hers. "He's a friend. That's all."

Without hesitation, Crew homed in on her, searched her face. Right there, they were locked into that connection she'd felt in the alley. The one that'd compromised her ability to "just be friends" with this mountain of a man. "Looked like more."

The growl in his words set her back a step. Frowning, she felt the gazes of Chapel's entire team. Embarrassment roiled hot. When had she ever made such a fool of herself? Right, then . . .

Apparently seeing her understanding, Crew gave a nod. "Stay with the team—"

"Don't tell me what to do."

"—they'll need your skills," he said, grinding out the latter part.

Oh.

He shook his head and strode into a closed room with the team where she'd seen a group of uniformed officers waiting. A move that said so very clearly that she did not belong with him.

A star doesn't need the moon to shine.

Dad's saying had always made her feel better.

But not this time.

"We've got a lead on where they took Vale," the Turk said as they crowded into the small Command center.

Crew tucked aside his disappointment regarding Foxtrot's mixed signals and took a seat where he could see the screens while he rested his leg. Havoc sidled up to him and sat, giving him a morose look. As if he mourned Foxtrot's absence too.

Chapel nodded. "Via Majid's connections, we were able to track the van that left here with Vale through the city."

They watched the feeds of the van moving through one light or intersection after another. Past a bank, a park. A residential area. Then it pulled into a parking structure.

"That is a brand-new business center on the north side of the city. It's still under construction and vacant."

"No sign that they exited, maybe took another vehicle?"

"Negative," Chapel said, indicating to the monitor on the lower right. "Live feed."

"Let's get moving," Bennion said.

"That's the plan." Chapel eyed Crew. "I know you weren't expecting to work, but we could use Havoc's nose and your experience in tracking her."

Son of a heart attack. Told Ghost this would happen. "We're here," he muttered with a shrug, knowing it was no good fighting it. "Use us." Besides, had to admit—being mission focused gave him a healthy diversion from the confusion that was Foxtrot.

Fifteen minutes later, they'd geared up with tac vests, weapons, and comms. They were soon en route via two of the Turk's armored vehicles.

"Am I the only one who noticed this Felicity Vale is the spitting image of Gatlin's hottie?"

Chest tight, Crew grunted. "Not my . . . anything." Irritation clawed at him. When Havoc threw his head back at him, demanding some attention, Crew smoothed a hand down the thick, muscular neck. Somehow knew his partner felt the same frustration over the woman. "Foxtrot is Vale's stunt double."

"If you don't—"

"Leave it," Crew growled, and even Havoc withdrew from that. He knew he wanted her, but he wasn't so sure she knew what she wanted. The way she'd pulled her hand from his when the punk showed up . . . then the way she'd sobbed into his chest, then punk-boy's . . . Her appearance could stop a guy in his tracks—that was obvious. But it was her inner warrior that knocked his feet out from under him. That was hot. That made him want to defy every vow he'd made to steer clear of distractions.

That smile . . . holy Moses, her kisses, feeling her soft curves against him—curves that were toned and—

A thump to his shoulder snapped him up. Havoc barked and came up, focused on Rush Bennion for the "assault" on Crew's person.

"Dude, where's your head?"

Crew scowled. "What?"

"You've been twitching the selector switch the last five minutes."

"Whatever," Crew growled, absently glancing at his M4 even as his thumb hit the switch again, moving it to FIRE.

Doggone.

"Hey," Bennion said loudly for everyone to hear. "I think Foxtrot has fried your brain, brother. Not sure you're going to be any good for us tonight."

Crew thumped the guy's gut—and hit his tac vest. "Shut up."

"Good thing he has Havoc," one of the other guys barked.

He was slagged. This was why he didn't date two-leggeds and stuck to canines. He tugged the bill of his hat, avoiding Chapel's probing gaze in the rearview mirror, and tapped the schematic on the device strapped to his arm. Again reviewed the layout of the building they were going into. A basic familiarity with the environment helped him focus better on Havoc and his behavior. Five stories. First level held a lobby, cafeteria, store, café with street-side access, and two main halls that jutted in both directions from the lobby. Four elevators. Rear stairs. The other levels were all mirrors of each other with four offices hugging a conference room. Two main halls as well. And a maintenance room.

"ETA in two mikes," Chapel called.

Crew did a chamber check on his M4 and a press check on his Sig, then ran his hands over Havoc's harness to make sure all was well. His Malinois slapped a paw on his leg. "Ready to get some?"

With a low whine, Havoc shifted. Rose onto all fours.

The SUVs swung into the parking structure. No sooner did darkness descend than tires screeched to a halt. Even as he wondered what was happening, Crew saw the beat-up van parked on the far side. Damocles and the Turk's men deployed from the SUVs with expert precision.

Pulse amped, Crew hopped out and let Havoc have the lead.

"Don't touch it," Chapel called. "Let Havoc clear it."

In other words, the team leader suspected it was rigged with explosives. Like old times . . . But he prayed this time didn't take a limb with it.

Just Turkey, eh, Ghost?

Crew nodded to Chapel, and as the team backed up a few paces, he drew Havoc closer. "Havoc, seek." And with that, he walked the perimeter of the van, letting the Malinois haul in draughts around the tire wells, the doors, the front bumper . . . with each second that went by without a break in behavior, Crew grew more relaxed. Realized how much he'd missed working the dogs. Around the back and still no hit.

Taking out the KONG, he backed up. "Clear."

The team moved in, opened the van, and found it empty. Chapel signaled the local authorities, who moved in and started processing the van. He and Bennion conferred, then the team leader glanced at Crew. "Send in the dog."

They were sending Havoc in first. Which meant him. Made his gut tighten, since he'd been out of the field for over a year. But he wasn't going to be a weak link. He just prayed Havoc was up to this, too. The dog hadn't missed a beat so far. Shouldn't be a problem.

Sliding his selector to FIRE and reaching for Havoc's lead, he slid Vale's shirt from the protective sleeve and presented it to Havoc. His partner hauled in the scent even as Crew unhooked the lead and caught the harness handle. Havoc's tail thwapped hard against Crew's tac pants, nearly spinning up for liftoff. He gave a nod to Chapel, who tugged open the door.

"Havoc, seek-seek!" Weapon tucked into his shoulder, Crew slid through the opening, trailing his patrol explosives detector dog through the unfinished hall. Floors were still concrete, paint sprayers blocked doorways, and walls were nothing but sheetrock.

Havoc zigged into one space, then rushed back out, into another.

Behind him, Crew could feel the team packing into the hall. Some likely banking right down to the other hall.

Crew kept pace with Havoc, letting him do his thing. In the lobby, he spent a lot of time around a blocked-in reception desk. Nose pressed to the floor, then tracing up the side of the desk.

Angling in, Crew saw— "Blood."

Havoc was focused now, his 100 million sensory receptors snatching scents and processing them. Crazy smart and entirely more reliable than the human 6 million. And the part of the dog's brain that processed and analyzed the scents was forty percent larger than the center in the human brain.

He zigzagged down the far hall, then circled back to the

desk . . . sniffing low and slow the door with the universal sign for stairs. There, he sat.

"Got a hit," Crew called over his shoulder.

Chapel and Bennion flanked the door, the latter pushing it open as Crew let Havoc dart inside and followed him.

"Entering south stairwell." Chapel's voice carried smoothly through the comms.

Havoc advanced up the stairs. One flight . . . two flights . . . he moved to the next level, then backtracked. Sniffed at the door. Stared at it, giving Crew sidelong glances as if to say, "Slow, human. You're too slow."

Crew opened the door and Havoc bolted onto the third floor. Only half the rooms on this floor were blocked in, but no taping or mudding. Havoc slid through a narrow space that had no drywall—a space too narrow for him. He muttered an oath, slipped between two steel supports, then angled around to the other room. Weapon out, he stepped around the corner and moved into the room, a decent level of certainty it wasn't rigged or Havoc would've alerted.

There, he spotted Havoc spending a lot of time on a bag, a water bottle, some litter, and a shoe. Crew backstepped until he could see through the sliver Havoc had slipped through and spotted Bennion. "Got something."

In seconds, the guys converged.

But Havoc wasn't done. While Chapel and the others dissected what was in here, Crew kept pace with Havoc, who seemed to have detected something. He zigzagged, narrowing the scent cone as he trotted down the hall, picking up pace. "Chapel."

Havoc went to the south stairwell and stared at it, then to Crew. Back to the door.

"Got something," Crew called over his shoulder. Once he heard the team thudding closer, he opened the door.

Pop-pop-pop!

"Contact!" Crew comm'd as he signaled Havoc back to

himself. "Taking fire, south stairwell. Third level." Boots thudded behind him, but he was already moving up the stairs, hugging the walls and seeing his Belgian Malinois flying up the levels, ignoring the shots.

The enemy was having a hard time trying to lock on the lightning-fast dog coming at him.

Crew pushed himself up the levels, weapon tucked in his shoulder as he peered down its stock to the target. Fired once. Twice. Short bursts.

"Damocles, report of helo incoming," came a heads-up.

When he saw a burst of daylight shove into the stairwell, Crew didn't want to lose sight of his dog. "Havoc, down! Stay!" It took him five seconds to pitch himself up the last flight to him. Mind racing, processing that a chopper was landing on the roof. That shooters were outside the door that had thudded closed.

Even as he clipped the lead back on Havoc, he felt Chapel and Bennion crowd in behind him.

"Fifth level," Chapel intoned in the comms. With a firm pat, he slid past him. Then Bennion, who swung to the other side of the door and readied himself.

Chapel flicked open the door.

Light and bullets shot in. Bennion fired, advancing into the open. Crew followed with Havoc, assessing what he saw—a bird, four men and Felicity Vale, whose screams and cries were drowned by the rotor wash.

Wind shoved and tore at the operators even as the helo's engines whirred louder.

"Havoc, *fuss*!"

The Malinois tore across the roof and clamped onto the leg of a man whose scream mingled with the deafening noise. He aimed his weapon at the dog.

Crew's gut dropped when he realized the helo was lifting off. Havoc still had the man. "Havoc, *aus*!" He sprinted forward, firing at the bird, praying like crazy he didn't accidentally hit Vale, but more desperate for his dog to release. The drop would kill him if they got out over the city. "Havoc, *aus*!!" But just as the din ate the screams, it ate his words. *Merciful God, help!*

"Havoc, *aus, aus*!" He was almost there and his dog was still thrashing on the leg, using the deck to gain traction. "*Aus! AUS!*"

In a heartbeat, the bird swung away. Up . . . Up

"Haaavoc—*aus*!"

The man kicked Havoc, who fell away taking a chunk of calf with him. Blood spraying.

Crew skidded up under the dog, nearly going over the edge of the roof as eighty pounds of Malinois thudded into his chest. Knocked him off balance, his foot slipping off the edge of the roof.

Hands clamped onto him. Yanked him back. He crashed into whoever had saved him, his hands a vise around Havoc. Face buried in the Mal's thick neck. He rolled to the side, so whoever was behind him could get free. He shifted and found Chapel staring at him, shaking his head.

"The two of you—freakin' psychos."

10

ÇIRAĞAN PALACE KEMPINKSI HOTEL, ISTANBUL, TURKEY

AN HOUR AGO, THEY'D BEEN INSTRUCTED TO PACK THEIR SUITCASES and bring them down to the ballroom. Jets were inbound to fly the cast and crew back home and buses were lining the street to deliver them to the airport. Kerr was already planning alternate sites with their production and set coordinators. Set crews were taking copious notes on the palace and filming every possible angle so they could replicate it for scenes with Felicity and Mark.

If Felicity was ever found again.

Vienna had her gear down in the lobby before anyone else, but within the hour, they were all standing around. Chaos seemed the order of the day, so she stepped up and helped coordinate travel. She got the first twenty on the bus—including the producers, Mark, and the directors—headed out. Tackling the list, she lined up the next group. She'd go with the last one. Each trip out to make sure things were going smoothly, she'd eye Chapel's armed men. Patrolling the grounds should've given her confidence that they were safer, yet they challenged her confidence that safety would ever be restored.

"Okay," Vienna said, stepping back into the ballroom. "Group 2—you know who you are—grab your suitcases and let's get loaded."

"This is crazy," Baako hissed as he stalked to her. "You should have been in Group 1. For that fact, so should I have."

"Well, we weren't." The knot at the base of her neck was tightening. "But you're in Group 2, so out you go."

"Why are you being like this?"

"Baako, please. Just get on the bus."

"Come with me. It's too dangerous and I don't want you to get hurt."

She recoiled "I can't—you know that. Iris is injured, so I'm helping. I'll be okay, Baako. Really." She nodded to the line seeping into the ominous night. "Now, hurry up. If you're not on that bus, I can't promise your flight will still be there."

The guy faltered, and she was glad. It showed he cared. That he wasn't just jealous or irrational, which is how he'd behaved since Crew had stepped onto the set back in L.A.

She gave him a shove. "Go. Please. Save me a seat on the jet."

"This is wrong."

"Maybe, but it's the only plan we have. Go." And he did. She heaved a breath and glanced at her list again. Eyed Iris, who'd sprained an ankle getting away from the gunmen. The girl looked completely wrecked.

"How are you doing?"

At the new voice, Vienna turned.

Nora Glace crossed the foyer, having emerged from the Command room, the door slowly closing behind her.

"Okay, I guess . . ." She shoved her hair back. "Just another thirty and one more bus, and we'll be out of your hair."

"Not in my hair, but I'm glad they're able to move so quickly."

"Thanks to the Turk."

She arched an eyebrow.

"Any word on the team?"

Glace's smile was a little less genuine. "Yeah. This isn't new to them."

"Right." *But it's very new to me.* "Have they found Felicity?"

"Not to my knowledge, but comms chatter is kept to a minimum for op-sec."

Piqued voices near the door to the buses drew her attention. Baako was there, arguing with one of the guards.

"V, c'mon, girl. You're too important. Get on the bus."

She shook her head. "If you aren't on the bus in two seconds, I'll tell the driver to leave you."

"That's cold," Baako said. "You know I'm just watching out for you."

"Time's up—hey, guard—"

"A'ight, a'ight." And he was gone.

"Hey, I know it's not any of my business, but what's with you and him?"

Vienna frowned. "Baako?" She shoved her hair back, noting the knot on her temple was even more tender now. "Close friends. Worked several gigs together. Nothing more."

Nora ached an eyebrow. "Nothing?"

"*Nothing,*" Vienna ground out. "I don't date guys I work with. Or really . . . anyone."

"Including Gatlin?"

The answer stalled on her lips. "Well, he decided that, didn't he?"

"Glace!"

Nora pivoted and looked to where a guy popped out of the Command center.

"They're coming back and you're needed."

She touched Vienna's arm and hurried toward them. "What's coming?"

"One through and through. MWD team went down."

Vienna's heart jarred in her chest. MWD team—that was

Crew and Havoc! No no no. That couldn't . . . What did that mean, *went down*?

She moved toward the door, but the guard there stepped into her path. Didn't say anything, but his grim expression and his hand over the trigger well said he didn't have to.

Even as she faltered, she spied through the window at the far end the bus pulling away and the third one easing to a stop. "Okay, Group 3. Let's go!" Even as she made the announcement and the people were moving in that direction, she spotted Iris hobbling across the open area. Her heart ached for the young woman. "Iris, what are you doing?"

The PA hobbled aside, letting others pass, and balanced herself against the wall. "My tablet—I left it in my suite on the sideboard. It has everything on it. I can't leave it."

"*I'll* get it." She pointed to the door. "You get on the bus. Hey, Franklin."

The boom operator jerked toward her from the line.

"Help Iris get on the bus and tell them to wait two minutes for me!"

"Sure thing."

She took a step, then faltered. "What suite?"

"Two-twenty-eight. Off the escalator, last room on the right. Oh—you'll need the code: fifteen-thirteen."

Vienna nodded and moved to the stairs. Took them two at a time, appreciating the invigorating workout. At the top of the landing, she glanced to the right and hurried past the three rooms to the last one. Which was 208.

Do what?

Vienna frowned. Maybe Iris meant to the left. About to move in that direction, she saw another wing bank off from this one. Saw the sign on the wall. 210-228. Her gaze traipsed down the long corridor. Allll the way down. "You have *got* to be kidding."

She hurried down the hall and found the room at the far end. She punched in the code. The lock disengaged, and she let herself in. Glanced around the room, on the tables. No sign of it.

Walking the room, she looked to see if it'd fallen in between cushions of the chair or settee. No luck. "C'mon . . ." she whispered. She looked under the bed, under a cabinet, on the window seat . . . even the bathroom.

The woman wasn't known for being absentminded, but she was frazzled and injured. They all had been shot at. That could make the most balanced person miss something.

After one last inspection of all the drawers, the closet, nightstands, she tried calling Iris, but it went to voicemail, so she decided to check the ballroom. Hustling down, she went into the ballroom—wow, it felt so weird empty—and looked at the table where Iris had been sitting. She scanned the floor around it. Nothing. Frustrated, she tugged back a chair—and it slid off onto the floor. "Aha!" No wonder it'd been missed—the tablecloth had concealed it.

Her own gear and suitcase were not in here anymore. Someone must've loaded them for her, thankfully. In a jog, she used the back service hall since it was closer to the buses. Her boots thudded loudly in the mostly concrete corridor, and she wondered for the millionth time how the team was doing. More accurately, how Crew was. Her conscience pinched, recalling the way he'd shut her down. Just as she'd done to him. She'd been out of the game so long, she wasn't really sure how to do this, how to like a guy but not lose herself, her sense of control. She stepped out the back, gave a halfhearted smile to the guards, then angled around the corner. And stopped cold.

Wait . . .

Where there should have been a bus . . . there was an open parking lot. Her heart gave a heavy thud. She wheeled back to the guard. "The bus." She thumbed in that direction, but the guy gave her a blank stare. "Where's the bus?"

The answer was obvious, but she didn't want to accept it.

"There should be a bus there! I was supposed to be on it!"

He shrugged, clearly not understanding or worse—didn't care.

No no no. This couldn't be happening. Vienna darted back inside, and this time raced down the hall. Came around the other side, and aimed for the door, as if coming this direction would give her a different answer. Realizing what she was doing, she slowed to a stop. This . . . this couldn't be happening.

Heart now pounding, she turned a full circle. They were gone. They were all gone.

Limping, Havoc trudged into the Command center, totally milking the sympathy tossed his way by the team. Crew had cleaned, sealed, and taped the bullet graze that would likely leave a scar.

"Tattoos and scars always win over the ladies," Chapel said as they made their way back into the command center. "Hey, Tahj—get on that phone the hostile dropped."

"On it, boss."

Chapel turned to Glace. "It sounds quiet. I assume the film crew is gone?"

She moved toward him with a nod. "Buses are en route to the airport right now."

"Good, good."

Crew was relieved to hear Foxtrot would be on a plane and headed back to the States within the hour. After what happened at that building, he sure didn't want her here. "Something is off—I know we said it wasn't private military or contract, but how many civilians do you know who have a Black Hawk at their disposal?" Someone touched his collar and he swatted at them. "Get off."

"Would you please sit down!"

He started at the demand from Nora Glace. "What—"

"I need to look at your neck."

"I'm good. We sealed it."

"The amount of blood on your shirt is concerning."

"Neck wounds are eager bleeders—"

"Sit down, Gatlin," Chapel instructed. "It won't change this conversation."

With a huff, Crew planted his backside in a chair. Refocused. "The guy Havoc took a chunk out of was in uniform."

"Noticed that," Bennion said.

Nora cut Crew's shirt.

"Hey!"

"It was already ruined," she huffed, cutting it away. "You need stitches."

"Benn used the gel."

"It's not holding." She went to work stitching.

"And I'm glad for your dog—if it weren't for him and the guy having a desperate need to shake those powerful jaws, he wouldn't have freed himself of his phone. Now, we have a way to find out who we're dealing with. But . . . too bad your boy couldn't have dragged him out of the chopper rather than drag us over the side of the roof."

"He tried, and nearly gave me a heart attack doing it." Crew said, patting Havoc who stretched out at his side, gnawing his KONG. Never forget how his gut dropped with each foot the helo rose, Havoc dangling from the guy's leg.

"Do we have IDs yet on the shooters from the hotel?" Chapel asked, hovering over Nazari.

"Nothing yet, boss," Cage Macklin, a curly-haired grunt with more muscle than height said. "The Turk promised us access to his systems once we get back to his base."

"Keep me posted," Chapel said.

"Boss," Tahj Nazari called, "got the phone unlocked. Take a look."

Relieved of his shirt, Crew gritted around the pinch and tug of the thread sewing up his raw flesh. Thought about that near-death encounter with a six-story drop. Remembered the fight in the alley with Foxtrot. He eyeballed Glace. "She got on a bus?"

Glace didn't falter or look away from her work. "Yep, the PA was shellshocked still, so your girl took over."

He wanted to object to the "your girl" thing, but then again, he didn't. In fact, kinda liked the way that sounded.

"She stepped in and organized everything. Got the cast and crew herded off. Baako gave her grief about staying, but then the coward rushed onto the bus." Glace huffed. "What man leaves a woman behind after what just happened?"

"Someone who trusts she has the skills to take care of herself."

Glace tucked her chin and glowered. "Would you leave her behind?"

"Not as long as I had breath in my lungs."

"Exactly." She snipped a thread, then reached for gauze. "But you're right—she can take care of herself, and apparently everyone else. Quite a trooper. She was part of the last group that left right before the team returned."

"Good." So why was he disappointed? It was good she'd left.

"She asked about you."

His heart skipped a beat. "Yeah?"

"If you need help finding a ring—"

An F-bomb ignited the air and spun Crew to the others. "What'd you find?"

Chapel had a grim expression. "Nothing good."

"What?"

When Glace patted his shoulder, telling him she was done, he came to his feet, feeling his gut tighten and the prosthesis pinch. Hiking those stairs in the building had worn him out.

"Put it on the wall, Tahj," Chapel instructed.

The video had a whiteout opening, then swung to a man in all black, his face hidden behind a balaclava, only his eyes visible. He held a sword in one hand.

Crew moved closer, massaging his leg.

"We are Abna' Suria and we fight against the Great Satan that is the West. You have killed our men, raped our women, slaughtered our children, dropped bombs from drones because you are cowards. And now, you sinful infidels would think to say what we can do in our own country?" The camera panned to Vale. Beaten, bloodied, she sat gagged and bound. "We will pay blood for blood. End this whore's life."

Crew wasn't surprised at her condition, but he quickly realized the backdrop for the video had been that building. If they'd been five minutes earlier . . .

"We do not answer to the infidel on how our country conducts its business. The lamb does not tell the lion where to hunt. To this end, you will not vote to impose sanctions on our country and cut off our heads. If you do, your daughter will lose hers!"

"What is he talking about?" someone groused.

"Holy Moses," Crew said, struggling for his next breath. "That's not . . ."

Chapel glanced at him. "What?"

"The choice is in your hand, Horace Wolffe, and the judgment for your actions is in mine. Fail us and you fail your daughter!"

"What're they talking about? Whose daughter is Felicity Vale?" Tahj muttered.

"They think they have Foxtrot."

A gasp came from behind. "No!"

The word hauled the oxygen from the room, even from Crew's lungs because he knew that voice. Numb, shocked, he rotated and spotted Foxtrot standing in the doorway, face white as a sheet. "What're you doing here?" he demanded stalking toward her. "You were supposed to be on a bus—the plane!"

Her gaze was hooked on the screens where Vale was on full display in her battered condition. "They . . . they think it's me."

"Hey. Right here." Crew got in her face.

She blinked, her gaze hopscotching from the monitors to his chest. Color finally rose into her cheeks.

"Hey," Chapel said with a half laugh. "Put a shirt on, Gatlin.

You're making it impossible for the girl to breathe." He touched Foxtrot's shoulder. "You okay?"

She flicked a scowl at him. "No, I'm not okay!" She pointed to the screens. "Men kidnapped Felicity because they thought she was me!"

11

ÇIRAĞAN PALACE KEMPINKSI HOTEL, ISTANBUL, TURKEY

Rattled, Vienna couldn't tear her gaze from the screens where a bloodied and beaten Felicity stared back. Men in black ceremonial garb stood over her with swords, threatening her.

No, not her.

Me.

Black-bearded and hair tied in a queue, Chapel angled Crew and Vienna to face him. "Break this down for me. Don't leave anything out, even if you think I already know." He gave a nod.

Mouth still dry, Vienna felt sick to her stomach. "I . . . I am a stunt and body double for Felicity Vale. We have such a strong resemblance that we're often mistaken for each other. On more than one occasion, her boyfriend kissed me instead of her."

Barked laughs echoed around the room, the operators clearly amused.

"Crew, you need name, address and serial number to take the guy out?"

"Quiet," Crew said firmly to the guys. He eyed her. "She's got nothing on you."

Last time he'd said that, she'd smiled. This time, however . . .
"Regardless, Felicity is in that"—she again glanced at the screen
and felt her throat constrict—"situation because of me."

"No," Chapel said, a finger to her shoulder. "She's in that
situation because those men are intent on perpetrating violence."

"Against me," she growled. "Me! Vienna Foxcroft, not
Felicity Vale. And that girl is in trouble—danger. They will kill
her because they think she's me!"

"Slow your roll, Foxtrot," Chapel said in a low, controlled
voice. "Nobody's going to get killed because we will interdict."

"You can't promise that." Vienna drew back, not missing that
he'd called her 'Foxtrot' like Crew. "Don't pander or placate just
because I'm a woman."

"Wouldn't dream of it, but I am looking for you to find your
calm." Chapel gave her a slow nod of understanding.

Right. Only then did her own echoing voice register in her
thoughts, right along with the way the room had gone quiet, the
men avoiding looking at her. Except Crew. Now wearing a black
tactical shirt, he stood next to her, his expression inscrutable. Yet
there was emanating off him a sense of assuredness and
strength, that she took a minute to soak in. Reinforce her
reserves, which were low.

"Let's circle back," Chapel said. "Your dad—tell us about
him."

Stomach squeezing, she glanced at Crew. Recalled what she'd
told him. Remember this man before her had told Crew
something that made him step back from her. She focused on
Chapel. "I think you already know—"

"As I said," Chapel interrupted, his tone hardening with his
expression, "tell me even if you think I know."

Not sure she liked this man, she had to remind herself that
personal feelings didn't matter. Getting Felicity back did. Vienna
couldn't live with herself if the actress died because of her.

"Can we have a sec?" Crew said, stepping in.

"No, I'm okay—" Her phone buzzed in her pocket, and she

drew it out, saw the screen, and froze. Bounced her gaze to Crew. "It's him—my dad."

He placed his hand over hers. "Can that wait until we've gotten things sorted?"

Disconcerted at the thought of not talking to Dad, she hesitated. Eyed the screen, then Crew. "He can be hard to get hold of . . ."

Chapel was there again. "We have a very tricky situation here. You want Vale back alive, yes?"

He seemed to be setting her up with that question, so Vienna held his gaze.

"Then we protect her by protecting the intel. Keeping what we know close to the vest for operational security." He indicated to the phone. "If you answer that, say nothing about Vale or my team. Clear?"

The man's order—that's what it was, wasn't it?—made her want to defy it, him. But that smoother, calmer presence, the one that invited her into its warmth gave her the courage to reconsider. She met Crew's gray-green eyes, hoping for direction.

He stared back, steady, confident. Gave a nod to her phone.

"Did you not hear—"

Crew shouldered into Chapel. "Hey, man, back off. Give her space to think."

"You're edging into dangerous territory, Gatlin," Chapel warned, then acquiesced. Stepped back. "Since, I know you can pick the best mutts and trust them, I guess that transfers to the two-legged variety."

"And I guess that includes me, since I'm the original mutt."

"Your words." Chapel cast her a long look before moving to the others.

Alone with her, Crew eased closer and eyed the phone. "Put it on speaker."

"I . . . it's a personal call."

"Not anymore," Chapel countered.

The world was spinning out of her control. "O-okay." Hoping she hadn't waited too long to accept the call, Vienna swept her thumb over the speaker icon. "Dad . . .?"

"V! Oh, thank God!" Thick relief sailed into the air along with his jittery laugh. "I was so worried. We got a call that the hotel was attacked, and then you weren't answering . . ."

"Sorry." Again, anchoring off Crew, she swallowed. "I'm okay. It's been . . . crazy." Her thoughts erupted over the truth that her dad could save Felicity's life. He was a good man, so he'd want to do that. If she just told him, maybe he could stall the vote or . . . fake it or something. Or—

Crew's hand folded over hers, like a blanket that soothed her stress and fears. He gave a slow shake of his head.

How had he read her rampaging thoughts? She fought the urge to groan, realizing she was tired, stressed, and scared. Didn't trust herself. Maybe she wasn't as strong as she'd thought . . . "Dad, I—things are kind of crazy right now. Can I call you back, maybe in an hour or so?"

"Listen, I want to send a jet for you. Right now."

"N-no." Her pulse stampeded over that thought. "I'm—"

"It is not safe for you."

Crew nodded, as if he wanted her to let her dad send the plane, but that'd mean . . .

"Dad—I'll call you back. Love you." She ended the call and rolled her position into a nearby chair. It was probably the smarter thing to do, going home, but . . . Bent forward, she stuffed the heels of her hands against her forehead. How was she supposed to think or figure out anything when she couldn't even use logic and reason instead of emotion to talk to her dad?

"I know that was tough . . ."

"Hearing his voice, his worry," she moaned into her arms, "I couldn't help but think he'd help, that he'd want to save Felicity."

"Of course he would."

Vienna sat up and found him squatting next to her. What he

didn't say hung in the air. A thick, heavy truth that she didn't really want to acknowledge, but knew—of course her dad would want to save her, but his role on the Security Council would complicate, possibly inhibit, him from doing so.

She groaned. "I don't know what to do."

"That's what we're here for," Crew said with a smirk.

"This is my fault."

He scoffed. "Because BotoxBunny looks like you?"

"No, be—"

Havoc was there. Went on his hind legs and leaned across her, elbows digging into her thighs. She laughed and lifted her arms, not sure what to do. The big lug leaned back and thrust his head up at her—violently. Thumping her chin. "Ow!" But then she gave him a hug—from the back—remembering Crew said he didn't like to be crowded. Guess this posture allowed him to get some free loving and not feel closed in.

"Okay, jealous beast," Crew said, motioning Havoc off her lap. "Off." He cocked his head toward the team. "We need to run some intel and work through this. Ready?"

She stood and considered the area where tables and monitors were heavily attended by the dozen or so operators. *I am so out of my depth. And clearly not strong enough.*

A gentle touch at the small of her back made Vienna's abdominal muscles twitch as awareness spread up her spine. But she couldn't beat down an overpowering wave of unease. "I don't belong here."

Crew edged into her periphery, his hand still on her back as he looked at the Command area, too. "It's a lot when you're not used to it."

"You can say that again." She peered up at him—and saw the white bandage sticking out from under his shirt. "You're hurt?"

He adjusted his ballcap and grinned at her. "That concern I hear, Foxtrot?"

She gave him a playful push.

He smiled at her. "C'mon."

Chapel lasered his blue eyes on her. "Ready to tell us what you know?"

That really sounded like a challenge, as if she'd deliberately held back earlier. But she reminded herself that he wasn't the enemy, even if he was a jerk. "My father is Horace Wolffe—billionaire, owner of several large tech and security firms, and a six-term senator. A year ago, he was named an ambassador to the UN and assumed a seat on the Security Council. He told me there was a big vote coming up. They're poised to levy sanctions against Syria."

Chapel's intensity only seemed to grow as he absorbed the information. "And do you know which way your dad intends to vote?"

"No, but it would seem that if these terrorists are desperate enough to kidnap Felicity—thinking she's me—then they believe he's going to vote against them and put sanctions in place. It would fit with his track record."

His gaze seemed to flicker, barely. "What do you know about Vale?"

Full of herself? Wanted Crew? She doubted he wanted to know the standard information—beautiful, bad taste in men, except for her interest in Crew, paid more for her purse than Vienna did her car. "We look alike—a lot but—"

Crew coughed-cursed a "bullspit" into the pause.

"—that's where the similarities end." Though she tried to hide her smile, she couldn't. "I really wish it'd been me because I know how to defend myself. The only thing Felicity can defend herself against is a bad latte."

"Well, for Gatlin's sake, I'm glad it *wasn't* you. He can't handle another loss."

"And I'm with Gatlin," Bennion said. "I saw Vale—she doesn't even come close." He gave her an appreciative look. "We saw the surveillance footage of you taking down some of the terrorists."

"Beg off." Arms folded, Crew adjusted his stance. "Any word on where that helo landed?"

"Not yet," Chapel said, nodding around. "But there's the SUVs. Pack it up and let's get relocated to the Turk's Command base. Foxtrot, you're with us until the plane's ready."

"What plane?"

"Private jet to get you out of here."

Outrage charged through her veins. "Do I have a say?"

"Negative," Chapel said. "We have an op to conduct, and you're not an asset, so that means you're a liability."

"Well, don't spare my feelings."

"Glad we understand each other."

12

ISTANBUL, TURKEY

THE TURK'S TACTICAL CENTER WAS SOMETHING STRAIGHT OUT OF the future or some epic spy movie. A series of concentric rings delved into the ground and were composed of steel grates, bulletproof walls, and some poly-alloy metal that the commander—the only name supplied for The Turk's right-hand man—said would protect them in the event of a nuclear blast.

Which was good considering the glower Foxtrot had seared Chapel with at the palace hotel.

The lower level had sunk-in stations where personnel in dark-green uniforms were working fastidiously, poring over intel, feeds, and comms. SIGINT, HUMINT, COMINT . . . all rolling into this area.

In a soundproof conference room, the team all huddled at the windows, watching the goings-on.

Havoc's hot breath bloomed over the bulletproof glass that slanted out over the lower hub. Crew shifted around and sat on the end of the conference table, chair swiveled out to face the glass wall. Havoc glanced over his shoulder and Crew tossed the KONG, which the Malinois caught and lowered himself to the industrial grade carpet and went to work gnawing it.

"Dude acts like he didn't just rip off a guy's calf," Tahj said.

"Work is his play," Crew said, noting Foxtrot sliding into the chair near him. "There's a reason MWDs are called 'force multipliers.'"

"How much longer are they going to keep us locked up in here?" growled Bennion.

"This is a Tier One TAC," Chapel said as he folded his arms and watched the goings-on below. "Give it—"

"Sorry for the delay," came the baritone voice of the commander as he entered with three lieutenants. "There has been a lot to sort out. We'll start with the most basic—as Mr. Chapel just stated, this is a secure facility and as such, those without the appropriate clearance will not be allowed on the floor."

Crew was pretty sure that eliminated only one person in this room—and she was sitting at his right.

"My apologies, Miss Foxcroft," the commander said, "but you will need to remain either here or in the living quarters for the time being."

"I understand," she said, but there was a clear mark of insult in her words.

"Sergeant Gatlin, your—"

"My clearance should be up to date, but not a problem," Crew said with a wave. "I'm staying with her."

Foxtrot set a hand on his elbow in silent objection.

"Actually," the commander said, his gaze lingering on the way Foxtrot touched Crew, "your dog and your handling of him at the business complex made you both clear assets. Mr. Badem is very impressed and has asked that you remain available, regardless of the status of this team—"

"Regardless of our status?" Chapel demanded, frowning.

The commander ignored the interruption. "We would appreciate your cooperation once the location is determined to effect a rescue of Felicity Vale. Mr. Volken will keep you updated on our progress." He indicated to a man with blonde hair and a too-eager smile.

Havoc let out a low snarl, his hackles rising. Crew hesitated, looking from his dog to the man. *Always trust the dog,* he'd long said. But this guy was the Commander's right hand.

Acknowledging the commander's request felt like a betrayal of both Foxtrot and Damocles, but this wasn't some movie or novel where someone with no real negotiating power could demand to be involved. Besides, if that look Chapel shot him was any indication, their sidelined status wouldn't last.

After Crew was escorted to a walled-in courtyard where Havoc could relieve himself, he and the team were led to an accommodation wing with its own access code and entrance. Most of Damocles claimed rooms and bunks, then hurried to a dining hall—which was four long tables, a serving station, and a window in a wall that opened to what looked like an industrial kitchen. Through it, on the other side was a more open area that appeared to be a full-scale cafeteria.

"Is it just me, or are we basically locked down?" Foxtrot asked, her voice quiet and worried.

"Yeah . . ." Yet the casual attitude of the Damocles team as they grabbed some chow said they weren't worried. Of course, Chapel also hadn't come below yet, likely taking up his displeasure over their "status" with Badem himself. If the guy was even here. Crew hadn't seen him since the attack.

Foxtrot bunked in the same room with Glace, and that worked for Crew, who took a bunk in the room opposite theirs. The living quarters reminded him of the dorms at AIT, which had been a step up from the ones at Basic. This quad branched off to four quads that were anchored by a main living area with a TV, couch, and dinette. It was much larger with nicer furniture and rather than a microwave struggling to boil water, the wing had the cafeteria and a wall of self-serve sandwiches, fruit, and dessert. The whole place was next level, making him wonder what happened in Badem's TAC that they provided everything a growing operator needed.

"You going to eat?" Foxtrot asked.

"No appetite." Crew tossed his ruck on an empty bunk. "Going to the gym."

"I'll come with."

"Why, so you can give me another beat-down?"

"Promise?" she demurred.

Crew chuckled as they entered the high-tech facility. He gave a low whistle as he led Havoc to a treadmill. He tethered his harness, then set it to 4.5 miles per hour. Havoc gave him a lazy, irritated glance as he slowly worked into a full trot. Crew did a short run on another treadmill, then moved to the leg press. Even as he worked different muscles and gave careful consideration of his stub in the prosthesis, he maintained a keen awareness of Foxtrot. He let Havoc off the treadmill and gave him some water. The workout had been enough for the maligator to slump onto a mat and veg out.

Crew moved to the pull workouts, then the battle ropes, noting Foxtrot didn't seem that engaged in her workout. Not like the intensity he'd witnessed in L.A. It was like she'd run out of steam. She'd been to Hades and back. The girl needed time to process. Maybe she needed someone to process it *with*. More than that, someone to keep her in the fight, because this thing with the vote, with Vale being taken, was far from over. He had no doubt about the fire that burned within Vienna Foxcroft, even if she doubted it. Just had to remind her of the blood pumping in her veins.

Had to admit . . . she was lightyears better than Rina. Ironically, this was the first time he'd thought of Rina since meeting Foxtrot. Quite a switch. It'd been his pattern to rule out every woman he encountered because of some similarity, no matter how loose, to Rina.

Crew grabbed the boxing targets and slid them on his hands, then tapped them together. "Hey."

From where she sat on the leg press bench, she glanced over her shoulder, then let the weights slowly thud down. "This your way of trying to avoid another humiliation?"

"Gotta save face somehow," he said, tapping them again and waving her over. "C'mon, Foxtrot. Show me what you've got."

She slid on a pair of gloves from the locker, then stretched her arms and warmed up her elbows and shoulders as she made her way over to him. She bounced a little, but she still wasn't up to par when she threw the first punches at the targets.

Crew angled in and sideways, backed up and to the left. Moved in. All forcing her to react and land her punches into the padded targets on his hands. But they were soft. "C'mon, Foxtrot."

A cross, right hook, uppercut, left.

"Soft," he taunted, "too soft."

Nostrils and eyes flaring, she paused. Then was back on the balls of her feet, moving. Punching.

"C'mon!" Crew shouted. "*Hit* the freakin' targets!"

Chin tucked, she was close to hopping, both on her toes and her anger. The punches were more solid, but a couple glanced off the targets. Nearly found his face.

"What is this, kindergarten?"

She growled. Threw herself forward. Punches coming rapid-fire, but the toll of the attack, her distracted thoughts were leaving head shots open.

"Better," he said. "Protect your face!"

She punched and rounded. He saw what she intended almost too late as she leaned back and drew that leg in, chambering it. A half second slower and she'd have cracked his jaw.

He barked a laugh. "Nice try."

Crew crouched and ducked. Felt her foot dust his ballcap—which went askew. Blinded him to her next kick. Holy spinning-hook-kick, Batman!

Her instep caught him across the head.

He stumbled back with another barked laugh and a sharp

awareness he'd unleashed her beast. As he staggered, she dove into him. Drove him back onto the mat. He cursed himself, the targets strapped to his hands inhibiting his ability to fight back. She locked her legs around his waist. Arms came around his shoulders.

In a split-second, he tore the targets off his hands. Whipped his torso back, slamming her against the mat with a hard thud. Heard her grunt—not in pain but angry determination.

No freaking way was she getting him in a rear-naked choke. Shoulders up, chin down, he used his cross hand to intercept her right wrist. Clamped down her left hand between his left bicep and underarm to prevent her from using that arm in a choke and drove his whole body to the underhook side. Got his head on the mat. Worked to wriggle and get his hips on the mat, too. Released her wrist, knowing she'd come to the top.

As any good grappler would, she did—swung up to mount.

Crew drew in his legs into a half guard, his feet finding her abdomen. He saw her eyes, saw the brightness in them and her flushed cheeks from the effort.

She leaned into his feet and sagged. Slumped back onto her knees and patted his thigh, signaling that she wasn't doing anymore.

Did he dare trust the beast within her to really yield?

But Foxtrot lowered onto the ground, crossed her legs, and bent forward, head cradled in her hands.

Crew hauled himself up, one leg tucked under him, the other bent at the knee. He hooked an arm over that and stood guard while she worked through it. Shoulders and torso weren't bouncing, but the veins in her neck and hands bulged. He touched her arm, just letting her know he was there. She wasn't alone.

"Frode died . . . because of me. They all died because of me."

Yeah, had a feeling this was what had been sapping her strength and inner fire. He wouldn't let her vanish down this vat of dung. "They died because—"

"Don't." Her head snapped up.

Crew lifted his hand from her arm.

Green eyes blazed. "Skip the platitudes, okay?" She all but dared him to counter the command. To speak up.

He didn't. Knew better. Somehow knew her better than he knew the guys in the other room.

She lowered her gaze to the mat, morose, and shook her head. "And it's still not over. I've killed a man . . ." Sorrow knotted her brow, tears pooling her irises into a sea of green. "That's never okay."

Just keep your trap shut. Let her talk. He wanted to tell her it might not be okay but sometimes it was necessary.

She narrowed her eyes and looked past him. "I'm not sure I could ever do what you do. All these years, learning martial arts, learning how to fight, to be street smart . . ." She swallowed. "But when it's real, when it's . . ." She shoved her fingers into her hair and jerked it back. Held it there. "I can't stop hearing his neck crack."

And like the word and what she'd had to do to the man trying to kill her, Foxtrot's voice cracked.

Crew shifted in closer. Slid an arm around her shoulders as she battled through more tears. "I hope you never stop hearing that."

She jerked up, nearly headbutting him. Her face contorted in revulsion. "How can you say that?"

"Because that is your tether on morality, that sound stirs in you revulsion and it will always remind you that a life—a person—God placed on this earth, ended at your hands. We can debate the ethics of combat and killing—and we'd have to take a deep dive into King David, a onetime shepherd turned warrior—a role God ordained for him, yet the blood of those he killed—at God's instruction—kept him from building God's Temple. Remembering that sound will help you weigh what you do the next time you're faced with a similar situation."

"*God?*" she scoffed. "Are you kidding me?"

Yeah, kinda saw this coming, too. She relied a lot on her own strength . . . but not much on God's.

"You really believe in God?"

"I do," he said calmly, firmly.

"How can anyone—look at the world!"

Sad for her limited view, for the blame she placed on the Maker's shoulders, he nodded. "Yeah, we've made a mess of it, haven't we?"

"How? How can you believe in Him?" She shifted around to face him, her expression borderline defiant, but also . . . desperate.

Past the pitched words, the knotted brow, he saw the wounded heart below those features. He shrugged, not to be demeaning but because there was no other answer for him. "God makes sense." He tugged long threads from the padded targets.

She laughed. "How? In what world?"

Just like in sparring, he could handle the punches. This wasn't about him, about being offended, this was a heart and life on the line.

Crew swiveled his backside around and propped himself against the wall, twisting the threads the way he did for paracord loops for his gear. "A few years ago while on mission with an Israeli strike force, one of the guys on my team made some derogatory comment about the Israelis. And it just got me thinking about history, looking back through thousands of years and straight up to the present, if what some say—that God doesn't exist, that they aren't God's chosen people, then why on earth does this *one* race *always* have other countries trying to wipe it out? Babylonians, Seleucids, Romans, Persians, Muslims, Germans . . ."

Foxtrot stretched out on the mat, staring up at the ceiling. "Maybe . . . but Jews have been at war with Arabs since their inception."

"Lazy," Crew teased as he watched Havoc low-crawl over to Foxtrot and slump next to her, aligning his spine with her side.

He twisted and tugged the cords. They were short, so not a bracelet. "It's easy to say, 'it's always been that way,' but you can't just write off an argument with a broad generalization."

He adjusted to straighten his leg and let his thigh rest. "Beyond people groups, look at our planet alone—the exceptional conditions that make life happen also allow us to see the universe—way out across galaxies and past planets. One degree off, and we wouldn't see it. Or the properties of our sun—right distance, right orbit, mass, location, galaxy—to *nurture* life rather than obliterate it. Then there's the laws and constants of physics that conspire in a mind-numbing way to make the universe hospitable for life. Just too much there that's unexplainable about how they came into being, how there is so much order amid the chaos." He shook his head, staring out of the gym.

"But I think the singular thing that most erased any doubt about God for me"—really baring his soul here, wasn't he?—"was when I was lying in that hospital, side shredded, leg missing below the knee . . . wondering why I wasn't dead yet. Learning of the mind-blowing brilliance of our bodies, their ability to self-preserve, heal all . . . Then being in rehab, seeing the difference one minor thing between my situation and another guy's had him a near vegetable and I was learning to walk again."

Stretching his neck, he exhaled heavily, then went on. "Mess up that precarious, delicate arrangement of our minds and our body, and it's lights out." He shook his head, then snapped his gaze to hers. "Our DNA has *one hundred trillion cells* in a chemical alphabet that is a meticulous, detailed set of instructions on what Crew Gatlin looks like, what he likes, what makes him totally into the firestorm that is Vienna Foxcroft."

Her gaze held his for a long time, thinking, then she looked away. "That must've been miswiring—maybe that explosion did mess up your head."

"If anything, it made me smarter. More determined to get

what I want." Okay, maybe that was too obvious. He twisted the cords into a loop and tied it off. "My point is that you can't throw a grenade in the air and when the dust settles, you have an industrial complex housing thousands and worth millions. Explosions don't create, they destroy." He tapped his leg. "Losing Larry taught me that."

"Who's Larry?"

"My leg."

Foxtrot lifted her head and frowned at him. "You *named* your leg?"

"No, I named my shin, ankle, and foot that were vaporized in the explosion. Thought about having a funeral for him, but there was too much paperwork, even though he'd been cremated."

She rolled onto her side, propped her hand beneath her head and studied him. "How can you laugh and joke about it?" She took the thread loop. Eyed it.

"Doesn't help if I'm mad about it."

Havoc rolled onto his back with a moan and stretched his paws over at Foxtrot, earning a laugh and drawing her back down. She held up the paracord loop he'd made and slid it onto her finger—a ring.

His gut twisted, tightened. Holy Moses . . . "Does that mean we're engaged?"

She wrapped an arm around Havoc and stroked his side. "Well, me and him, maybe." But then the fur-missile leapt up, trotted to the side, and retrieved his KONG. He returned and set it in front of Foxtrot, staring at it—snout a half inch away—as if it might sprout legs and escape.

"You realize he and I are a package deal, right?"

"Do I dare throw this?" Foxtrot looked at Crew for direction.

He reached into his go-bag and drew out the tethered KONG. "Toss this."

Even as he handed it off to her, Havoc's eyes darted up—and locked onto the new KONG. Ears swiveled to attention. Eyes went all melty as he eased back, snout closing in anticipation of a takedown.

Foxtrot tossed it and Havoc tore across the gym after it.

As Crew retrieved the black KONG, a shape appeared in the doorway—and a curse erupted because Havoc nearly collided with him. Twitching back, Bennion let another curse sear the air, likely convinced Havoc was about to turn him into mincemeat. Huffed and glowered at Crew, who was probably laughing a little too hard. "Chapel wants y'all topside. If I let you live that long."

13

ISTANBUL, TURKEY

"Baako." In the conference room, Vienna stared at the pictures laid out on the obsidian table that stretched the length of the room. Next to his, there were images of two others: Iris and one of the crew, Magnus Goldblum. Finger touching each one, she finally looked at the two formidable men in the room. "What's this about?"

"That's what we want to know," Chapel said as he and the commander moved from the wall they seemed to be protecting. "You recognize these three?"

"You know I do." She resented being asked questions people knew the answers to—it felt like a complete set-up.

The commander's blue eyes bored into her as he motioned them into chairs. "Please name them, Miss Foxcroft."

Vienna looked to Crew who didn't seem any less annoyed but he nodded, telling her to play the game. "Baako al Masry, Iris Greene, and Magnus Goldblum. Would you like their rank and serial numbers, too?"

Chapel considered her, then moved to the far side of the room and indicated to a young man in a TAC uniform who tapped into a tablet, which transformed the far wall into a series of screens.

Her breath backed into her throat as she found all three—Iris, Baako, and Magnus—staring back at her. Each with one live camera and one screen that looked like a display of their vitals. Magnus's looked as if a kid had gotten hold of an Etch-a-Sketch.

"I don't understand," she said, dragging her gaze back to the commander, then Chapel. "They're *here*?" She eyed Crew, who looked ticked as he edged forward and adjusted his ballcap. "But they caught the private flight."

"That was our belief as well," the commander said, "until we got a call from the Çırağan stating these three had shown up there. We sent a team over to retrieve them."

Vienna sat next to Crew, frowning at the commander. "I don't understand—how did they miss the flight?"

"According to your friends, a weapon appeared in a bag," Chapel said, his voice gravelly. "All three claim the bag did not belong to them, but they were the last ones in line. Authorities could not prove who the bag belonged to, so they were released but missed the flight and returned to the hotel, hoping to find you or the team so other arrangements could be made. Ms. Greene said you had her tablet, so she couldn't access booking records."

"I-I do." She touched her forehead, remembered how it'd all played out. "She'd hurt her ankle, so I offered to grab it for her. By the time I'd finally located it, the bus was gone. They'd left without me." She scowled. "But . . . *weapon*?"

"Problem is," the commander said quietly, "when there's a weapon found in a bag at the airport, incident reports are filed." His expression went stony. "There isn't an incident report, or any report related to these three." He cocked his head. "What do you know about them, the Egyptian especially?"

"The Egyptian?'" she balked. "He's a good friend. We've done three films together. Same with Iris—but four films. Magnus is a boom operator or something. I'm not sure. It's impossible to know everyone on the crew." Her mind swam at the implication the commander and Chapel were insinuating. "What're you saying?"

The commander seemed too at ease in his authority. "Just that—no report of a weapon. The bag said to have held the weapon? Doesn't exist, at least not according to airport security."

Crew leaned forward, hands fisted over each another on the table. "What does security footage show?"

Chapel gave an impassive glare, then sighed. "Shows them getting off the bus, last of the film personnel to enter the airport, then once they approach the security line . . ." He shrugged. "Conveniently glitched."

"Wait." Vienna couldn't believe what was happening here. "Are you saying . . ." It was too hard to process, impossible to speak. "Are you saying they're *lying*? Why? They wouldn't—especially not Iris. She's a sweet, mousy production assistant. She wouldn't have a weapon."

"What're their stories?" Crew adjusted his ballcap and earned a hard nudge at his elbow from Havoc, who seemed to detect their stress. He smoothed a hand down the Malinois' neck.

"Ms. Greene states she was last off the bus to be sure the others were taken care of, and that Mr. Goldblum stayed to help her with her luggage. While he was getting those from the bus, Mr. al Masry demanded to know where you were, why you weren't on the bus."

"Took him long enough to notice," Crew muttered.

Chapel gave a grim nod. "Al Masry says he never saw the bag, that he had his gear duffel and suitcase. Mr. Goldblum is distraught and claims he only carried what Ms. Greene instructed him to, outside his own."

"This is ludicrous," Vienna said, trying to grasp this, and more—the reticence of the men in this room to believe Baako and Iris. Magnus she didn't really know, but . . . she couldn't fathom that. "Why would any of them have a weapon?"

"People who've had their lives threatened sometimes don't react with logic but desperation."

Vienna dropped back against her seat. "I don't . . . This doesn't make sense." She leaned forward again. "Look, I know Baako—even Iris. They wouldn't . . . If they said they didn't do it, I believe them."

Chapel squinted at her. "Do you really? Do you *really* know them? You've been lip-locked with Gatlin here, but do you really know him?"

"Hey," Crew said in a low warning.

Feeling nauseated, Vienna looked at the table. "Your suggestion that someone is lying, that maybe they're all lying doesn't make sense. Why? What would they gain from that?"

"You." It was the commander's man Volken who spoke that time.

She'd nearly forgotten he was there. "Why? What do I—"

"Abna' Suria." The commander sat across from her. "They want you, and they have pretty far-reaching tentacles. If they've managed to corrupt your friends—"

She barked a disbelieving laugh.

"—then we need to be very cautious. You need to be very cautious."

"But they have Felicity." Her heart skidded across his icy glare. "They don't know about me . . ."

Unless they *had* corrupted one of her friends. And if that was true, they could have told the terrorist group they had the wrong person.

Which would explain why they came back. She was going to be sick.

". . . the unexpected return of these three means it's vital we get you out of the country now."

"Agreed," Crew gruffed as he nodded.

"Good," Chapel said. "You'll take Ms. Foxcroft to a small private airstrip where one of the Turk's private jets is waiting to ferry her out of country. We want you and Havoc to be sure she gets on that plane, but the commander and I agree you're needed here to find Vale."

Crew faltered. "I . . ." He gave her a sidelong glance, his jaw on his shoulder, then back to the commander. "Negative. The threat against Foxtrot is too pervasive. She needs someone to protect her."

Vienna would've argued she didn't need anyone to protect her, but she really did not want to be alone right now.

"We have—"

"No." Crew's jaw muscle jounced. "I go with her. End of story. No way I'm letting you put her on a plane with strangers whose loyalty I cannot verify."

The commander scowled. "Stand down and hear me out, Gatlin. We have a potential lead on Vale. You and your dog are needed here."

"Negative, I'm staying—"

Vienna touched his arm. "Hey. It's okay." She nodded to the commander. "It's a private plane."

"And there will be a security detachment handpicked by the Turk."

When Crew lowered his head, she knew he couldn't argue with the logic of him staying to find Felicity.

Vienna lowered her hand to her lap, nervously twisting the rope ring he'd made in the gym. Happy, for once, to let someone else work the conflict. He hadn't made the ring for her . . . but she'd picked it up. And he hadn't objected. Putting it on her finger . . . that had meant something to her. She'd tried to put it on casually, not draw attention, but he'd been all over the simple action. Asked if they were engaged . . .

That wouldn't be so bad, would it?

You don't even know him. As Chapel so clearly pointed out.

But she did know Crew Gatlin. Something about the man seemed written on her soul. Eyeing the corded ring, she wondered how she'd gone from 'not dating' to *this* in the space of what, two weeks?

"I'll be okay," she said.

Crew's jaw muscle jounced. "I don't like it." He looked at her. "I should be there for you."

She managed a smile. "You know where I work . . ."

With a huff, Crew adjusted his ballcap. Expelled a thick breath. "Fine."

The commander finally surrendered. "Before we get you to the airstrip, we need you to do one thing first—eat a meal with them. Play dumb. Don't tell them you're leaving—it's too risky. While you're eating, let them talk. We'll be monitoring it to see if anyone reveals any intel we can use to determine who is compromised."

"Compromised." She'd known that was the inference, but hearing it out loud . . .

"You're using her as bait?" Crew barked, starting to rise. "Not happening."

"*Vital*," the commander argued, eased forward, crowding Vienna's personal space. "Understand this, Miss Foxcroft—you know them as friends and coworkers, but one of them is *not* your friend. Possibly not even named Magnus, Iris, or Baako."

"Foxtrot," Chapel said, his voice dark and lethal, "Crew said you lost a friend during the Çırağan hotel attack. That right?"

Frode. She swallowed. Nodded.

"Remember that one of those three is responsible for his death. One is colluding with the same terrorists. And since these three are here, that means the Abna' Suria know they have the wrong person. It's very likely Felicity Vale is already dead. They want *you* now. *That* is who you're turning the tables on." He shouldered even closer somehow. "Gatlin told us you're strong, so while we know we're asking a lot, we are confident it's within your skillset."

He'd said that? Vienna met Crew's gaze, stomach in knots as she thought of the lethal game she'd been swept into. Street fighting, wearing a harness to stunt double another was one thing . . . but knowingly walking into a room where it was promised someone in there wanted to hand her over to a terrorist organization . . .?

The instinct to take his hand, siphon off some of his tanker-deep strength, feel grounded, safe . . . not this swirling vortex of darkness and fear, was huge. Which was insane—since when had she ever sought a man for strength?

But . . . why would that be bad? Hadn't Dad always said he was stronger with Mom than without? Couldn't it work the other way? It wasn't one person's strength superseding another's, but rather a buffeting, a strengthening . . . iron sharpening iron.

Then again, were she and Crew even at that point?

As if hearing her roiling thoughts, he hooked his elbow back and his large hand dwarfed hers. Cocooned it—*her*—in that constant reassurance he always seemed to exude. Tenacious belief in her. One that said she could do whatever she wanted, and he'd be there. He drew her hand to his side and held it there.

A strong, persistent—and cold—nose thrust her arm up. Demanded attention. Havoc's amber eyes locked onto her. His paw snapped onto her leg. Claws dug in. A vow of commitment, loyalty. Just like his handler's.

"Whatever you choose," Crew said, his voice deep, low, "Havoc and I have your six."

14

SECRET TACTICAL CENTER, ISTANBUL, TURKEY

You can do this—you're an actress. Pretend. Fake it. As if the camera's rolling.

The elevator doors opened, and she stepped into the corridor of the lower level, sensing Crew and Havoc at her heels. When they'd left the conference room, the commander and Chapel said to act natural, not ask questions but let them volunteer information. The commander promised they'd have eyes on the entire conversation. All she had to do was be a conduit.

Right. A conduit.

That conduit, however, seemed clogged with the nauseating realization that one of those three was betraying her. Setting her up. And she hated that somehow her thoughts landed on Baako as the culprit.

"Hey." Crew's word was more breath and grunt than actual word, but it was enough to draw her around. "You okay?"

Shifting aside, she angled toward him but stopped shy of facing him. She looked down the passage, feeling chilled. "I . . ." Turn right and she'd be in the cafeteria. Could she even eat without getting sick? "I-I don't think I can do this."

"Your choice."

"They're my friends. I worked with them. Baako and I were close . . . I don't . . ." She deflated. "How can this be happening? What if I screw this up? What if I tip them off or do something stupid?"

Crew edged in closer, his chest against her shoulder. Though he had Havoc's lead in hand, he adjusted his ballcap. Craned his neck to bring those gorgeous eyes closer.

Mercy, he was a beautiful man.

"How's it working?"

Vienna frowned, mind whiplashing. "What?"

"I'm distracting you."

With a groan, she rolled toward the passage to start moving again.

"Just kidding." He caught her arm and tugged her back.

This time, she went into his arms willingly, put her forehead on his chest. Breathed in that willingness.

"I'm worried I'll blow this, or they'll read through me. I thought they were my friends, and now I have to play spy to figure out which one is trying to hand me over to terrorists!"

"No." Crew cupped the back of her neck and held her close, his mouth at her ear. "That's not on you to find that out. The guilty always betray themselves eventually. You're just giving them space to do it. Dig deep and find that core strength you're always flashing." Two fingers beneath her chin tipped her head until she met his gaze. Then his mouth was on hers for a long, languorous kiss. He left a trail of kisses along her jaw, then back to her mouth for another deep one. "Now," he said, his voice husky. "Just sit there and think about that kiss."

How did he do that—tangle her mind into a dozen knots?

"What, did you think it was memorable?"

He smirked around a hooded gaze. "If it isn't, we can keep practicing."

She laughed, loving that he always knew how to make her

laugh. Kept her on *terra firma*. Then she groaned again. "I'm not a spy or an operator. I'm . . . fake."

"You pinned me on the mat and stole my manhood. That's not fake. That's hot."

Vienna cocked her head at him. "Do you know how to encourage me *without* flirting?"

His brow rippled and a frown tugged at his trim beard. "That's a thing? If so, I own that failure."

Laughing yet again, she thumped his gut and he gusted out a breath as she turned to resume course. Havoc barked, coming up on his hind legs, ready to play, too. She took a step, then glanced over her shoulder and gave Crew a rueful smile. "You can distract me any time."

"Hold up—what?" He drew her back to him. "Let's practice."

She extricated herself. "Later, Soldier-boy."

"Vienna?"

The laughter, the merriment, the joy, the headiness of that kiss evaporated at the sound of Baako's voice. Stilled, Vienna gulped a breath and stared wide-eyed at Crew.

He leaned in, which probably looked like a kiss from Baako's point of view. "You got this, Foxtrot. And if it's easier, I can nibble on your ear while he's conning you."

"Stop," she sniffed but the laugh never quite made it to her throat because she'd turned and saw Baako scowling as he slowly came toward them.

Havoc let out a low snarl, his head down, his hackles raised.

"Leave it," came Crew's gruff command. "Or should I command him to attack?" Crew whispered into her hair.

"Baako!" Did that sound too piqued? "What're you doing here?" Sensing the fortress of safety and sexiness at her back, she moved toward her friend, remembering the commander said to keep in the lounge. "I thought you got on the plane?"

Standing with his hands on his belt, Baako couldn't hide his dark expression or the feral hatred toward Crew. "Tried," he said, glowering at Crew again, then looking at her. "So were you. What happened?"

A warm touch found her back. "Want me to get your food tray?"

That was a very deliberate move, one to remind Baako that Crew had staked claim on her heart. She glanced up and smiled at the very nice view. "Please."

"Preferences?"

"Edible."

Crew gave an affirming nod, then headed toward the serving line.

"Sure got cozy fast with GI Joe," Baako bit out.

"Oh." Vienna motioned to Crew, where he was juggling two trays and doing his best not to let Havoc yank them out of his hands. "Did you want him to get you a food tray, too? Does that make you feel better?"

Eyes wide, Baako scoffed. "Hate much, V?"

"*Hate?*" she balked. "You're the one in my face because I finally found someone I like." Okay this definitely wasn't going the way it should. "Look." She pushed her hair back and turned toward a table and chairs. "I'm sorry. I've been under a lot of stress and scared and then getting left behind, I just . . ." Her gaze hit the woman nearby. "*Iris?* You, too? I thought you were both long gone by now."

Iris teared up. "It was so awful."

Okay, wasn't expecting that. But it was a lot easier to work with than Baako's strangling jealousy over Crew. "I . . . I have your tablet. Want me to go get it?"

"I don't care about that stupid tablet," Iris said around sniffles, then she shuddered. "That's so ridiculous—I need that tablet. It has everything on it."

"I'll grab it. Hang on." Vienna jogged out of the room, grabbed the tablet from her ruck—recalled what Chapel had said about taking necessities. She'd have to do that later. Back in the cafeteria, she slid the tablet over to her friend and started to see Magnus. "Oh, hey. I didn't realize you were here as well."

He sagged. "Do not get me started."

She regained her seat, noting that Crew had tracked her every step.

Behind her came Magnus, who took the spot next to her. "Hey, Vienna."

"Magnus, what happened?" She glanced around. "Is everyone here? Did the plane not take off?"

"Oh, it took off," Iris seethed.

Vienna wasn't known for emotionality, and she really wasn't sure what to do with it. Normally, she'd give her friend room to cry. But they needed information. "I was so scared when I found your tablet, then discovered the buses gone . . ."

"I'm so sorry about that—Kerr had called and was giving me information. I was writing it down when the driver pulled away."

And she shouted for them to wait two minutes!

Crew set the tray in front of her. "Drink? Soda, water . . . I think they have coffee . . ."

"Water, please."

"Thankfully, the security team was still around, so . . . " Iris said, her gaze following Crew as he moved away with his dog. She leaned forward and wrinkled her nose. "Tell me you broke your no-dating rule."

Vienna felt the heat scorching her cheeks. "We're not—" She wanted to say they weren't dating, but . . . how many times had they kissed? And what was on her finger from their time in the gym? Maybe being open would help Iris feel comfortable enough. "I don't know what we are to be honest." She twisted the thread ring he'd made. Didn't really mean anything. Just was . . . cool. Clearing her throat, she tried to brush off the embarrassment. "Anyway . . ."

Crew returned, handing her a bottled water, and pulled out the chair next to her.

Which Havoc helped himself into.

"Hey, Meatball. That was for me," Crew grumbled, earning a laugh from Iris and Vienna. Naturally, Baako threw him another glare.

Havoc leaned toward Vienna, sniffing her, sniffing her tray.

"Off," Crew instructed, then leaned on the table with a hand. "I'm going to take him out. Be back in five."

Vienna's heart skipped a beat. "Sure." He was leaving her alone? Couldn't that wait? "Okay."

He clicked his tongue and left with Havoc, who leapt off the chair and trotted after him. Why did it seem her brain had gone with them? What was she supposed to do or say?

"Who is he that he was playing soldier with the security team?" Baako asked, dropping into a chair across from her. "He's not just a dog handler."

"That's exactly what he is," Vienna countered, seething with irritation. "He was a handler in the Army but an explosion"—*he will hate you if you mention his leg*—"got him discharged. That dog is a military K-9 that saved his life in Afghanistan, now they both work for a ranch in Texas." She glowered, pulse whooshing in her ears. "And what am I doing explaining him when he has done nothing but protect me this whole time, while you rode a bus and missed a plane?"

"How do you know we missed the plane?" Baako demanded.

"Deductive reasoning—how else would you be here? Lord knows it's not because you have any desire to protect anyone but yourself. Aren't you the one who got on the bus and left me at the hotel?"

"You told me to go!" Baako said.

Yeah, and she'd told Crew to leave, too. Which man stayed? Which man had always been there for her the last two days?

"She chose the better man . . ." Bennion had told Baako at the hotel.

She really had, hadn't she?

But that wouldn't help them here, would it? "You're right,"

173

Vienna said, stuffing down her irritation. "It's been a long few days. I'm sorry . . ."

"Why are you apologizing to him?" Iris said. "He hasn't done anything but look out for himself and accuse everyone of everything."

"V said she'd get your tablet, and you let her, but then you can't even hold the bus for her?" Baako growled. "And him"—he flung his hand in Magnus's direction—"and he does nothing but follow you around like a lost puppy."

"He was helping me with the luggage, and all you could do was blame and accuse me!"

"He had them all! What was I supposed to do?" he hissed. "He's probably the one who had the gun bag anyway."

Magnus looked aghast. "What? Why would I have it?" The man looked ready to cry. "I just wanted to help Iris. That bag—I don't know where it came from. One minute it wasn't on the belt, the next it was."

"What're you talking about, man?" Baako said. "You put it up there. I saw you."

"You're out of your mind," Magnus countered. "I think you put it there."

"What? Why?"

"Because . . ." Magnus blanched, then looked away.

"Hold up. Is that comment because *I'm Egyptian*?"

"Foxtrot." Crew's bark sliced through the tension with expert precision. He stood in the doorway with Havoc, who was emitting a low snarl. "The commander wants you."

On her feet, she glanced at the food tray and snagged the roll. Strode toward Gatlin. "I could kiss you for that rescue."

"Promise?"

"V!" Baako shouted. "What are we now, chopped liver?"

Vienna glanced over her shoulder but was saved from having to respond when one of the commander's men summoned Iris, Magnus, and Baako to follow him. As the others stood to leave, she eyed Crew. "That was about to get ugly."

"No kidding. I nearly told your buddy chopped liver was an upgrade for him."

"Be nice."

"Why? Guy treats you like you owe him." He rolled his shoulder, adjusted his ballcap. Noticed she was still watching him. "What?"

"You looked like you'd like to go a few rounds with him."

"If by rounds you mean .223 caliber rounds . . . yeah."

"You'd *shoot* him?" she balked as they moved through the corridor to the bunkrooms.

"*Neutralize* is the term."

"That means kill."

"And?"

"Hold up." She swiveled around in front of him and planted her hands on his abdomen. "You would really kill him."

Crew's gaze lasered in on her and any of that lightheartedness that she'd come to love and expect from him vanished. His hands were on her hips. "I'd do whatever it took to protect you, Foxtrot."

Was this real? How could he feel that way? She nudged his ballcap back a little to see his eyes better. "You're serious . . . But I don't have four legs."

He smirked. "But the two you have are very se—"

"Gatlin, Foxcroft," Bennion said from the end of the hall. "Let's move."

It took them forty minutes to reach the airstrip and it was about forty minutes too fast, in her opinion.

How do I stop this?

Nerves akimbo, she sat in the SUV while two of the security team went with Crew and Havoc into the private jet.

Things had been on fast-forward since stepping into Istanbul, and it seemed everything had irrevocably changed—her life, her outlook, her belief she'd never get married. With thirty creeping toward her with vengeance and stealth, her siblings married, she had given up on a happily-ever-after. And while she might've found a man worth slotting into that empty place in her life . . . they were about to go their separate ways.

And she really did not want that to happen. She could give him her number, but what if he didn't call? Okay, so she needed to get his number. What if he maybe gave her the wrong number? Or never answered her calls? Was he the type who had dalliances when he'd deployed? Was that what he was to her?

Okay, *this* was why she didn't like the dating game.

"Ma'am," the driver spoke over his shoulder.

Vienna started. "Yes?"

"He's waiting for you, ma'am."

He? She glanced to the plane and saw Crew standing on the landing, waving her over. Wind tore at her as she crossed the tarmac. Hunched, she shouldered against the wind and the ramping whine of the jet engines as the pilots readied for takeoff.

She climbed the stairs and met him. "All clear?"

"It's like a five-star in here. Havoc doesn't want to leave." He motioned her inside and followed her.

"Wow," she said, not really caring how nice it was or wasn't. She wandered down the row of seats. Not near as nice as the jumbo jet they'd come over on, but it was definitely upscale.

"Hey, you okay?"

At Crew's question, she turned and found him parked on the arm of a chair. "Yeah." She scooted past him, avoiding his eyes, avoiding saying much more.

He caught her hand. Held it and her, though she tried to keep moving.

"What's wrong?"

She finally stepped back until she stood in front of him. Should she tell him? Admit how strong her feelings were for him? With his gorgeous eyes, firm planes of his face, the muscles that knocked a girl senseless on the man. The guy who didn't hold punches during sparring, who treated her as an equal?

"I'm scared." It was mostly true.

Crew cocked his head. "About what?"

Being in a situation where he wasn't there to fight with her.

"I don't like this any more than you do."

Her gaze flicked to his, surprised. They started watering. "What if they find me?"

His nostrils flared. "You're strong."

"Yeah . . ." She traced his beard, heart hammering. "But I'm stronger with you."

"Holy Moses, Foxtrot." He pulled her closer. Crushed her to himself and held her tight.

Easing back, she stared down at him. "I want to stay until you can leave."

The way his eyes moved over her face told her he was considering it. Working through if that could work. "There's too much risk with the three at the TAC."

"I don't know why . . ." She cleared her throat. "I'm not weak. I just . . ." Why couldn't she come out with it, say she liked him? More than liked him. For pity's sake—she couldn't even think of the right word. But she'd never met anyone like him. Never would again, she was sure of it. He was . . . *Made for me.*

"Read you loud and clear, Foxtrot."

She framed his face. Had this crazy idea that this would be the last time they'd see each other. Kissed him.

"Mr. Gatlin, we're cleared for liftoff."

Crew came to his feet and nodded to the security officer, who moved back out of sight. He caught her hand. Fingers pressed the back of her hand while his thumb slid along her palm to her ring finger.

No. To the cord ring he'd made.

"I like which finger you put this on . . ."

"It fit perfectly."

"Kind of like us."

Stunned that he'd say that, that he'd voice what she'd been harboring beneath uncertainty and fears, she nodded.

"Well, when this is over . . . maybe we could make this . . . nicer."

She drew in a quick breath. "I—"

"Sir."

Crew growled, then seemed to need to stem his anger and glanced to the side. And something happened in his posture, in his eyes. He shoved forward, bending to look out one of the portal-style windows.

"What's wrong?"

"Hey!" Crew barked over his shoulder. "Security!" He straightened, a gun suddenly in hand.

"What—what's wrong?" She craned to look out the window. Saw the SUV on the tarmac. Two guards . . .

"Incoming. Radio your team." As Crew whistled, bringing Havoc to his side, the guards were hustling out of the plane, weapons up as they moved.

Vienna's gaze finally found the problem. Two large flatbed trucks with gunmen trounced across the swath of green that separated the road from the runway. "Oh my . . ."

"Out, go," Crew barked. "Now!"

But even as he said it, the cabin door closed and she felt a pull on her body as the plane started taxiing.

"No!" Crew shoved himself toward the front. Tried the cockpit door—locked. "Augh!" He banged on the door. "Stop the plane!"

"Why stop? If we can take off—"

"RPG," Crew said indicating to the window. "We have to get off this plane."

"How?" Vienna's panic cracked her word.

"C'mon," he barked as he charged toward the back of the jet, winding past the main seating area, then through a small dining area.

"Where are we going?" Was it safer at the back?

"Jets of this size sometimes have—"

Bullets pinged and cracked against the plane.

"Down!" Crew barked but kept moving.

Crouching, she navigated the gangway, hearing windows crack. Thumps against the hull. "What are we doing?"

"Cargo access in the rear. Hopefully there'll be a door in the fuselage." He scrambled up to the lavatory door.

"In the bathroom?" Vienna balked.

Crew yanked open another panel, revealing access to the cargo hold. "C'mon—in."

"Are you—" She clamped down on her objection and threaded her way into the tiny lavatory and followed him through the opening. Surprised to find what seemed like a small room, she glanced around.

Crew and Havoc scrambled to the side where they indeed found the cargo door in the wall—fuselage. He managed to open it, a red light erupting above the door. "Let's go."

Light punched its way into the dark hold, and she squinted, momentarily blinded. She slowly saw the tarmac rushing below them.

"Are you crazy?" she shouted over the din.

He sat on the edge, Havoc next to him who seemed excited and ready for an adventure. "Just like a stunt."

Except there were no pads to fall on. Right. She knew how to take a fall. She angled into the side, still nervous. Still wondering if this was nece—

Crack! Boom!

A whistle screamed from behind.

Feeling a strange vacuum suck at her ears, Vienna glanced over her shoulder. Saw an eruption of flames barreling at them.

She turned. Toed the edge—

The fireball roared straight at them.

Vienna sailed into the air.

15

PRIVATE AIRSTRIP, ISTANBUL, TURKEY

PAIN SCORED HIS HIP AND SPINE AS HE THUDDED TO A STOP IN THE ditch. Fire and smoke billowed out, blanketing him and the air. His head thudded against the ground. Dirt rained down. Howls came from his three—the corporal screaming. The others who'd been patrolling him. Smoke. Fire. Blood. His leg . . . Nausea roiled. He glanced down . . . his leg was missing . . . blood seeping into the dirt.

"Gatlin!" Ghost grabbed his tac vest. Hauled him forward. Marvel barked frantically but stood guard.

"My leg . . ." He breathed. "Tourniquet—I need a tourn—"

"*Crew! Hey!*"

He blinked. Smoke billowed overhead, blocking the sky, framing—"Foxtrot." Not Ghost. The terror of the minefield vanished, depositing him back in the present. The plane attack.

Havoc nipped at him, as if telling him to get his head in the game. Get moving.

Man. What'd just happened?

He jerked up, shaken that he'd flashed back to Afghanistan. Situational awareness hauled him with a hard punch back to the present. Gaze sliding over the scene—the plane was a roaring fireball, drifting on the tarmac and providing cover for them—he caught Foxtrot's sleeve. Pulled her to the side. Something . . . something wasn't right. Felt the very reassuring lick of Havoc's tongue against his cheek and beard. What was he missing?

"You okay?"

"Yeah." Staying low, he glanced over his shoulder. Saw hangars, smaller buildings. Large containers. "We have to move." He shifted to his nine, toward her. "There." He indicated to the buildings. "Go go . . ."

When he came up, that thing he'd been missing, the thing nagging at him, erupted with a vengeance. Pain. His leg, the prosthesis was digging into his nub. It hurt like crazy, but he had no time to pamper discomfort.

Die later, Gatlin.

Palming the ground, he pushed himself upright. Growled as pain stabbed straight up his femur and tangled the muscles.

Arms encircled him. A hand on his abs.

He tensed, irritated he needed help. Humiliated—*that should be my job, supporting* her, *not . . . this*—he bit back a curse as he struggled to stand.

"Still need soap, I see."

Guess he'd let that one slip out. Jaw tight, he struggled to get vertical. Relocate that center of balance on a prosthetic leg that must've taken some damage. Tightened his core and hooked his arm around her shoulder.

They were moving, run/stumbling toward shelter. He wasn't the most graceful elephant in the circus, but at least he wasn't down.

She peered over her shoulder. "They're coming."

Twenty more yards gave them cover. Crew braced against the side of a building and clenched his jaw, tugging out his SAT phone. Muttered another oath when he saw it'd shattered in their dive from the moving plane. "We're on our own." Not having the phone also meant he couldn't track Havoc if they got separated.

"What about the security team?"

"Likely dead. That was a lotta firepower coming at us." He grunted and tried to make sense of what was happening with his prosthesis. "Doesn't make sense—how can they use you if they nearly killed you?"

"What?"

"We're missing something," he gritted out, holding his leg and grimacing.

"Are you injured?" she asked, crouching and huffing.

"No." He lifted his leg and noted the way his boot had movement to it. "Think my prosthetic leg is damaged."

She knelt in front of him and reached for his pant leg.

"No!" Crew pivoted away, gun held center mass in a safety position. "Leave it."

Green eyes looked up at him. "If I can fix it—"

"Later. We need to keep moving before they find us."

"Crew—"

"I said leave it," he growled and limped around, painfully aware of the instability that forced his core to work overtime.

She straightened and frowned. "Let me help. You can't move—"

"It's not safe. We need to—"

"What're you afraid I'll see?"

Me. It felt like a Gatling gun thundered in his chest. "Nothing. Just—"

"I saw it on the plane, remember?"

Tires squealed as voices erupted to his ten.

"Go!" Crew shoved her around. Stumbled to get his foot under him. Cursed himself, his weakness, his disability. Cursed this whole freakin' trip. Just wanted to get home. Marry the girl. Make her his.

Smoke my brisket—where had those thoughts come from?

Maybe that cord she'd slipped on her ring finger. The one he'd suggested they glam up later.

What the heck are you doing, Gatlin?

Foxtrot was a half step ahead of him when she glanced back before stepping into the open. Since he had the weapon, he should take the lead. He moved to the side even as hands reached around her. Hauled her out of reach.

"No!" Crew brought the weapon to ready and shoved himself forward, foot tangling, but he remained upright. "Havoc, *fuss!*"

The fur-missile launched at the guy who'd grabbed Foxtrot, but it was too late. He already had her. Another man pawed at her, dragging her into the back of the truck while the remaining returned fire.

Fire tore through his right shoulder. The force of the impact made him sway, but he focused. Advanced, firing. Adjusted his aim and targeted the one who'd shot him. Once, twice, three times.

The guy shifted. The bed of the truck clipped the back of his legs. He canted out of the bed. Dropped like a bag of rocks and lay unmoving on the concrete.

Crew hurried forward, firing. Saw Foxtrot fighting. The girl was some serious stuff, throwing right hooks, left, kicking, deploying her unique skill set. Her eyes found him for a split-second. Saw that terror. The split lip.

Fury licked through Crew. Drove him forward, firing. Havoc gave chase, but the distance was growing. Running, Crew did his best to avoid a tire. Stumbled. Cursed. Reacquired. Fired again.

Havoc flew at the vehicle, but the truck banked hard right and the Malinois missed. Glanced off the edge. He skidded on the concrete and came around as wheels screamed around the corner.

"Augh!" Crew pushed himself, biting through the pain. Working to find a new center of balance that did not feel like the world was tilting. If he focused too much on the pain and the awkward gait, he'd lose them. Slow down—mentally and physically.

He made the corner fifteen seconds after they'd cleared it . . . and found . . . nothing. An empty street. He cursed again, knowing she'd chastise him. "Havoc, *hier*! *Fuss*!" He jogged, the pain pushing itself further into his awareness. Demanding attention. "Havoc!" He hurried down the road, not slowly. Eyeing each road that jutted off it. Each one empty. Each one . . . proof he'd failed. "Havoc!"

He pivoted and slammed his fists into the side of a corrugated building. "Augh!" He pummeled it. Planted his hands on the aluminum. "Augh!"

Get your sorry carcass moving, soldier!

Foxtrot didn't have time for him to lose it. Neither did Havoc. He had to get his head back in the game. Find them. Keep moving until the stupid prosthesis fell off him if that's what it took. Learn something from Havoc who went after, kept going till the mission was finished, the package secured.

Foxtrot. They had her.

Crew adjusted his ballcap and used the building to get himself back together. He bent and grabbed a handful of dirt. Pulled his shirt away, packed it in the wound, grimacing. The slick warmth sliding down his back told him it was a through-and through, and he did his best to pack that one, too, but it was a little too low. Okay, plan . . . just keep moving. Find a phone, a way to communicate with Chapel.

About every two mikes he called out for Havoc, trusting his partner. Knowing he'd trail Foxtrot until his paws fell off it that's what it took. Which would tick off her kidnappers, so he just prayed he didn't find a furry corpse along the way.

Already did that once. Had a plaque and collar in a shadow box at his house that he'd hung in his living room. Didn't need another. That wall already gave him enough grief.

He stretched his neck, kept moving. Winced at the fire in his shoulder. The ticked off aches in his lower back and hip from the clumsy gait. In the sleeve he felt the nub slipping. Couldn't be blood . . . a blister?

Warehouses gave way to low-rent apartments . . . which gave way to a small market. Even as the thick smells of food and waste assaulted him, Crew had the daunting, sickening awareness that he could be moving in the wrong direction.

God . . .

He paused, leaning on a plaster wall. Fisted his hand at the myriad pain signals pulsing with each heartbeat. With a tired exhale, he fought the headiness that came from blood loss and significant trauma. The body had a way of violently protecting itself.

A woman emerged from her stall, scowled at him, and shooed him away.

Swallowing, he tucked his gun into the holster at his side and backed into the alley. Diverted his path and decided to keep to the shadows. Bloodied, pants scorched, he would draw a lot of undue attention. But the darkness swooped in. Made it hard for him to see. Made his already-fuzzy vision swim. He tripped over something. Nearly face planted. Caught himself on a trash bin. Felt something nasty squish between his fingers.

Son of a . . . With a growl, he shook his hand out. Thought to just sit down. It was a lost cause . . . he was wandering in the dark. Literally. Figuratively.

God, help me . . .

He forced himself to get moving. One thing was certain—he wouldn't find anything here. Plodding along, using walls and fences for support, he didn't give in.

A distant bark echoed through the dingy street.

There were a lot of dogs in a crowded city, but that—that was Havoc's insistent bark. "Havoc!" He worked himself into a fast walk, then a trot. He nearly tripped over a curb. Steadied himself and planted one foot in front of the other. "Havoc, *hier*! *Fuss*."

Walking like a drunkard, he cupped his hands over his mouth. "Havoc! *Hier*, boy."

The effort of shouting, of moving on swelled through him. His brain felt the pulse of the next heartbeat. Heard it in his ears. Nausea roiled up his gut. His hearing protested, clogging the din of the city.

Another bark, followed by a few more, yanked him around. "Havoc!!" He lost his balance. Slumped against a wall as the edges of his vision battled his will to stay coherent. Sweat dotted his brow. "No," he argued with his body. "No . . ." He dropped hard against the sidewalk.

Foxtrot . . . I'm sorry . . .

Brakes groaned and a vehicle squawked. Shapes swarmed toward him, shouting.

Combatants!

Unable to hear them, he sure saw the weapons. Tried to lift his own.

"Easy," he heard a deep voice say.

Eyes unfocused, Crew growled. Wasn't sure but that . . . Was it Chapel?

A hand patted his face. "Hey. Back with us. You here, Gatlin?"

He grunted. "Yeah." Remembering his mission, alarmed that he was down, he struggled to get up. "Foxtrot . . ."

A pinch came at his shoulder, then two—three?—men hoisted him up. Carried him to a vehicle.

"No!" Crew slammed his hands against the side of the vehicle.

"Gatlin, it's us—"

"I know—Havoc. He's nearby. Tracking . . . Foxtrot."

"Get in the SUV. We'll track Havoc."

Track . . . right . . . the GPS microchip. "My phone"—he felt them maneuvering him into the SUV—"was destroyed in the explosion."

As the vehicle lumbered away from where they'd retrieved

him, Crew let Bennion bandage his wounds, cover them so at least he wasn't leaking heart fluid everywhere.

Tahj handed him water, then slid an IV into his arms to pump liquids in.

"What happened?" Chapel asked from the front passenger seat where he was working on his phone, likely bringing up the tracking app.

Crew pinched the bridge of his nose. Tried to focus. "They, uh . . . they had two trucks filled with fighters. Targeted the plane. We escaped through the rear cargo door in the fuselage. Explosion did a number on me." He guzzled the water. Felt life flowing back into him. "We hoofed it to the hangars, but they found us. When they took Foxtrot, I ate some lead. Tried to track them . . ."

"You covered twenty klicks," Benn said. "I'm impressed."

"Don't be," Crew growled. "I lost my objective and my dog."

"Got him! Turn right. Two blocks." He glanced back at Crew. "That's some pretty epic tracking—twenty klicks and you were within a half klick of your dog."

"How'd you find me?" he asked, realizing twenty klicks was a lot of ground to search.

"Someone called local authorities about a man at the market with a gun and covered in blood."

Crew huffed. Remembered the woman scowling at him. Realized that was also the same time he'd asked God for help. "Wasn't thinking clearly—should've avoided the market."

"Here," Chapel said, pointing to the next turn. "Still moving, but slow."

"Then he's injured." Angling to see better through the front windshield, Crew scanned the creepy area. Looked like a . . . "Cemetery." He shifted to the side. "Let me out."

Even as the vehicle slowed, Tahj slid the liquids pouch between Crew's shoulder and the bandage. They eased to a curb.

He lumbered out, wincing at the various spots in his body

that screamed for attention. "Havoc," he called, his voice echoing over the open area. "Havoc, *fuss*."

A whimper came from the far right. Crew turned in that direction and moved. Heard the guys behind him. He negotiated row upon row of what looked like concrete bedframes marking the various gravesites. "Havoc . . ."

"There," Chapel said, slowing to a stop.

A shape limped as it moved, taking a break every fourth step. "Havoc, here, boy."

The head came up. Ears in the shape of equilateral triangles swiveled in his direction. For several long seconds as Crew headed toward him, Havoc panted. Eyed him. Then turned, lifted his snout into the air, and started moving again.

"Stop him," Benn hissed.

"Water, IV, and bandage—now. Get them." Crew jogged toward his Malinois, who hesitated again, half looking but also not. This was his "stay away, I mean business" side-eye. "Easy, boy." Crew moved to his side. "Good boy." He smoothed a hand over his spine as he lowered himself onto the edge of one of the concrete forms. "Good boy."

As Crew's fingers neared that wound, Havoc bared his teeth in a snarl.

"Message received." He heard one of the guys approach. "Slowly," he warned. "Don't want to scare him off." He rubbed his boy's ears, relieved when Havoc lowered his back end to the ground and whimpered. Adjusted so he didn't hurt the wound, then sat there. Trusting. Taking a break.

Crew did the same thing to Havoc that Tahj had done to him. Did a quick field dressing of the wound, ran an IV, then bandaged it up with a liquids bag, knowing Havoc wouldn't stop. He'd kill himself and try to end them.

"You're going to let him keep tracking in that shape?" Chapel asked.

"He's no different than me," Crew said as he secured the bandage, "except he has four legs and a fur coat. He's still trying to track her, so we need to let him do that. For as long as he can. Especially since we don't have any other leads. The wound slowed him, but I don't believe it's life threatening. Just like I did, he ran out of juice."

"Follow in the truck?" Chapel asked.

Crew nodded. "Slow and steady. I'll keep the window open, so he knows I'm there."

"Think he can still find her scent? It's been a while . . ."

"They can pick up scents that are weeks old and buried six feet deep." Crew smoothed a hand over Havoc's head, earning a very pleased smile in those amber eyes. He gave him some water and his boy inhaled it. "If anyone can find Foxtrot, it's Havoc."

As if to confirm his words, Havoc stood. Shook his spine, likely not sure what was strapped to him, swiped his tongue up Crew's cheek, then started limping along again.

"Benn, trail the dog," Chapel ordered.

"On it." Bennion slung his M4 and fell into a lope behind Havoc, who slanted the guy a glance but trotted on, moving in a zigzag and letting the scent hit his receptors.

Back in the truck, Crew watched from the rear passenger seat. *We're coming, Foxtrot. Hang on . . .*

16

ISTANBUL, TURKEY

I'M GOING TO DIE.

If she stayed in this truck, she would not make it out of this alive. Hands and feet bound behind her, held down in the bed of the truck, she felt every thud of the wheel that had clearly gone flat. The holes and bumps punched against her ribs, and having two grown men sitting on her did not help.

There had to be a way out.

Recalling the courage that had kept her alive when they'd been shot at that night at the hotel, Vienna planned. The second these men lessened the pressure, she needed to roll. Hook her arms down so she could slide her legs through and bring her hands to the front. Use her tied feet as a battering ram. Hop upright. If worse came to worse—and it likely would—jump. Even if she broke something, at least she'd be alive.

But then what?

They'd slam on the brakes and race to recapture her. They'd be faster sans no tied legs.

So. Figure out how to get free of the ropes.

Right, because that was so easy to do. In her gigs, the ropes were always done in a way that she could easily extricate herself. Not so in real life. Why couldn't these guys be careless and tie them loosely? The deck of the truck dug into her shoulder when she tried to shift.

The man muttered and struck her side. The blow knocked the air from her chest, which made her cough. Earned another strike. She bucked, unwilling to be their punching bag. The pressure on her back eased marginally. Enough to inspire her to keep fighting. She wasn't going to vanish without one heckuva fight.

The truck slowed.

Vienna hesitated, listening, trying to get her bearings on what was happening. Freed of the weight, she hiked herself up and flopped onto her back, strain pinching her shoulder joints. Though she saw men standing over her, she wasted no time hooking her arms under her, hiking her knees up and slipping her feet to the front.

Apparently stunned at what she was doing, the men finally unfroze. Kicked at her, nailing her side. She recalled her stunts and rolled into them with as much force as she could muster, considering her hands and feet were still anchored behind her.

Rolling adjusted her view, and she saw two more men there. She swung her hips and drove both her boots at them. That, combined with the truck lurching to a stop, threw them off-balance. One flipped over the side of the truck. Angling to the side, she again drove her feet at the guy.

A gunman bent toward her.

Vienna pulled her knees to her chest and shoved them into his face.

With an audible crack, he flipped backwards.

A few more kicks and she found her feet. Used her bound hands to hold the side and vaulted out of the truck. She landed, her footing awkward because of the ropes, and she pitched forward. Spotted a stack of barrels and dove for it. Rolling, she reached toward the ropes at her feet. Came up and managed to free them.

Free! She was free. Now to get out of here!

Shots rang out, then someone hurled Arabic into the mix. She leapt up and raced between two rows of massive, concrete structures. The bottom halves were square and supported domed cylinders. She had no idea what they were, but they were big enough to conceal her movements. So, she ran for all she was worth, diving between them and turning left then right, avoiding a straight line that would make her an easy target.

She rounded a corner and found herself in the open. Skidding to a halt, she nearly lost her balance on the gravel surface.

"Get her!" A man erupted from the upper level and aimed a gun at her.

Vienna sprinted to the left—wrong direction, wrong direction—and then banked right. Ran between two more. She looked back—don't look back!—and wrenched her ankle. Crying out, she realized her mistake. Clamped her mouth shut. Rolled around the next corner.

Straight into the business end of a rifle.

Slamming on her brakes, she again skidded. Lost traction and landed hard in the gravel. Scrambled backward.

A voice came from behind.

She glanced there, only to find the stock of the rifle crashing into her temple. The force knocked her back. Groaning, vision blurring, she fought for purchase on consciousness. Couldn't—

Crack!

The second blow dropped her into a well of black.

Warbling noises plied her from the thick grip of an ebony void. Moaning, she shifted—and her head exploded with pain. She cried out and her vision finally found the searing white of the daylight. Another yelp as she strained around the brilliance that made even the backs of her eyes hurt.

Hand up to shield her throbbing head from the light, she blinked rapidly. Saw a shape there. In the split second as he leaned closer, her surroundings came into sharp focus. First above—the man in black tactical gear and even darker eyes, his malice a rival for his clothing. Second—around him the gravel piled high. Third—the hard surface digging into her back—wood.

A box. I'm in a box. A coffin!

Rectangular with a lid—that Mr. Malice was closing! He sneered as he and another of his kind forced the lid closed.

"No!" she shouted. She threw out her hands to block it. Used her feet too. No way they were going to bury her alive. She would not die, not like this. "Stop!" She pushed upward, her core, legs, and arms burning as she fought the men forcing the lid down. "NO!" Her shoulders came off the bottom. "Augh!" She shoved.

Another blow to the head dropped her back.

Thud!

With a whoosh of acrid air, the lid dropped hard.

Vienna screamed. Fought. Kicked. Even as she heard a succession of *thunks* into the wood.

Nailing it shut.

"No!" She banged and kicked. Heard what sounded like rain thumping the wood. Then a roar. Dust plumed into the box.

She coughed. Gagged on the thick dust. About died for the way her vision wobbled beneath that bellow. She kicked. Tried to stop him. A feral scream unleashed itself from her chest as she pounded on the ceiling. "Noooo!"

"Dude, you sure about this?"

He understood their doubt, borne out of ignorance. But their lives had never depended on a four-legged hero. His had. "One hundred percent."

"It's been two hours."

"We might as well be going in circles," Nix said from the back.

"But we're not. Each turn Havoc takes is intentional. Don't doubt him."

Again, Havoc took a break. Moved to the side of the road and sat down, tongue dangling way past his jowls.

Once Chapel slowed the SUV, Crew grabbed the water and medkit, then exited the vehicle. Went to his boy's side and knelt, heart heavy. "Hey, bud."

Havoc gave him a couple of side-eyed pants, then slumped down. Laid on the rocky area, his ribcage rising and falling rapidly.

Fist balled, Crew set a hand just behind his front shoulder joint, felt the fast but steady pace of the heart there. Even as he went to work changing out the IV and checking the wound, he took his time. Tried to give him what he needed, be there for him. He believed in this psycho-traitor who'd been smitten with Foxtrot just as much as Crew. *I know you'd die trying to find her . . .*

But . . . it was also Crew's responsibility to protect him. Even from himself. Wondered if he should sedate Havoc and take him back to the TAC. *If I were you . . . I'd keep going . . .*

He set out the water, then extended some treats.

Still laid out and panting, Havoc eyed him. Didn't lift his head.

"Dog's had it," Benn muttered.

"Shut up," Crew snapped. Knelt beside Havoc and finished the dressing. Tucked in the new IV beneath it. He'd gone through the first one pretty fast. The second almost as fast. This one, he hoped, would last a little longer.

"Think he lost the scent?"

"No." Crew stared out at the city. He couldn't believe that. Wouldn't. Even if Foxtrot was dead, Havoc would find her scent. Track her.

"Thinking we should call it a day?" Chapel's words were unusually soft and careful. Supportive.

"I . . ." Crew roughed a hand over his face as he sat next to the dog. If they took him in . . . Foxtrot was gone. Dead.

"I know what you're thinking . . ."

Doubt it. Crew slid him a glower, daring him to even attempt to get a bead on this.

Chapel crouched behind Havoc. "But if you're honest with yourself, you know that if he keeps going, you're going to lose them both."

Crew tightened his jaw. Smoothed a hand over Havoc's skull.

"I can make the call for you."

"Just try," Crew growled.

Havoc lifted his head, keenly attuned to Crew's anger. He adjusted his position and sat up, head bobbing as he rapid-fire panted. Then dipped his snout toward the water. Lapped it up. Then some more. His gaze swung out to the distance as he continued panting, one paw tucked under him.

Crew stared at his four-legged hero. Ached for him. His loyalty was unparalleled. Gently, he petted him. Dug his fingers into the one spot Malinois fur thickened—around the neck. *You were there for me, boy, and I'm here for you.* His tenacity worthy of those inches-long canines. All he'd been through . . . All this guy would put himself through to protect his own. Everyone knew working dogs would drive themselves into the ground to protect their own. Put their own lives at risk to save their handler or person.

Crew had experienced that firsthand. Probably wouldn't be here today if it weren't for this eighty-pound Malinois if the lug hadn't negotiated a deadly minefield with the QRF behind him, leading them to Crew before he bled out.

While there was a line that even Crew knew existed, where human life outweighed that of any animal as God ordained, he also knew that God commanded mankind to look out for animals. You don't exactly give naming privilege to someone without a connection or shoulder of responsibility, but God had Adam name the animals. That created a kinship.

Crew had been in combat with this guy. Had his life saved.

Now it's on me to return the favor. Protect you—from yourself. Because he'd do this, wouldn't he? Track until he dropped dead.

"Okay," Crew breathed. "Yeah . . ." He balled his fist. *God, have mercy . . .* Foxtrot. *Forgive me. Protect her.* Tears burned at the back of his eyes. He gathered the supplies and stuffed them in the kit. Handed them off to Benn, who trudged back to the truck.

"Want us to carry him—"

"No." His rage crackled through the eerily quiet street and Crew regretted his harshness. "He'll shred you," he added as he dug out the vial from the medkit. "Just . . . once I have him, help me up."

Crew shifted closer, hating this. Knowing if things were different, if Havoc hadn't been shot, he could do this all day long. "Okay, bud . . . Don't hate me, but this is for your own good." He drew the dose from the vial into the syringe, then aimed the needle at Havoc as he'd done many times. "Easy, bo—"

With those lightning-fast reflexes, Havoc bared his teeth at Crew. Snarled.

"Hey—"

A demon bark-snap. The whole slithering tongue, touch-me-and-you-lose-that-hand business came with a searing little reminder on Crew's thumb and the meaty part of his hand.

He yanked back his hand, dropping the syringe. "Hey! No!" He shook out the stinging reprimand.

"Want us to hold him—"

With a bark, Havoc hopped onto all fours. Faced in the direction he'd been going twenty minutes ago, slanted another bared-teeth snarl at Crew, as if condemning him for trying to drug him, then gimped down the road.

"Think he knew?" Benn asked.

"No doubt," Crew said, wiping the bloody bite marks on his pants. "He could smell the chemical in the syringe." *And my roiling emotions.*

"Load up. Let's move!"

They trailed Havoc again, the Malinois hauling in scents and still processing them. At one corner, he took a long time, deliberating, smelling the air and ground.

"He lose it?"

"No." *But I'm about to.*

"Hey," Chapel said, his voice rough and businesslike again. "We've got a problem."

Crew looked at the boss. "Yeah?"

"TAC got a lead on Vale's location. We need to head back."

"Drop me here," Crew said pointing to the road.

Chapel stared at him. "You're in no condition—"

"If Havoc keeps going, so do I."

The boss almost smiled. "Figured you'd say that. TAC is sending over a car for you. They'll continue on with you and Havoc."

Two klicks delivered them to the rendezvous point where a security guard met them with another SUV, food, and equipment.

"Hey. Stay frosty," Crew said to Chapel. "Good luck."

17

ISTANBUL, TURKEY

HELLO, DARKNESS, MY OLD FRIEND . . .

Vienna sniffed a laugh, fought off the tears. It wasn't funny, not really. But maybe it was. She couldn't tell anymore. That concussion Crew had worried about earlier, the one she'd rebuffed? It was here, in full force.

Crew . . . She pressed her hand to the ceiling, which only reinforced its smotheringly close proximity.

It's a gig. Just pretend it's a gig.

But gigs had outs, safety measures. EMTs standing by if something went wrong.

This . . . this had nothing. Just Death waiting on the other side.

She cried out again. Banging her fist against the top. Dust dribbled into her face again, making her cough.

Right. Use up all the air.

Ha! Did that even matter? It wasn't like anyone would find a box buried in some chemical plant in the middle of Turkey.

Havoc could.

Could he? She wasn't sure. Movies sure made dogs out to be

crazy-smart, do things that were, ultimately, unrealistic. But wasn't it based off some morsel of truth? She had no idea what Havoc could or couldn't do. But she desperately wanted him to be that hero dog. Wanted Crew . . .

A sob choked her. Nobody was going to find her.

She banged her fist against the top again. Felt like something was crawling over her skin. *It's not real. It's not real.*

It was so small in here. So . . . tight.

Her chest was tight. *I can't breathe. I can't breathe.*

Heels of her hands to her forehead, she growled. "I can breathe," she whispered. Had to calm down. Relax.

But the box rubbed her left elbow. She shifted—hit her right and her left that time. As if the wood was closing in.

What if it was collapsing beneath the weight of the gravel they'd used to bury her alive?

Panic rushed in with a violence, ardent, screaming at her that she would die alone. That her martial arts could do nothing here. She was powerless, not in control. With no air, no room to move, she would die with the dust, dirt, and spiders. She would never be found. The Abna' Suria had won—they'd gotten her. Now, they'd get their way. Force her father's hand, change the vote.

And I die.

"Augh!!" Vienna arched her spine. Kicked. Thrashed, screaming, kicking. "Help me!" She rammed back and forth, as if she could dislodge it. Or make enough noise so that someone could hear. Or disturb the rock.

Only the dust and creaking wood responded. Plied another cough from her.

She covered her face. Felt the tears sliding down her temples. Shoved her hands to the side. Pushed. Screamed. But calm rushed in. She drew in a breath—one that felt obviously heavier than the others. "Focus, you imbecile! Find a way out." So . . . what? How could she get out? The box . . . Were there hinges?

They'd be along the side, right?

Blind in the ebony void of the box, she traced her fingers along the edge. Reached overhead . . . nothing, no hinges—

Something sharp pricked her finger. She sucked in a breath, then remembered the thumps as they sealed the box. Nails? Okay, this was one nail . . . her fingers kept moving along the lid. No more. No way removing one nail would help her. Even if she could remove them all, she couldn't stop the lid from collapsing beneath the weight of the gravel.

But what if she used the lid to angle the dirt away? At least she might get air. Right? Was that even realistic?

She had no idea, but she couldn't stay in here.

Vienna tried pushing the nail back, but it only dug into her finger deeper. Hissing, she stuck her finger in her mouth. Need something firmer. Her boot! But the soles were a rubber material. It'd just go through that, too.

With another growl, she hit the roof.

I need out of here. "I can't do this!" As her voice bounced back at her, she heard Crew's words from the last time she hadn't thought she could do something. *"Just dig deep and find that core strength you're always flashing."*

He believed in her. Unlike anyone before him.

Okay. Deep breaths. She could do this. She would. Making herself relax, she felt her muscles unknotting. Was intentional about resting her hands on her core, just as Crew had said, though he'd been talking about something else. "Okay . . ."

Though she opened her eyes, she saw nothing. Just pitch black.

"Now what?" How did this help? "It doesn't." This did absolutely zero for her situation, except made her feel like a live skeleton in a coffin.

Panic returned with a vengeance. Her hands went to the side. Breathing became difficult. She punched the board. Hard. Harder.

Die in peace? No way. Death wasn't going to have an easy delivery. Not with her. *I'm going out kicking and screaming.*

Vienna punched again. Kicked. "Help me!" she screamed.

Logic told her she was using up air.

Desperation told her it would only make a fraction of a difference.

She shifted onto her side, scooted toward the bottom. Planted a hand on the side as she drew her knee up. One . . . two . . . She drove her heel into the board.

Pain jarred up her leg.

Not close enough. Huffing a breath, she shimmied closer. Repeated it. One . . . two . . . She slammed her heel at the wood.

Crack!

Vienna sucked in a breath—and regretted, it, dust blooming through the air. She coughed but felt renewed hope. She shifted, wanting to be sure if that lid came down, she wouldn't be forced into a prone position. Again, she nailed the wood.

Crack! Groaaan.

Shifting, she heard it splinter. Fueled by her victory, she did it again. And again.

The wood surrendered. Buckled.

Even as she jerked her hip back down, the lid shifted.

Oh no.

The lower end collapsed. A glimmer of light dared stab its way into the darkness. In the split-second before the lid gave, she shoved her hands up. It tilted and dropped onto her legs. Rock and gravel followed.

Though somehow the glimmer of light remained, Vienna realized she was now crushed. Air lazily drifted in . . . but it was a struggle to breathe it in. She hadn't freed herself but made the situation ten times worse.

18

ISTANBUL, TURKEY

"He amazing dog, yes?"

Crew eyed the TAC driver, a guy who wasn't bulked or tatted up, but there was this quality about him that warned not to underestimate the man. And that feeling he'd had, the way Havoc had growled at this man—Volken—back at Command had put Crew on edge. "Yes."

Brown eyes sparked. "I want dog for team. Commander tell me no."

"When we succeed and get the girl back, use that to convince the commander you need one."

The man barked a laugh and slapped Crew's shoulder. "Yes-yes. Good-good." He tossed a bag to him. "Eat. Be happy."

In the bag were what looked like three wrapped sub sandwiches. But the aroma drifting from them said they were much more. His stomach growled as he pulled one out and unwrapped it. "What is it?"

"*Kokoreç,*" the man said with a jut of his jaw. "Turkish food. Lamb, vegetables. Yum-yum. Volken knows good food." His jolly laugh could make him a rival for Santa.

Maybe he'd been wrong about the guy. Either way, Crew was starving and the sandwich was sealed, so he bit into it and groaned as the flavors bounced across his tongue. First bite he savored. The rest, he devoured. Yes, indeed—Volken knew good food.

"Look-look," Volken said, indicating through the window.

Havoc had stalled out at a spot, digging his snout deep into tall grass. He went in a circle, relieved himself, then moved on a few feet, scenting again, then lifted his head and swiveled in their direction.

"I got you, bud." Crew grabbed one of the sandwiches and exited the vehicle with the supplies for Havoc. He limped over to his dog and bent down.

Havoc sniffed his hands and licked them—and it sure wasn't to apologize for nearly taking a digit or two earlier.

"Good," Crew said as he tore off a chunk sandwich and let Havoc inhale it. Then more. The food seemed to revive him. "That buy me back into your good graces?" IVs were good, though low, so he replaced it. Inspected the wound. Good for now. Then gave him water.

After some more water and a fluids bag check, Havoc was OTG again. About a klick later, he was trotting along like it was a walk in the park—a painful one with that limp —but then he snapped to the side. Worked a spot in the road. More than one car honked at them for blocking the street, then swung around them, narrowly avoiding hitting Havoc.

Crew muttered an oath and wanted to take out their tires.

"The girl we find," Volken said, "she pretty?" He stabbed a finger at Crew. "Your woman, yes?"

She's a lot more than "pretty." Crew glowered. "Just keep your eyes on the road, on my dog."

"I make you angry. Much apology."

"No worries. Just"—Crew wagged out the window—"the dog."

"Yes-yes. We good." The man nodded, his mood ever merry. "I have wife. Three girls."

Goodnight, he did not care what this guy had except a bead on Havoc. Who . . . "Hold up." Crew stilled, watching the Malinois. "Slow down . . ."

Scenting again, Havoc stood in the middle of the road, glancing up the street, then down.

"Something wrong?" Volken asked, his smile not quite fading.

Crew leaned forward, recognized that sign from his boy. "No, this is good."

"He has something?"

"I think so."

In response, the driver lifted a phone, and it was like everything snapped into place. "Commander, possible we have something." The man nodded, muttered something in their language, then hung up.

Anticipation thrummed and Crew did his best to stay out of Havoc's business. It wasn't a false read . . . He unbuckled and slung his M4 on. "Follow us." Even as he exited the vehicle, he noted Havoc trot away to his two. Moving side to side. A focused zigzag now. Head up, swinging side to side.

Crew hustled to track with him. Felt his gut cinch when he heard the *hauk-hauk-hauk* of Havoc hauling scents to the back of his throat to process them.

With a glance to the vehicle, Crew signaled him to stay close. Then limp-jogged toward his dog. *C'mon, buddy . . . you can do this.*

They moved down a road. Then another. Banked right. Crew could smell the seawater now. Were they really that close to it? He ignored the pinch and slurp of his sleeve, knowing he was going to need some serious rest and care once this was done. He just prayed he didn't spawn an infection that would cost more of the leg. Adjusting his cap with one hand, he slid his M4 to the low-ready with the other.

Ten minutes in, Havoc was moving faster, though it really seemed painful for the guy. Crew wanted to pull him aside, get him to rest, but he would probably get another sharp reprimand from the dog, who was technically his superior. And then that reminded him about Ghost's warning.

Slowly, the scenery changed from residential to bustling restaurants to . . . Hold up. He glanced at his device and noticed they were trekking on a parallel course with the water . . . straight into an industrial sector. What the fluff?

He squeezed the rim of his ballcap and glanced back at the vehicle. Saw Volken on his phone.

But Havoc didn't falter. He kept moving, the cone narrowing with each klick. This can't be right.

"Mr. Crew," the driver called from the window. "Commander talk to you."

Crew huffed and glanced back. Saw the guy holding the phone out the window. Backtracking, eye on Havoc as he did, Crew had to wrestle his irritation into submission. "Yeah?"

"Mr. Gatlin, it would seem you are nearing an industrial sector, in particular one owned by some very influential and powerful people."

"You and I both know I don't care about that."

"Some of the facilities you're approaching have very hazardous material. It would be wise—"

"What would be wise is to stop wasting my time. Havoc has a hit. I'm following it." He tossed the phone back at the driver. "I appreciate your help, but I don't need it. If you want to rat me out to your boss, then we part ways here."

With a hop, Crew hustled up behind Havoc. Let his boy take the lead. "Please find her," he muttered, wondering what the driver would do. All the gear was in there.

Tires crunched behind him.

Crew smirked, relieved, but didn't bother to look back. He was going to—

Havoc lurched into a run. A gimpy one, but it was fast. In fact as Crew rushed to keep up, Havoc flew down the street. Past gated drives with hazardous materials signs.

"Seek-seek-seek!" Crew shouted after him, desperate to encourage his boy. Frantic to find Foxtrot. Hope zinged through his veins when the Malinois whipped around and backtracked.

Crew held a hand to the SUV and stood there, waiting for Havoc to find where he'd dropped the scent. Snout down, he trekked crossways over the road. From one facility on the right to another on the left. Then back. "C'mon, c'mon . . ." He had no idea what they'd face here, what dangers would present themselves, but he knew one thing: the nose knows.

The SUV door opened.

"Stay in the car!" Crew shouted, watching Havoc and scanning around them to check their surroundings. One side had a glue factory. Another polyurethane. Thankfully the road was empty, the facilities shut down. Guess it was after five.

But steps soon approached.

For Pete's sake, the guy could throw off Havoc. "Hey." He glanced back just as he saw the guy raise a weapon and aim.

Shock slammed Crew. He snapped up his weapon. Fired a short burst. Dropped the guy. "Holy—"

Havoc barked.

Whipped Crew around. He saw his boy sitting at the gate of the factory on the right. A hit.

"Havoc, stay." Crew sprinted back to the driver, verified he was dead. Patted him down and found a standard cell phone. Not the one he'd used to call the commander. He hooked his arms under the guy and dragged him back to the SUV. Didn't need any surprises or bystanders interrupting him. He stowed him in the back, grabbed the SAT phone from the console in the front, then parked the SUV to the side. Locked it.

Back at his partner's side, he eyed the gate. Thought about calling the commander, letting him know his guy had been a mole . . . but something in his gut told him to hurry. The fence was standard—chain link, six feet. Another day in the park for Havoc.

Crew called his boy back, then glanced down at him. "Ready?"

Havoc was on all fours. Let out a keening whimper.

With a nod, Crew rushed the fence with him. "Hup!"

When Havoc went airborne, Crew moved under him. Gave an upward thrust that assured the fur-missile cleared the fence. He was already in motion, scaling it himself as he watched Havoc land. Yelp. Then hobble, not putting his right rear hock on the ground.

Crew bit back an oath as he dropped to the ground, his own right leg yelling at him. "I feel your pain, bud." He motioned to the facility, shaking his head at the massive concrete silos. "Seek-seek!"

The first command had barely left his mouth before Havoc took off. No hesitation. No faltering. He darted down the first row. Backtracked, then resumed course. To the far end. Then to his three.

Crew was there and rounded the corner. Saw nothing but gravel mounds.

Tail going a hundred miles an hour said that Havoc had the scent. Strongly.

Crew shifted his gaze again to the gravel mounds. "No no no . . . tell me this isn't—"

An excited repetitive bark hauled him around the far side. Havoc had lowered his front to the ground, barking excitedly.

Crew rushed there. The six-foot tall mound was a formidable foe. But if Havoc said she was here . . . He crouched and started digging, but the more he did, the more it just seemed to slide. From one side to the other. "Augh!" He was getting nowhere.

Havoc was digging, too, the gray gravel quickly turning red.

"Havoc, *aus*. Leave it."

His boy whimpered and sat, didn't want to obey, but he did. Had to. He'd shred the pads of his paws.

Hands bloodied, Crew slumped. It was hopeless.

Air defied her, the weight of the lid forcing her breathing to remain shallow. Her head was throbbing. She'd told herself to calm down. To relax. But she'd panicked. Then put her hope and trust in herself, in her skills as a martial artist. That wasn't necessarily a bad thing, but it was . . . shallow. Like her breathing.

Vienna closed her eyes. Slow, silent tears slid from her eyes. Down her cheeks. Into her ears, tickling. Of course. She shuddered a half laugh, half cry. Couldn't wipe her tears, couldn't address the tickle because her hands were pinned beneath the board. Elbows aching, she knew even if she could shift her hands, it would mean her immediate death. The rocks would exert their weight against the lid, which would crush her chest.

Again, tears streamed out. She choked a sob, which made everything hurt more. Reminded her of the very limited room she now had. And clearly nobody was watching the site, or they would've come, right? So that proved the terrorists had intended for her to die here all along.

So . . . she was going to die . . . She should make peace . . . With no voice recorder, she would just have to will the sentiments into the air. It was silly, but somehow it gave her a modicum of calm.

Dad . . . please vote for the sanctions. Make them hurt. Make them fix their very broken system.

Next should probably be her brother, maybe her sister. Perhaps even Baako for his treachery. Or was that Iris? But the only face and name that came to her were that of a very handsome, mind-numbingly honorable operator.

"Crew . . ." She groaned. *I find the right man and I'm going to die before I can tell him.* Gosh and his dog. A laugh squeezed through her chest. "Havoc . . . you goofy, intense boy . . . take care of him . . . for me." Her lungs burned. "Oh, Crew . . ."

Tears rushed free in a torrent as she shuddered and shook. "God!!" she sobbed. "I don't want to die." It was hard to talk around the tremors and the dust. "Please . . ." She worked to stem the tears. To control her breathing "C-Crew says You make sense." Continuing their trek into her hair, tears streamed unabated. What he'd said about the planets, our bodies . . . his life-altering moment.

That's what I'm having . . . isn't it?

Assuming I survive.

"God . . ." She swallowed heard. "If you're there, like he said . . . I'll believe it—" Was it so terribly selfish to say she'd believe in Him if He saved her? Was that fake? She strangled another sob. "I don't care!" Desperation drove her and she shook her head, hating her weakness, her inability to be strong, to believe in something so daring as God. She had this strange, squirrelly feeling that the reason God made sense to Crew was not just because he'd lost a leg. But what he hadn't lost . . . Life. A chance to be there for others. To operate with Havoc. *To be there for me.* "Let me live, God. And I'll do that, too."

Even as she spoke the words, Vienna realized the selfishness of it all. The focus on herself. Even she knew God said to love others. More than yourself, right? What bargain could be made to persuade a God like Him to save her?

I'm not worth it.

She lay in the suffocating silence, accepting the non-answer. Heaviness, and pain held her hostage, she scoffed. *See? He—*

Light shattered the darkness.

Air rushed in, warm and heady.

Vienna drew in a breath that wasn't a thousand-pounds heavy. Saw an opening. Then a snout thrust into the gap, sucking in big draughts. It stanched a laugh from her. "Havoc!" she breathed, savoring the dusty air.

"Foxtrot! You there?"

"Yes!" she cried, relieved, shocked. Mind racing, reeling. Exhaustion and adrenaline collided into a volatile cocktail in her blood, making her feel hysterical. "I can't move."

"Hang on. I'm coming!"

She would. Oh she really would. "Hurry." Not that there was danger, but that she was desperate to be out of here. To be free. Afraid the cave-in would happen again. That it'd kill her instantly this time.

"Watch yourself," Crew shouted. "We're going to dig out the gravel."

"I can't move," she warned him.

A giant claw dug into the space and unloaded the burden from her. She heard the steel teeth grating over the wood and drew in a breath, realizing how very close that was. Moments later, he was there, hauling out the rocks. With each moment that passed, with the ore rocks removed, she worked to free herself. Get out of here.

God, please . . . Don't let this be one massive "Psych!"

The claw returned. Pulled out more rocks. Now she could move her legs a little. She tried to shove the lid but found no strength. Panic gouged what little courage had found her.

"I'm coming down," he said. "Hang tight."

Others were there, too, working. Shouting.

Crew dropped in, boots shifting as he steadied himself to the side. "Vienna."

Something about her first name on his lips closed her eyes. *Don't cry. You're stronger than that. It's over.* But the way he'd said her name—that mirroring desperation, the concern, the affection—it'd broken something loose in her. Something that had been lodged wrong in her heart. In her life.

"Vienna!"

"Yeah," she said around a thick throat. "Just get me out."

"Working on it, Foxtrot." He bent down and reached for the lid.

"Yes," she said with a frantic chuckle, "put those muscles to use for something good."

"Hey, they worked for getting your attention. That was a win in my book."

She huffed a laugh, then coughed.

He managed to pull the lid up and reach around it. "Grab my hand."

It took everything in her to move her arms, to ignore the ache in her biceps. Pray she hadn't broken anything. Her tremoring hand reached for his.

Crew snagged it. Braced. Hauled her up. She struggled, fought not to be dead weight. Sagged into him as his arms cocooned her. "You okay?"

"Yeah . . ." She hated the whimper that snuck into her words.

His hands were moving, doing something, and she really didn't care what— "Don't let go."

"Never." He pressed a kiss to her temple. Looked skyward. "Pull us up!"

Even as she held on, aching arms wrapped around his neck, she buried her face against his neck. Sensed them being hoisted from the gravelly grave felt . . . surreal. Poignant. Symbolic.

He shifted, and she felt the purchase of ground beneath their feet. Didn't let go.

Neither did he. He angled over her. Cupped her head. "Sweet Lord . . ." he whispered and there were other words she didn't hear.

Shuddering a breath, she sighed into him. *Mine, too.*

"I was so scared you were gone."

"You found me." She smiled at him, exhaustion dripping from every pore and threatening to pitch her back into the box. The thought made her take a step to the side. She saw the hole. Stumbled away more.

Havoc was there, wedging between her and Crew. He nudged her hand. Licked it.

"That's who you need to thank. Nearly killed himself tracking you."

Vienna petted him, but then looked at Crew. "My heroes."

Crew gave her a cockeyed grin, his expression going crazy soft. "I like the sound of that. A role we're proud to fill."

19

ISTANBUL, TURKEY

Exhausted, wrecked, Crew fought the desire to jump behind the wheel of the SUV the commander's men had arrived in and tear off. Get him, Foxtrot, and Havoc out of Dodge. Hole up in some spot where the terrorists and the world couldn't find them. He watched the TAC agents talking with local authorities, who had already interviewed Foxtrot and Crew.

Strength seemed to have fled his body, leaving behind aches and pains. "I think I could sleep for a week."

"A *month*," Foxtrot murmured, letting her head thump back against the headrest. Scratches and cuts lined her arms and face. Her lips looked dry, cracked.

He nudged the water bottle in her hand. "Drink up."

She eyed him for a long time, and there was something in her gaze that he couldn't quite sort. A split lip, bloodied cheek, slightly swollen eye . . . Foxtrot had never looked more beautiful. A softening, though he couldn't really say the woman with him had ever been 'hard.' Tough as nails, high octane, serious . . . yeah. His speed in every way that mattered.

She released him from her visual grasp and took a sip of the water. Seemed to appreciate it, then gulped some more. Sat up and rested her forehead on the back of the front passenger seat. Then slanted him a glance. "I can't believe you wrecked your car saving me."

"One—not my car. Two—I missed the safety briefing on driving bobcats. Three—it wasn't like there was much room to maneuver with all those concrete silos." Thankfully, he'd gotten the ruck out of it and the authorities were willing to drive them to the TAC. "Mostly, that vehicle was the least of my concerns when you were down there suffocating."

"I approve of that line of thinking."

He grinned. "Good." His gaze hit the rope ring hugging her finger . . . It was now frayed, dirtied, and bloodied. Bore marks of her fight to stay alive in that box. He took her hand, swept his thumb over the rope ring, then lifted it to his lips and kissed it. "Thank you." Gently, he set her hand back on her own lap.

"For?" She leaned forward with a furrowed brow.

"Fighting to stay alive until my slow self got there."

She smiled, then sighed and took another drink. "I—"

Havoc's loud snore invaded the moment and made them both laugh.

Foxtrot peered over her shoulder at him, chin resting on the seat back. "Did he really nearly die looking for me?"

"Refused to quit." Crew showed her the bite marks. "We decided he needed to be sedated and taken back to TAC, so I went to give him the injection. Psycho nearly bit my hand off. Next thing I know, he's OTG again. Ticked off at me."

She craned her head to see over the seat where Havoc was getting more liquids and some pain meds. Not doping him up—which always made Havoc come unglued—but helping him relax a little. "He's amazing."

"Don't forget the two-legged warrior involved in that intervention. I mean, I took a bullet"—he pointed to his shoulder—"damaged a twenty-five-thousand-dollar prosthetic leg and foot"—tapped Larry's replacement—"hiked all over—"

Foxtrot slumped closer and rested her head on his shoulder—thankfully it didn't hurt or maybe it just felt too right to have her there that he didn't care. "You saved me." She slid her hand in his. "I would've died . . ."

"I wouldn't have let that happen." He dug into the ruck and drew out the SAT phone Chapel had given him and scrolled through, searching for either Chapel or the TAC. Tried not to think too much about how dope this felt, sitting here with Foxtrot, her curled against his side.

"You know this is crazy, righ—" A yawn swallowed the rest of her word. "We've only known each other three weeks . . ."

And yet it felt like a lifetime. In a good way. "Don't you know—I excel in crazy. Have you met my dog?"

The *sniff-sniff-sniff* of Havoc's cold, wet snout tracked over Foxtrot's head as Havoc smelled her hair, earning a laugh. Foxtrot reached up behind her and petted Havoc's ears.

Crew found the number and hit the green phone icon. As he lifted it to his ear, he heard a low growl emanate from the back seat.

Crew jerked his gaze back to Havoc. "Hav—" His gut tightened when he noticed the Malinois sitting up, head swiveled to the rear. Ears like radars as he let out another low rumble. Then he spotted what had triggered his psycho's alarms.

The pair stalked down the road, clinging to the shadows. Posture indicated weapons at the low-ready.

He cursed and ducked. "Havoc, *aus.*"

"Go ahead," Chapel's voice crackled through the phone.

"Trouble. Can't talk." Even as he heard Chapel reply that he understood, Crew tucked the phone in the upper arm pocket.

"What d'you see?" Foxtrot breathed.

"Two terrorists. Incoming." With his stealth skills, he rotated around. "Nice and slow, down on the floorboard." Crew pressed his back to the seat and slithered down, feeling Foxtrot's knee in his spine. Angling to face the left rear passenger door, he brought his weapon to a ready position, guiding the safety off, and aiming at the window. Heard another barely audible growl from Havoc. "Be ready to bail," he breathed to Foxtrot.

Gravel crunched as the men passed the SUV. One hesitated, the sound of rock grinding beneath shoes warned Crew this one had likely turned to the SUV.

Slowing his breathing, he tilted his head toward the weapon. Stared down the sights as a chest came into view. *Keep moving . . . keep moving . . .*

They reached for the handle.

Crew rested his finger on the trigger, ready to deal with this guy. With the threat they posed.

Clunk. Thunk. The door handle disengaged.

The light would come on and they'd be exposed.

He firmed his grip and applied pressure to the trigger.

"Over here," came a distant voice.

The man at the door skated a glance over the vehicle. Strained his neck to look inside.

Go away. There's nothing to see here . . . these aren't the droids you're looking for . . . and I really don't want to kill you.

After another bark from the other guy, the first turned and left.

Crew eased up, monitoring the guys as they moved toward the TAC agents and the local law enforcement. He fisted his hand and drove it into the interior light on his side. Then hers. He eased up and did the same for the front. When he glanced to the rear one, Foxtrot read his thoughts. Snaked over the back and broke that one.

"Havoc, hup," Crew slapped the seat and the dog was there without hesitation. He nodded to Foxtrot. "Out your side. Like glue to the truck."

"And go where?" Her voice had a tremor to it.

"Across and down," he said, sliding over the seat and leaving no room for personal space. Pointed to the narrow alley on the opposite side of the road. "Down that road. Bank left. Keep moving."

She looked at him over her shoulder. "Is this ever going to end?"

"Not sitting here." He nodded. "Go."

Every muscle, limb, and joint protested as he climbed out of the vehicle. With a hand signal, he brought Havoc to his side. Eased the door to just enough so it didn't draw attention.

Ahead, Foxtrot moved fast even though she had a noticeable limp. Which matched his and Havoc's. Quite a trio, they were. But they were able to move quickly, and rounding the corner he breathed a little easier, not having a shout or shot erupt behind them.

He felt like he was a seventy-year-old man hobbling down th—

Crack-Crack!

Barked shouts peppered the air.

Pop-pop! Pop pop pop!

With a gasp, Foxtrot turned to him but didn't stop. "What was that?"

"Signal to double time." He urged her onward. Shrugged into the ruck with his other arm and focused on just moving, negotiating his prosthetic foot that had more wobble than stabilization. Kept track of his force multiplier trotting ahead of them, focused and intent. Tugged the phone from the pocket.

"Didn't we just do this?" Foxtrot huffed as they switched to the other side of the road.

"Had to up your training for nighttime ops."

"Good to know."

He jogged with Foxtrot and Havoc, trailing her to cover their tracks and numbers. "Still there?"

"Yeah. We're tracking you. What happened?"

"Located Foxtrot at a chemical plant. Must've had surveillance because we've got some heat on us again."

"Okay, listen up. Head to the docks. Board the Long Circle Bosphorus Tour by Public Ferries. We'll intercept you on the water."

"Good copy. See you there." He pocketed the phone again and focused on their route, their position in relation to the water. "Left," he said, guiding her around the corner.

Tsing! Crack!

Sparks flew off the fence. Crew ducked but felt the violent kiss of that bullet hiss past his ear. Felt another punch into his arm. *Crack!* "Augh!" It hit him just right that he spun. Slumped against a wall and kept moving. Extracted the phone from the pocket and it crumbled in his hand. Felt the burn that the ricocheted bullet left on his bicep. It'd have a wicked bruise, too. "Son of . . ."

Foxtrot looked at him, brow furrowed.

"I didn't say it," he growled.

"Wasn't worried about a curse word."

A car swung onto the road behind them.

"*Run*! Toward the docks." He broke into a sprint. "Right." Veered in that direction. "Right!" Down an alley. Diverted behind a tenement building. "Slow slow slow," he murmured, drawing her to the side and into the shadows.

Breathing labored, she gulped air. Her gaze skated to the side, monitoring him, his position. Adjusting as he moved.

Crew took her hand. "Just two lovebirds out for an evening walk." He was glad for the darkening day.

"Enjoying the humidity and odor of spent bullets."

"Talking my love language, girl." He kept Havoc close as they moved through the darkness and edged around the corner.

Lights spread over the buildings and cars lit up the street.

Releasing her hand, Crew stepped back and moved in front of her, pinning her to the wall. Drew his weapon to a low-ready. Signaled Havoc back and hooked a leg around to gently guide the dog behind him. He tried to minimize his visible imprint and felt bad for crowding Foxtrot's space. Felt her hands on his dorsals.

The car wasn't even doing two miles an hour, scanning and scouring for them.

Foxtrot's fingers crawled up his back to the bandage there. Traced the edges of it. She seemed to pause there, and then her forehead pressed into his spine. It was nice. Comforting. Which was whack with her behind him.

Car. He tensed. *Car's gone. Move!*

"Wait." Crew stepped out and angled to see as far down the street as he could see. Checked his six. "Okay," he said, never taking his eyes off the road. When he felt her at his side, he started in the opposite direction the car had gone. Crossed over. Through the buildings, he saw the glimmer of water in the distance.

They banked right and headed that way.

"The docks . . ." Foxtrot whispered. "Why are we heading there?"

A half dozen paces more and she nodded. Huffed out, "Catch a ferry."

"That's the plan." He grinned down at her. "Someday, when we're not running for our lives—"

"So this *will* end?"

He took her hand again. "It will. I promise."

"I'll hold you to that. So . . . when it's over . . ." Her gaze slid to his, speculative and curious.

Was she imagining a future for them as much as he was? Who was he kidding? He hadn't been thinking about that. And yet . . . he couldn't fathom a future without her. Strange how that worked. But maybe it was too soon for that kind of convo . . . "If you could travel anywhere, where—"

"Greece."

He chuckled at how fast she'd answered that. "That's not far from here. Once this storm settles, we should go together."

She eyed him as they walked, and he wondered if he'd overstepped. All this excitement and adrenaline had thrown them together rather violently. What if that's all it was? Holy Moses. Talk about an adrenaline crash. Yet he had this powerful realization that this op wouldn't last forever and one thing he knew for sure—even if it'd only been a few weeks—he didn't want them going their separate ways.

"Whoa." Foxtrot pushed him sideways.

Crew faltered. Tripped over something. Staggered back and slammed a hand against the wall. Barely finding his balance. "What the—"

"Quiet. Back." She clapped a hand over his mouth. Lost her balance and fell into him. "The corner. Black car."

Anger cracking, he slid a look around her. Saw the vehicle. The two men sitting in it. The streetlight throwing illumination on their faces. Man. He'd been so distracted with the idea of 'them' he lost situational awareness.

"Sorry. Did I hurt you?"

Ticked with himself for not being more alert, he shook his head, watching the car.

"Is it them, the guys hunting me?"

"Possibly." He cocked his head to the right and started that way. "C'mon."

Down the street, they banked left. Slid down another block, confirmed they were out of sight of the black sedan, then hustled toward the docks.

"You need a shirt that isn't covered in blood, and I'd love some clean clothes." Then she let out a soft groan. "I should just jump in the water—I'm covered in dust and dirt."

"Maybe you could find another number like what you wore at the Turk's event."

She shot him a glance. "You liked that . . .?"

Was that bad? What did the lilt in her question mean? He adjusted his hat. "Kinda hard not to." Should he have not said that? Things these days left a guy dancing on eggshells, afraid to say the wrong thing. But he wasn't going to lie.

"Well, you looked pretty hot, too, but I think I prefer your more natural, every-day look."

"What, sweaty and bloody?"

She laughed. And man, he liked her laugh. There wasn't

much—anything?—he didn't like about Vienna Foxcroft. And she had a point. They needed to blend in and not draw attention. The closer they got to the Bosphorus, shops became more prevalent, along with tourist traps and sidewalk cafes.

"Here." Crew swung the ruck around and dug into it. Produced a credit card. "Over there." He nodded to a shop with linen shirts hanging along the sidewalk. "Grab a shirt for me and whatever you need."

"I look like a pig that's rolled in the mud."

"Prettiest pig—" He cringed. "That came out wrong."

"Uh huh." She snatched the card. "Better hope I come back."

"I'll find you if you don't."

"Promises, promises." Smirking, she stepped from the stoop where they'd stopped and made her way over.

Crew reminded himself this was about keeping a line of sight on her, not appreciating the view. But he was talented enough to manage both. He slid his gaze up and down the street, scanned rooftops, and when he sighted her again, she was pulling a shirt from the rack. Held it aloft—that wasn't for him, was it? Looked too . . . pretty. Did she even know what his size was?—then moved inside. His gut clenched, hating that he couldn't see her. Nobody else had gone inside, but . . . wasn't this taking too long?

"C'mon . . ." Another ten minutes passed and he'd had enough. Twitched forward. His foot hit the street.

Foxtrot emerged.

And he couldn't breathe. Grinned like a fool as she came toward him wearing a more casual version of the gown she'd worn at the ball. The navy cropped top accented her bare midriff—he could still remember the warmth of her skin, how her stomach muscles jounced at his touch—and the black pants she'd changed into were sensible. Explained what'd taken so long.

"You changed." *Wow, blinding flash of the obvious, genius.*

Foxtrot tucked her chin. "Yeah. They had rooms. Unlike

you"—she handed him the plastic bag—"I can't change out here."

"Well, you could . . ."

She swatted him with the bag. "Here. Change."

A groan threatened to escape when he pulled out the shirt for him. Off-white, two two-inch stripes down each side, and buttons that gave it a Henley style. "Are you sure this isn't a girl shirt?"

She scooped her hair up and put it in a ponytail. Did she realize how bare that left her neck? "It's a *nice* shirt and will look good on you."

"You trying to turn me into Fabio or something?"

"He has way better hair." She considered him. "And are you really being a child about a shirt?"

Fine. A means to an end. Crew gritted his teeth. Tugged off his tactical shirt with bullet holes, blood and sweat stains. Ripped off the tag from the shirt and threaded his arms into the sleeves.

Foxtrot drew in a quick breath. "You *did* get shot."

"I don't lie." He winced as he hooked it over his head. The buttons delved down the center of his chest and he secured those. Sleeves were absurdly wide, so he rolled them to his elbows.

Sniggering, Foxtrot shook her head. "Have you ever worn anything other than tactical shirts?"

"Not if I can help it." He jabbed the sleeves up marginally more and gritted his teeth at the way she mocked him. "Look, you give me a monkey suit—"

"Well, how do you think I feel in *this*?" she balked, motioning to the top.

Hold up. She didn't like wearing that, but she'd bought it . . . "Did you get that because I said I liked—"

"Aren't we supposed to be moving?" she said, turning away, hugging her waist. Hiding that midriff.

That was okay, he had a really good memory. "Lead the way,

Foxtrot."

"Just one thing." She reached up and freed his shirt buttons.

"What—"

"We're going to the docks where there's some heavy nightlife," she said, tugging up the collar. "If you want to blend in, this is how you do it. Didn't think I'd have to teach you how to dress, Soldier-boy."

Jaw grinding, he bit back his retort. It didn't matter. Clothes didn't matter. Staying alive did.

Eyebrows arched, she smiled. "That looked like it hurt."

"You have no idea. Let's go." He slung the ruck over his shoulder, clipped a lead to Havoc—normal people didn't let their dogs walk around a city off-lead—and headed to the docks. Ten minutes later, they negotiated the streets around the docks and spotted a ferry loading up. They waited till just before it was about to pull away, then hurried forward.

"No dogs!" the guy selling tickets said.

Foxtrot paled, looked at him with wild eyes.

But this was a route Crew had navigated many times. "Service dog," he said as he pulled up his pant leg. Revealed his prosthetic leg.

The guy faltered. "Yes, yes." He took the money Crew extended and waved them aboard.

On the ferry, Crew moved into the lower level. Shouldered against a corner. "Hang on," he said to Foxtrot. Watched the gangway for incoming trouble. Saw two cars pull up. Not good. Four men hopped out and jogged toward the gangway.

The ferry master must've seen them, didn't like what he saw, because he motioned to the girl now at the ticket booth and she closed the gate. He then pulled up the ramp. Despite protestations from the new arrivals, the worker tossed off the dock ties. Signaled the driver.

The horn blew and the ferry puttered away from the dock.

Crew stood watch there until they were out of jump reach,

and even a little longer. "Hey," he said, voice soft, guiding. "C'mon. We're okay."

For now.

"There's food. Let's get something and find a place to sit."

Crew realized then that though he'd had a sandwich, she likely hadn't eaten anything. Terrorists weren't worried about sustenance when burying people alive.

They purchased kebabs and water for them and Havoc, then found a table at the rear. He took in the bay, searched for the team. Saw a few yachts, some jet skis, sailboats and even some speed boats. None were the team that he could tell. From his pack, he pulled out the collapsible water bowl and filled it for his partner, while Foxtrot devoured hers. He sat sideways so he had a line of sight on the ferry and the water. Offered chunks of meat to Havoc, who refused them.

That's not good.

"C'mon, bud. Take some." He wagged it in front of him again.

Havoc jerked his head up and away. Slumped onto his side.

"He's not doing well," Foxtrot said softly.

"No," Crew said, looking around. Searching the waters. "He really needs medical attention. They should be here any . . ."

Something dark bounded across the water. No lights, but it was moving pretty fast. Watching that craft as it raced toward them, Crew packed the bowl. Released Havoc's lead. Swiveled himself around, his back to Foxtrot, weapon at the low-ready as the Zodiac approached.

"That them?"

"Or trouble." No way to know which just yet. It had no lights. Though he could see people aboard, they were in black.

Someone aboard flashed a light.

He expelled a thick breath. Reached back and caught her hand. "It's them." He moved to the side and waited as the boat came alongside. Bennion and Tahj were at the edge and tossed up a rope ladder.

Crew caught it and secured it on the edge of the rail, grinning at Foxtrot. "Ready to put those stunt skills to use again?" He leaned over the side. "I need a rope to harness Havoc." Another one sailed through the air even as Foxtrot hooked a leg over the rail and caught the rope ladder.

"Hey!" came a shout from behind. "What're you doing?"

Crew made quick work of creating a harness, hooking it over his shoulder and around his legs, then used a carabiner to hook it into Havoc's harness. He looped it around one of the posts of the ship, then climbed up onto the rail with Havoc.

"You can't do that!" the ferry worker yelled.

Watch me. "It's okay," he said as he began the descent. "It's what we do."

20

BOSPHORUS STRAIT, TURKEY

"Did they say anything to you?"

In a luxury cabin on the superyacht that apparently was one of many owned by the Turk, Vienna sat at a table as the commander, Chapel, and another man worked upstairs. She propped herself against the headboard and hugged a pillow. They'd been brought aboard, separated by Damocles, and medically treated. Since she was the least affected physically, she'd been released after giving Chapel her report of what happened. Mentally, however, she was a basket case.

They'd taken Havoc into surgery—the team had brought a vet with them, and the Belgian Malinois was having the bullet removed. She'd heard whispers of irreparable damage and permanent limp. Then she'd seen a doc stitching up the wounds on Crew's chest and back.

All because of me.

Wasn't the vote over? What had happened to Felicity?

Frode had been killed.

I killed someone.

The horribleness of the last week roiled over her. So

226

much for being tough-as-nails. The way Crew had handled it, run to the danger, not from it—well, except when ushering her to safety—had kept his head while responding to the threats, insuring she was safe. *Digging me out of that box . . .*

Tears weren't even there. She'd used them all in the box. When she'd bargained with God. Staring out the window, she peered up at the sky, the stars. Remembered how she'd prayed—begged—God would let her live. Now, here she was. Alone. Cut off from Crew and Havoc. From her dad.

God, I guess it's just You and me n—

A rap came at the door.

Vienna hiked off the bed and opened it.

Like the storm he was, Crew stood there, cockeyed in the passage. Head craned forward, half because he had to duck to fit in the gangway, half because he looked ready to collapse. She stepped back to let him in. "What're you doing here? You should be resting."

He trudged into the room, glanced around, looking lost. Like he didn't know what to say or do.

"You okay?"

He shrugged. "Figured if you were anything like me, you couldn't sleep either."

She gave a half smile, closing the door. "Yeah . . . How's Havoc?"

"Sedated. Surgery went well."

Why did this feel weird, awkward between them all of a sudden? "And your leg?"

"Temporary fix until I can get to the specialist. Not great, but it'll work. What about you? They cleared you pretty fast."

She bounced her shoulders, feeling sad, lonely. "Physically fine." Wanting to hug him. Which was weird. They didn't do that kind of thing.

"Mentally?" His gaze never seemed to find home, his hands twitching.

Like her pulse. "Mm, that's the question, isn't it?" Involuntarily, she shifted toward him.

He reached for her.

Compelled as if by a force of nature, she went into his arms. Let him crush her to himself.

Breath on her neck, he exhaled heavily. His arms and hands pressing her tightly into his hold. "Needed to know you were still here."

Heart stirring, she fought the tears. "Same," she whispered into his shoulder. She eased back and cupped the back of his head. Thought to say something but knew what would be better. She caught his mouth with hers. There was nothing soft or proper about it, and the connection was immediate. Electric.

As he deepened the kiss, he groaned, and she savored it. Savored being in his arms. Being with him. His urgency was next-level and she stumbled back. Thumped against the wall but he was there, chasing that kiss. Trailing kisses along her jaw and neck, pulling her back to himself.

But then he veered off, arm over her head and resting on the wall that held her up, his presence overpowering, taunting. He breathed heavily. "Whoa," he husked. Kissed her again.

Vienna's hands were somehow under his shirt as she pushed into the kiss and things heated again.

"Whoa." A few more kisses. "Whoa-whoa."

She faltered.

"Let's slow down . . ."

"Seriously?"

"Don't tempt me, Foxtrot." He nodded, his nose brushing her cheek as he breathed a kiss against her earlobe. "Light this fire, there's no dousing it."

She was very aware of the craven desire roiling through her. How she'd never wanted or done something like this . . . until him. Aware of his passion, hers, the roiling of the two, the cabin bed behind them . . . Where the heavy kisses could lead. How very much she wanted that.

Which was completely unlike her.

He straightened. Stepped back. Turned and dropped into the small chair in the corner. Cradled his head in his hands.

Suddenly chilled, Vienna hugged herself and moved to the bed. Sat cross-legged on the mattress. "I don't know how to figure you out. The mixed signals . . ." Did he want her? Or didn't he? Or was he like Brant?

No. He was not. At all.

He groaned loud and long. "I know. I know." He exhaled heavily and sat back in the chair, dragging his hands over his face. "My fault. I own that—haven't exactly been a gentleman."

Exactly. Complete opposite of Brant. And she hadn't really objected to moments of passion, so what did that make her?

Chewing the inside of her lower lip, she glanced at the comforter. Picked at a loose thread. Ha. There it was—*loose*. Did he think that of her? "I don't—" She shook her head. "That's not like me." Except thirty seconds ago, it had exactly been like her. She swallowed. "Sorry. I'm ashamed . . ."

"Don't be, Foxtrot. What's going on between us is . . . natural. But . . ." He bobbed his head, then he shook it. "I used to be footloose and fancy free with regard to sex, but I made a promise to God long ago that from then on, I'd keep it in the confines of marriage."

"From then on . . .?" Her heart hammered, hating that it sounded like there'd been someone else.

He deflated. "Rina." He roughed a hand down his beard. "I was different back then. She and I were living together. Next thing I know, she's pregnant. I—I didn't want that responsibility or . . . her." He grimaced. "I know it's terrible of me, but I couldn't admit it to myself. Being with her was . . . comfortable. Familiar. A habit. Not anything like you and I."

How could her stomach want to hurl one second and flare with excitement the next beneath these heavy confessions?

"She'd made all kinds of threats against me, against herself, saying she'd kill herself. Kill the baby. I grew numb to them, to her, knowing she manipulated me. But I couldn't walk away because of the baby. It was my mistake, I owned it." He gave a sharp nod. "I deployed—volunteered actually. She was ticked. There I am, deployed, and I get a bill she wanted me to pay—for an abortion. She'd already had it but wanted me to pay her back for it." He gave a slow shake of his head. "Guess I drove her away, but I felt responsible. So, I sent her the money." He removed his ballcap. Thwapped his knee. Put it back on. "A bad infection set in. Cost Rina her life."

"Crew—"

He held up a hand. "Hang on. It gets better." Tone acerbic, he roughed a hand over his neck and beard. "At her funeral, feeling like a serious piece of work, I hated myself and my selfishness. Stood there staring at her casket thinking if I'd just been more attuned to her needs, if I'd just put aside my frustrations . . . she'd be alive."

He went to the window and peered out into the night, then turned back. Propped himself on the ledge, massaging his leg. "Finally left the graveside, just wrecked. Get to my car and this Italian guy with a huge Boston accent walks up. Dude's drunk, gets in my face—thank God Ghost and Chapel were there to interdict—and shows me a picture. A *sonogram* picture. Tells me the baby was his. That *I'm* the reason *his* girlfriend and kid are dead. The girlfriend I'd been living with, supporting."

"Are you . . . That's awful."

"Didn't believe him at first. But he shows me this social media account they had together. Couldn't believe it. She was living two lives. Everything she'd ever told me had been a lie. I don't know why she stuck with me, except maybe she found some semblance of messed-up stability. All while she lived the glam life with Mr. Italian Stallion."

There were no words for that. It was just . . . evil. "I'm sorry, Crew."

"Nah." He returned to the chair near the bed. "I didn't tell you that for sympathy. Just don't want you to think . . ." His gray-green eyes found hers. He nudged up his ballcap. "I want you—us, *this*—more than I've ever wanted anything in my life."

She swallowed, scared and yet . . . exhilarated. Tears burned.

"I know guys have used you, but I honestly don't give a rat's behind who your parents are. They're not who I'm into. Who I want to spend the rest of my life with."

Surprise choked her. "Crew." She shifted to the edge of the bed. "We don't—"

"Don't give me that bull that we barely know each other." Earnestness carved hard lines into his face. "What we have, Foxtrot, this visceral, humming current . . . it's one of a kind. You can't put data parameters on it or define it by Days Accrued. All the time I was with Rina, I never felt anything like what I feel with you. What nearly drove me to compromise both of us a second ago. Where I deployed to get away from her, I couldn't get down here to see you fast enough just now." He moved to the edge of the seat, again kneading his leg muscle. "When I saw Havoc digging that mound . . . it nearly did me in thinking you were under there. That I'd lost you."

Tears welled in her eyes.

"I want you. *Us.*" He took her hand. Kissed her palm. "If I had a real ring, I'd propose."

"You don't need a ring to propose—"

"Is that a 'yes'?"

"You skipped the question."

"Because there's never been one when it comes to you."

"That's cheating." She sat back, though, startled at how she'd gone from "It's you and me, God" to this mountain of a man talking marriage. And her considering it! "I . . . I told God if he let me live, that I'd believe in Him."

Crew bent forward again, cupping his mouth.

"I'd no sooner spoken those words than you were there. And I just somehow knew that God was with me, but also that you and He were a package deal."

He smirked. "Absolutely. We both love you as you are and will never leave you."

"Love me?"

"Want me to say it again?"

Her vision blurred. "I do."

"Getting ahead of the game, aren't we?"

She sputtered a laugh. "You're terrible." Then she shook her head. "No, you're not. You're the best man I've ever known." She couldn't believe she was even considering the question he didn't ask. It felt a little hard to breathe, remembering another time . . . "You should know about Brant."

"Is this the guy I'm going to kill when I meet him, or should I start making a list?"

She wanted to smile but this wound had been buried so deep. "Besides you, he's the only one . . ."

The enormity of the secret she was laying bare seemed to register with Crew, who gave a slow nod. Touched her hand. "Before you go on, I want to make sure it's clear—I love you."

Heart thundering, she lifted a finger. "Hold that thought. It's only fair after you telling me about Rina that you hear my dark story." She shuddered, her emotions all over the place right now. "His name was Brant Kemp, and he was my MMA instructor. Young, enamored me, adored him, thought the world of the black belt master with World titles. We started dating, and it became very clear very fast that he knew who my father was. I didn't exactly advertise, so I was surprised he even knew about my father or his wealth. Apparently, Brant thought if he dated Horace Wolffe's daughter, he could get in with the billionaire—his real ambition was business and looking for ways to make money."

Crew kept his eyes locked on her, but she noticed his hand fisted.

"We were pretty good with sparring, and he even had me start teaching the family class at the dojo, which I enjoyed. Felt like he saw my skill, appreciated that. Things got . . . physical pretty fast." Heat charred her cheeks, and she couldn't hold Crew's gaze any longer, ashamed at how fast she'd fallen down that hole with Brant. "I saw things in him that bugged me, didn't like the way he was always wanting us to have dinner with my dad, but I convinced myself he was a good fit for me."

She scoffed. "Mom couldn't stand him—learned later he'd hit on her! Dad seemed to be okay with him. Also learned later my dad could tell I liked Brant, so held his peace. I rationalized myself into believing we were in love. We got engaged, and about then, I started feeling like he was my minder. He became super controlling, demanding. When I finally woke up and recognized the nightmare I was trapped in, I tried to break it off. He . . . beat me. Broke ribs and my jaw."

Crew was on his feet. Pacing.

Vienna knew she had to go on or she'd lose her nerve. "Threatened if I didn't go through with the wedding or if I left the apartment, he'd destroy not me, but my dad. My mom— whose entire career depends on publicity. That he'd videoed us in bed and would use it to blackmail my dad. For months, he held me hostage at his condo in New York. Raped me, trying to get me pregnant. Since he couldn't get my dad to accept him as a son, at least he'd get alimony or something. Child support." She shrugged. "I was his ticket to the easy life." When Crew didn't respond, Vienna wasn't sure what to make of his silence, the ferocity in his rugged features.

"I really will kill this guy if I ever meet him." He stood there, flexing and unflexing his fist. "Definitely explains why you hate men."

"I didn't *hate* them . . . just didn't date them." She peeked at him. "Until you crashed through all those barriers with your gorgeous Malinois."

His gaze was fierce, penetrating. Jaw muscle jouncing beneath that trim beard. He lowered his gaze. "I'm sorry that happened to you. You didn't deserve that. Nobody does."

"I can see that now," she said quietly. "Took a while to accept that no matter how rebellious I was in life, toward my parents, what he did was wrong. Good came out of it, though—my dad and I are closer than ever. And he's way more protective of me."

"Hold up," Crew said, eyes wide. "Is *he* the guy they found—"

"That story is exaggerated," Vienna said, feeling defensive. "Mostly."

"All the times I threatened to hurt him, and you didn't say he's already dead?"

"I don't talk about it because it just breeds rumors." She sighed and rubbed her temple. "My dad isn't a mafioso or don, nor would he hurt people. He's direct and rich, and there are those who don't like that."

Crew looked at her for a long time. "So if I ask for your hand, he won't take mine?"

She groaned at his pun. "That's awful."

"I've already lost a leg. I'd like to keep my remaining limbs."

Vienna tossed the pillow at him.

"So this Kemp is still alive?"

She faltered. "No . . ."

"Then he *is* dead."

"Pretty sure if he's not alive, that's what it means."

He smirked then seemed to sober. "I'm livid at what Brant did to you." He gave a cockeyed nod, then shifted to sit next to her. "And I think the reason you fell for him, justified him, is that—as twisted as he was in the end, he saw you. Saw you were a great fighter." He threaded their fingers and lifted hers to his lips. Kissed her fingers. "You don't need your father's wealth or your mom's fame to be amazing. You do it very well on your own. In fact, you excel at it. Own it."

Thud-thud!

Crew started awake. Head off the pillow, he took a second for his brain to register his location. Cabin. Not his. A weight on his arm held him down. He glanced there and froze.

No.

Foxtrot gave him a sleepy smile. "I'll get it." She stood and went to the door even as he came up.

When had he taken off his prosthetic leg? He swung himself to the side to hide it as the door opened. What in the world was he doing sleeping in her bed with her? They were fully clothed—*thank God*—but still.

"Topside," came Benn's amused bark. "Chapel wants to talk to you two."

Crew glanced there and saw the guy's smirk. Imagined where his thoughts went. "On our way."

"Uh huh."

She closed the door and arched an eyebrow at him.

"Freaking . . ." he hissed, hoisting his leg from the chair, and tugged up his pantleg. "How . . . what happened?"

Foxtrot opened a closet and drew out clothes that someone had set up for her. "I was telling you about my first gig when you started snoring."

Crew froze. Looked at her. "You're kidding."

"You were out. Hard. I tried waking you, but you just grunted and went back to sawing logs."

He'd never done that. Never been comfortable enough around others to sleep. Except in the field.

Armed with clothes, she wedged into the bathroom. "I promise not to tell my dad." She closed the door amid his objection and threat to throw his leg at her.

Ten minutes later, after a quick detour to check on Havoc, still sedated but not unconscious and healing fine, Crew strode into the conference room with Foxtrot. From where he stood amid computer and static displays, Chapel looked up. There was no little amount of chastisement in that searing gaze. "Hope you got *some* rest."

Man, word traveled fast. The innuendo was clear. "Sure did."

He tried not to look at Foxtrot, but his mind careened through the memory of waking up and finding her next to him. That beautiful face and pink lips. Auburn hair over her shoulder. The way she was on her side, curled into him.

"The op to save Felicity?" Foxtrot asked, folding her arms, a move so unlike her.

"A success," Chapel pronounced, moving to another station where he indicated to some images, including one of Felicity Vale after processing her. "She's en route to the States to receive medical care and be reunited with her family."

"Thank goodness," Foxtrot said, brushing her hair back. "And Baako and Iris?" She was on a roll, head in the game.

Chapel eyed the commander. "We'll get to that. First, you should both know that our interdiction to save Vale ticked off Abna' Suria. They've been breathing down our necks since."

That woke Crew up. He shifted forward. Planted his hands on his belt. "Is that why we had so much heat once I located Foxtrot?"

Chapel nodded. "That's our belief. Chatter has erupted and they're looking for us in force."

"Hold up," Crew said, his pulse jacked. "If they're looking for you . . . and our ferry rescue was anything but subtle . . ." He sat back and shook his head. "You're expecting them to hit us, this yacht."

Chapel held his gaze, then looked at Foxtrot. "Miss Foxcroft, can you give us some time? Breakfast is being served middeck. Gatlin can join you later."

She looked at Crew, surprised. Insulted.

Crew wanted to offer the platitude that whatever Chapel wanted to tell him, he could also tell her. But that's not how operations worked. Despite all they'd been through together, Crew had clearance and she did not. He couldn't argue that. "I'll be there."

Irritation flared through her green eyes, but she acquiesced.

Gave Chapel one long glower, then walked out and closed the door.

"Thank you for not countering me on that," Chapel said as he tossed down a tablet and moved to the other side of the room. At a desk, he eyed Crew. "Where's your head, Gatlin?"

"Excuse me?"

"I need to know your head's in the right place."

"My head's where it always is."

Chapel skewered him with a look. "Sleeping with her—"

"Hey." The insult burned. "You know me better than that."

"You were in her cabin and bed."

A groan churned through Crew's chest. "I fell asleep while she was talking."

Chapel faltered and grinned. "Not a great start to a relationship."

Man, he hated this. Wasn't going to endure a lecture. "I'm a handler now. My dog is sedated in the hold, so—"

"You're an operator, Gatlin. Plain and simple. And things are about to get real."

That sounded a lot like they knew more than they were telling him. "Read me in."

Arms crossed, Chapel let out a slow exhale, considering him. Deciding where to draw his lines. "Her buddies are aboard, and one of them is communicating with the terrorists."

Crew gripped the bill of his hat. Shifted it down. "Know which one?"

"Negative. Haven't been able to isolate it, even though we've got them under heavy surveillance. Staff onboard are operators, and there are listening devices. So give care declaring your love to Foxtrot."

Holy fluff. "You *bugged* her cabin?"

Chapel didn't meet his gaze. "We didn't want her aware because her last exchange with these three rattled her."

"She did great."

"So rather than put her under that stress again, we want her to be natural."

"Foxtrot already knows you suspect one of them."

"Maybe, but we need to play it safe, not tip them off. We've already interdicted three speedboats that were on an intercept. Those not dead are in custody, and they're trying to rout the contact."

"Why not just turn them over?"

Chapel's jaw muscle flexed. "Whoever did this is responsible for the death of one of my men. I want to know who it is. I want to deal with them."

"They'll just send more reinforcements."

"If they want to lose them, that's up to them. The Turk is fond of this yacht, so he has a pretty stiff response in the area. They won't reach us. He's giving me this time. And we don't want whoever is here knowing the game is up."

"Won't they figure out you're intercepting . . .?"

"Negative. One-way comms. Apparently they can send but can't receive," Chapel said, all business. "Be ready for a fight. Tahj is in the armory. Grab what you need and stay frosty."

Crew nodded, taking in the intel on the table. The images of the three members of the crew. The images of Vale and the location she'd been held. A board with intel on the terrorists. He looked back at the three. "You have a preference?"

"The woman," Chapel bit out. "It's always the woman."

He eyed the boss. "Sounds personal."

Chapel locked him in a visual dual. "Sorry about Rina."

Son of a brisket. "I want that deleted."

"Already done."

Crew didn't know whether to believe him, but he had no choice. No power here. "Uncool." He stepped back and moved to the door.

"Gatlin."

Irritated, he looked over his shoulder.

"Nice shirt."

Growling, he moved into the passage. Cursed himself for not finding a tac shirt. He'd put it back on last night when he'd headed to her cabin because she liked it and wanted him to wear it.

Go to Turkey for her. Wear stupid shirts for her. Holy Moses, what was next?

21

BOSPHORUS STRAIT, TURKEY

Sitting at a table with a plate of eggs, sausage, and fruit, Vienna stared out at the waters sparkling beneath the morning sun. It had ticked her off to be dismissed from the Command room when it was obvious they were going to talk more. Without her. She poked at some eggs, but they scooted away from the tines.

She huffed and pitched her fork down. Sat back and folded her arms. Noticed the host stood to the side, hands in front of him . . . legs spread shoulder-width apart. Not like a server at all. Head tilted to the side, she considered the man on the side of the room. He'd been cleaning tables—*clean* tables—the whole time.

If she happened to leave the dining room . . .?

Vienna tossed down her napkin and stood. Did not miss the way the hands of the host a few feet away fell to his sides. That was a very familiar stance. She went out onto the pool deck, both sides lined with leather couches, the far side a rail that hung over the water. She moved there. Gripped the rail, damp and chilled from the churning water and the early morning.

"Ma'am, I've been asked to have you move closer in. Waves are rough."

Vienna turned to him—the host from inside. "Waves."

His expression brooked no argument. He motioned to the side of the yacht. "Ma'am."

Not inclined to comply, she held the bar again. "I'm—"

"V!"

Her heart started when she saw Baako striding toward her. The craziest urge to suddenly comply came over her. That and keeping this host near. "Thank you." She moved in the direction he'd urged her a second ago. "Baako." What was he doing on the yacht?

He hurried toward her. Hugged her.

That was . . . weird. He'd hugged her before, but it felt wrong now. Not because of him—or maybe a little—but because . . . *I consider myself Crew's now.*

That was freaky. She'd never thought of anyone owning her. But that's not what it was about. It was . . . belonging.

He indicated to the couches. "I heard you've been running for your life."

Really? Had Chapel told them? "Yeah." She touched her temple. Saw the scratches and cuts on her arm. "They attacked the plane I was supposed to leave on." Instinct told her not to volunteer information. But what if Baako wasn't the one who'd betrayed them? He was her friend. Good friend. They'd worked together for years. That alone discounted him, didn't it?

Unless he was blackmailed recently . . .

Baako seemed genuinely upset. "I do not understand this craziness. It did not start until G.I. Joe showed up. I know that he got shot helping you, but if he had not come, you would not be in this mess."

She rolled her eyes. "What's happening has nothing to do with him, Baako, and you know that. Get over your jealousy. Crew and I are—" What? Dating? Engaged? She felt the rope ring she still wore. "He's the best man I've ever met. I really like him, Baako. I want to see where it leads."

"What of me, V?"

Was this really all about his jealousy? "You'll always be my friend."

"*Friend*. Bah!"

Vienna stood, indignant. "If that's how—"

"I am sorry." He was on his feet.

"Hey." Crew's decisive voice cut into the palpable tension. He joined her, and she noticed he didn't put an arm around her. Didn't act possessively. Also hadn't kept the cream shirt on that he'd bought. Somehow he'd traded it for one of his standard tactical shirts. "How was breakfast?"

Grateful for his presence and strength, for the way he trusted her to handle this, she smiled at Baako. "Tasteless."

"Vienna? Sergeant Gatlin?"

Vienna startled. "Iris!" After a hug, which also felt awkward, the warning of the commander still ringing in her head, she eyed the girl's foot, which was in a boot now. "How are you doing?"

The girl motioned to Magnus who was with her. "Good." She indicated to a table where plates of food waited. "Have you eaten? We were just going to dig in."

"That was my plan," Crew said.

It was? Vienna considered him, then mutely nodded.

"So what happened?" Iris asked as they put together two tables and sat down. "We overheard the soldiers saying you were running for your lives."

Crew ordered a meal from the host, a long look exchanging between the two, then focused on the table.

Vienna deliberately planted herself next to him, and gratefully, Baako didn't give her grief about her choice, but she saw his jaw tighten as he sat at the head of the table next to Magnus and Iris. "It was pretty scary." She shared a look with Crew, hoping he'd take the lead on telling the story.

"Terrorists hit the plane she was scheduled to leave on. We escaped."

"We?" Iris wrinkled her nose. "You said she was scheduled to be on it, but both of you were on it?"

Crew considered her for a hot second. "Yeah."

Wow, he was roaring alpha right there, not providing more information.

Chowing down, Iris seemed to enjoy the story as though she was reading a script. "So, what happened next?"

Vienna glanced at her, then the others. "You know, I really don't want to relive it. Suffice it to say, we ran for our lives. I got captured. He got shot. Havoc was shot. Then I was buried alive." Her hand automatically went to Crew's arm, and his steady gaze found hers. "He found me. And here we are."

"The ferry, though!" Iris exclaimed. "That was dope. I watched from my stateroom. That has to find its way into a script."

"That would be one film I would not want to work on." She grinned. "Right, Baako?"

He didn't quite meet her gaze and shrugged. "It's a paycheck. I'd do it."

His attitude surprised. What else would he do for money? Betray her?

"Me, too," Magnus said with a laugh. "Money and jobs are too few these days."

Baako frowned. "Just wouldn't want to be the one taking a bullet in the chest."

Iris chuckled. "Or be buried under gravel!"

Vienna went very still, realization—and fear—washing over her.

Shifting his arm, Crew took her hand in his. Slid his gaze to hers. "I need to check on Havoc."

"I'll come. I owe him my life." Anything to get out of here after what she'd just realized.

"How do you owe a dog your life?" Magnus asked, his wiry-gray hair askew around his pocked face.

"He tracked my scent and led Crew to me."

"So the dog found you," Baako clarified. "Not G.I. Joe here." Crew stalked away.

"He dug me out with his bare hands." And a bobcat, but that didn't sound as dramatic. "Where were you?" She hustled after Crew, not waiting for the response.

She caught up with him as he slid down the rails to the lower deck, and the sound of barking carried up the passage, making her smile.

"Hey, Meatball," Crew said as he rounded the corner into the medical bay.

Havoc's barking grew more incessant, and once she entered the room, she realized why—he'd been secured in a crate.

"Okay, okay. Hold up." He grabbed the collar and lead and bent to open the door.

Havoc shot past the door, nearly knocking over Crew who cursed, and bolted to Vienna. He tried to stop, but his nails had no traction. He slid straight into her legs. Pinned her back against a wall of metal cabinets.

Laughing, she bent and patted his sides. "Hello, handsome."

"Traitor," Crew groused as he trudged toward them and slid the collar on him. "Guess you're feeling better."

Havoc lifted his right paw and grabbed Vienna's leg, holding her close.

"That's supposedly a sign of love," Crew said as he clipped the leash on.

"Is that all it takes to declare love?"

Crew's foot came off the ground.

"Don't even try it."

Chuckling, he reached around her. Hooked her nape and tugged her closer. Kissed her forehead. "I want to see where it leads, too."

"Good." She peered up at him. "Now, trust me."

Crew frowned "I do tr—"

"What didn't Chapel want me to know? You told me not to give you the bull about not knowing each other long. Do me the same respect and don't tell me it's classified. I'm in the middle of this fight and can't execute the stunt without knowing the plan."

His gaze trekked over her face, taking her in. Weighing things. "I had no intention of keeping you in the dark, Foxtrot. First . . ." He nodded. "I think Iris might be the traitor."

Vienna faltered. "No—it's Baako."

He frowned. "No, you never told her about the gravel, yet she already knew."

Surprise washed over her. "I don't know how I missed that." She nodded to him. "Your gunshot wound—Baako knew you were shot in the chest, but we never mentioned that. And you can't see the dressing with that shirt."

"Good catch," he grunted in acknowledgement. "They both know more than they should. What about Magnus?"

She frowned. "What about him?"

"Exactly." Crew shook his head. "We're back at freakin' ground zero."

In the dining hall that evening, Crew couldn't relax despite the big band music pumping through the speakers. Had to work not to read into every gesture and word, no matter how small, that the three did. Thankfully, Chapel made it clear to everyone on the yacht that Damocles was in play as 'security' after the incidents.

He sat at a table that enabled him to have his back to the wall and his gaze on the room. Sat close to Foxtrot, arm around the back of her chair.

"You're hovering," she said softly as she tucked a piece of steak into her mouth.

"It's your fault," he said, noting the way Baako kept shooting glares their way. He kissed her nape. "Updos are notoriously cruel."

"For men without restraint," she said, a giggle snatching from her. "Stop. They're watching."

Cupping her face, Crew kissed her. "That's kind of the point." He grinned when she narrowed her eyes at him.

"You're taking this 'act natural' thing a little far."

"Oh yeah. Forgot we're working."

"How can you be so calm and sarcastic—"

"Chapel didn't want you to know what was happening because he said you'd be too stressed. Couldn't stay on task." His eyes held meaning, warning. "I told him you could handle it. Am I wrong?"

Noses barely an inch apart, she held his gaze. Touched his beard as a softness edged out the worry and fear, making her appear ethereal. "No." She gave a soft kiss, then sighed. "I think I'm falling in love with you, Crew Gatlin."

He let a slow smile slide into his mug. "Never heard anything more beautiful."

"Y'all good on drinks?"

Crew smirked at the intrusion of Benn, a nudge to make sure they maintained situational awareness. "We're good." He cocked his head toward the middle of the room. "Let's dance."

Her eyebrows arched. "You *dance*?"

"We call him Twinkletoes," Benn said as he moved to the next table where Iris was sitting with Nora Glace.

"Twinkle—"

"Bad joke." Crew threw a scowl at his buddy as he drew her to the open area.

Liked how easily she came into his arms, and how perfectly she fit there.

"They have to know we're waiting for them to make a move," she whispered into his shoulder.

"Mm-hmm," he murmured against her ear. "Just be ready."

"I'm not cut out for this stuff."

"D'you ever see Mr. & Mrs. Smith?"

She eased back and looked at him, frowning. "Seriously?"

"Remember when they'd figured out who each other were, and they did that dance?"

She laughed. "I can't believe you watched that movie."

Grimacing, he huffed. "Rina. But you're missing the point. They did that waltz—"

"Tango."

He grinned. "Whatever. And he disarms her."

"And she him."

"Yeah. Point is—she was as tough as he was."

"I'd argue more."

He smirked. "We're them."

Her hand slid up the back of his neck and she stroked his close crop. "I like that. As long as we don't have to kill each other."

He held her close, noting in their periphery that Baako and Nora were dancing now, too. "Agreed." Now Iris had conned Benn into being her partner. And Magnus . . . Where was Magnus?

Crew guided Foxtrot around the floor, turning her in a circle, taking in the perimeter. "Your weapon," he said as he slid his hand down her side. Not in some erotic move but for proximity to his weapon.

Though her expression tightened, she adjusted to reach the knife she'd secured at the rim of her top. Then her eyes widened at the same time he caught a reflection in the window.

Directly behind him.

"Magnus!"

Weapon in hand, he spun toward the man.

Havoc flew across the room. Broadsided the guy. Nailed him and toppled him into the nearest table. A shot cracked the air, and Crew's heart shoved into his throat. "Havoc, *aus!*" Even as he said it, he saw his Belgian Malinois lose his lock. He slid across the room with a yelp.

Benn, Tahj, and Nix converged on the guy, who had a gun. Whipped it around. Several bursts neutralized him as Crew rushed to Havoc's side, relieved when his partner lumbered back up.

"You crazy boy," he murmured, catching the collar. "All good." When he straightened, Crew saw Foxtrot rushing at him. He caught her and hugged her. Saw Baako and Iris. "Secure them," he ordered the hosts.

Stunned, the two gaped. Iris cried.

"How did you know where I was shot?" Crew demanded of Baako.

"I passed the medical bay when you were getting stitched up," he balked.

"And you," Vienna asked Iris. "How'd you know about the gravel?"

"I heard them talking about it," Iris sniveled. "They said you were in some plant that had gravel." She cried into her hands, then stole a look at the now-deceased Magnus. "I can't believe it . . ."

EPILOGUE
ONE MONTH LATER

A BREED APART RANCH, TEXAS HILL COUNTRY

"Gatlin, what's going on with all the new meat in the kennels?"

Crew smirked as he met Ghost's gaze across the training yard. "Catching up on my procurement quota."

Ghost adjusted his ABA ballcap. "You got handlers to work these dogs?"

Nodding, Crew thought of the candidates he'd scouted, the ones he'd talked to. "And a behaviorist—maybe."

"Did you happen to find someone for Jibril?"

Crew hesitated. Was he supposed to fill another position? "What's he need?"

"A wife."

Pitching Havoc's KONG down the training yard, Crew laughed. "Afraid that's above my paygrade."

"He's becoming an old maid. We need to get him out of my hair and books," Ghost grunted as he drew closer. "Want to throw some names at me?"

It wasn't a question or an invitation. That was the boss's way of demanding an update. "Sure. Outside the dogs we acquired from litters who are giving Khat and her puppy team a run for their money, there are some DoD dogs I'm watching in case they get dispositioned."

"Can't afford the high cost of health issues."

Crew understood the concern. Most dispo'd MWDs were retired due to health, medical, or behavioral issues. "I hear you—and I wouldn't dream of procuring a dog that's going to cost us more than it'd benefit ABA." He folded his arms. "What I'm watching for are the dogs sick of military life but have a few more operational years in them rather than turning someone's couch into a very large bite sleeve. They're perfect candidates for LEOs and contract work like ABA."

"It's a risk."

"Every dog is."

Ghost ran a hand over his shorn hair. "So, they're operational."

"Differing statuses but worth considering." Shrugging, Crew pursed his lips. "Remember the SEAL team that lost a dog in the Greater Antilles not long ago?"

"Cutter." Leave it to Ghost to know the names of the dogs. He huffed a laugh. "Don't ask me how I remember . . . or the handler's names."

"That I can fill in—Beau Maddox. DEVGRU, top-notch handler." He shrugged and swiped a hand over his jaw. "I'd love to see him working for the ranch, so I put a bug in his ear about ABA."

Ghost nodded. "Heard of him. Guy's got an attitude on his shoulders."

"What operator doesn't?"

"You."

"Yeah, well . . . I'm a special breed . . ."

Smile falling away, Ghost frowned. "I know someone on Maddox's team. Told me he's known to get sauced."

At that, Crew hesitated. "I hadn't heard that."

"Sobriety is non-negotiable."

"Agreed." He needed to change the subject. "Been trying to snag Davis Ledger's interest, too, but he's a no-go so far." Crew scratched his stubble, thinking. "Oh—Tsunami's twin."

A rare smile split Ghost's face. "Tsunami. That was an impressive dog." He squinted. "Twin was . . . Surge?"

Nodding, Crew was impressed again. "Yep. And Tsunami's double in every respect. Currently deployed, but I know the vet assigned to him. I reach out every few months, checking on him."

"Good. Anyone else?"

"A few, but it's hit or miss with dogs still working."

"Well, there's one nearby. Retired with his handler—Chaos."

"Wait. Chaos is *here*?"

Ghost inclined his head, then faltered. "Not at the ranch, but Hill Country. About forty mikes out. Kendrick Silva was his handler, and they're holed up together. He's in a wheelchair and as crotchety as they come, but I'm hopeful he'll realize he's in over his head and let us recycle Chaos before the dog ends up seized by Animal Control or worse."

"Working dogs need to work. It's in their blood; it's why they're so good at it."

Considering him, Ghost shook his head. "Ever think we're doing this backwards? Picking up the mutts, the MWDs nobody wants."

"Like me." Crew grinned. "It's unconventional, but it works. I think we're shoring up the kennels to be some serious stuff."

"Agreed." He nodded at him. "Glad you stayed aboard. With these options and plans, maybe Darci won't kill me for spending most of retirement on a dog ranch." He eyeballed Crew. "So what's happening with you and the movie star?"

"Stunt double, and we're figuring things out."

"You planning to marry her and follow her into the limelight?"

"No way. I don't belong there. I'm just one of your mutts who found home."

SIX MONTHS LATER

DELPHI, GREECE

Sitting on the edge of the cliff, the ruins of Delphi behind them, Crew wrapped his arm around Foxtrot's shoulders and pulled her back against him. Enjoyed the view of the rolling mountains that stretched down to the sea. They ignored the other tourists hiking the ruins, the votives, the temples. Just savored the time together.

Or he tried.

"This is beautiful," she said around a sigh. "I could stay here all day and be quite happy."

"As long as we're together . . ." Crew dug into his pocket and retrieved the ring, his heart rapid-firing a hundred miles an hour.

She glanced over her shoulder "What . . ."

Crew hooked his arm around her and presented the ring. "Will this do?"

Foxtrot sat up and whipped around onto her knees, facing him. Face alight. "Seriously?" She cupped her hands over her mouth and laughed, then dropped them to her lap.

The look on her face . . . was that anger? "Did I screw this up?"

"You haven't asked . . ."

Man, he loved this firestorm. "Vienna Foxtrot—"

"Fox*croft*."

"I'll propose how I want to propose."

"Get on with it."

"If you'd stop interrupting me . . ."

She pressed her lips into a line and arched her eyebrows.

"Vienna Foxtrot, will you be my partner in life, my wife?"

She wagged her finger—which still had the rope ring on it—for him to install the new, vastly more expensive piece there.

He gripped the rope ring and tugged.

"Hey!" She yanked away her hand. "No takebacks." She extended her hand again. "C'mon."

"You want me to put this on with the other?"

"Always knew you were smart." Again, she waggled her fingers at him. "C'mon."

Crew winged up an eyebrow. "You haven't answered yet."

She gave one of those lazy smiles that said a kiss was incoming, and he was all for that. Accepted the languorous, perfect lip-lock.

"Yes, Crew Gatlin. I will marry you."

He slid the sparkling doorstop on her finger and kissed her palm. She giggled and, though that wasn't her standard fare, he liked it. Liked the giddiness so evident on her face, and that he'd put it there. Again, she kissed him. Leaned into him and he caught her into his arms and rolled her to the ground. Deepened the kiss and thought of where this would go . . . in time. Not yet. But he would savor these pre-tastes.

A wet snout shoved between their faces. Havoc's tail wagged so hard, he nearly fell on them.

She laughed and nudged him aside, then looked at her watch. With a gasp, she sat up. "We need to go!"

"I thought we weren't stressing on this vacation."

"We have a reservation at To Patriko Mas, and it was not easy to get. Also, I am not going to miss my chance for some homemade baklava." She scoffed. "Are you kidding me? I have priorities, Soldier-boy."

"You're killing me here, Foxtrot."

She stood and extended her hand. "C'mon. Wasting time, Gatlin."

Arms crisscrossed and clasped with Crew's, she braced and helped him upright. Two hours later, they were showered and headed to the high-end restaurant with its killer views. Nerves jouncing, Crew was surprised when they didn't have trouble getting Havoc into the restaurant. Weird. He almost always had to convince them to let him in.

They negotiated the inner part of the restaurant, people startled to see his dog trotting past the linen tables. Up the stone steps. It was strange, but the higher levels they climbed, the less crowded it was. Made no sense. These were the best tables. When they reached the upper terrace with the killer views, he was surprised to find it empty.

"Huh," Foxtrot said, frowning at him. "Maybe they just turned the tables or shift."

Crew had long ago learned to listen to his instincts, and he knew something wasn't right here. The host delivered them to the corner table. Alone. It'd be nice if it weren't so wrong.

"Excuse me," Crew asked the host. "Is the restaurant closing soon?"

The woman smiled. "No, of course not." And she walked away.

"You feeling what I'm feeling?" Foxtrot asked as she sat to the side, letting him take the seat that gave him the best line of sight on the path. The rail hemmed in the terrace and afforded an unobstructed view of Greece.

"Yeah . . ."

But the server arrived, took their order for appetizers and drinks, then disappeared.

Foxtrot wagged her engagement ring in his face. "You did good, Soldier-boy."

"Well, Soon-to-be-Missus-Gatlin, I'm glad you approve." He leaned in and kissed her. "Surprised you wanted to keep the rope ring."

"Of course. It's our story." She hugged her own hand.

They ordered their meals and the appetizers were soon delivered. They dug in and sat, tranquilly holding hands and taking in the scenery. For him, that was Vienna Foxcroft.

"You know," she said with a satisfied sigh as she shifted her attention back to him—then froze. Slapped a hand on the table. *"Daddy?"*

Do what?

Even as Crew turned his head, he felt the swarm of new bodies. Came to his feet, bringing Havoc upright as well. Though he expected his partner to snarl, the Malinois just sat.

Six-one and roughly 220 pounds, billionaire Horace Wolffe stalked up the terrace steps, flanked by two take-no-bull bodyguards.

Holy Moses, I am dead.

"What's this I hear?" the man growled. "You asked my daughter to marry you without talking to me?"

Gut sinking, Crew held his ground. "With respect, sir. I called three times." Wouldn't mention those calls went unanswered.

"You saying I ignored your calls?"

"Nega—" Military lingo wasn't appropriate here "No, sir. Can't infer anything in that except that I made the calls."

"Daddy, stop," Foxtrot said rising from the table. "It's oka—"

"It's not okay."

No way this guy was going to ruin their vacation and engagement time. "Sir—"

"No. Enough." Horace Wolffe held Crew's gaze for a long time. A very long, uncomfortable time. "I owe you an apology, young man."

Uh . . . what?

"I'm protective of Vienna after . . . certain events. When some stranger calls and says he wants to talk to me . . . and V says she wants to marry a man she's only known for six months—"

"I under—"

"I wasn't amused."

"Wasn't funny, sir."

The man grunted, considering him again. "Agreed." His gaze swung to Foxtrot's. He took her hand. Eyed the engagement ring. "Not bad."

Nope. Wouldn't let that bug him. Would not be cowed.

"Stop." Vienna pushed her dad. "It's beautiful and all I want. Well, him and Havoc, too."

"Hav—oh, the dog." Mr. Wolffe sidestepped and glanced down at Havoc. "This the infamous war dog?"

Laid out on his side, bored with the encounter, Havoc rolled back, lifted his leg, and bared his belly for the billionaire.

"Worthless traitor," Crew muttered.

Horace Wolffe laughed. Stuck out his hand. "I like you, Gatlin."

Crew eyed the man's offering. "If I shake yours, will I get mine back?"

With a raucous laugh, Wolffe grabbed Crew's hand and yanked him into a shoulder hug. "Welcome to La Familia."

Gear up for the next A Breed Apart: Legacy thriller, *Chaos*, by Ronie Kendig and Steffani Webb, releasing January, 2024.

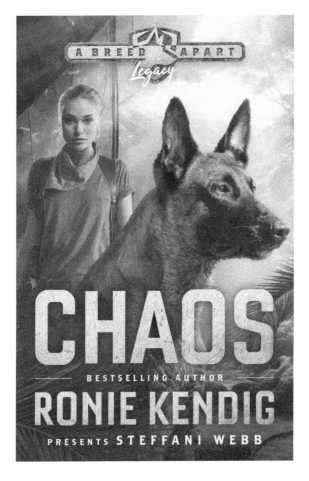

Buckle up for an edge-of-your seat trek through the dangerous jungles of the Philippines in this enemies to lovers, forced proximity, alpha hero, sunshine versus grumpy romantic thriller!

When Rio Silva is told her aunt and uncle are missing in a Philippine rainforest, she knows there is only one answer to finding them: the retired military working dog her dad entrusted to her. Chaos, however, has a mind of her own, a lot like Rio.

Worse, she'll have to trust arrogant and bossy former Army Ranger, Cathal McGowan if she hopes to get them back.

The last thing Cathal McGowan needs is to be shackled with a young, pretty teacher with no combat experience as he leads them into the dark heart of the rainforest. But she has heart—he'll give her that. And he has the experience she needs to rescue her family.

Putting everything on the line, Rio and Cathal struggle to navigate the terrain, as well as their emerging feelings for each other. But the closer they get to mission success, the more things aren't adding up, including who might be behind the disappearance. It's not long before they realize the rainforest holds greater perils than deadly vipers . . . and the biggest danger of all might be their hearts.

Keep reading for a sneak peek at *Chaos*!

CHAOS

A BREED APART: LEGACY BOOK 2
PROLOGUE

TWO YEARS AGO

UNDISCLOSED LOCATION, IRAQ

Sweat dripped down his face. Down his back. The heat almost suffocating under the sixty pounds of gear strapped to him. And dirt. It was flipping everywhere and invaded every inch of. . .everything. What he wouldn't give for a day back in Kildare right about now.

Instead, First Sergeant Cathal McGowan gripped his M4 as he led his Ranger team down dusty streets of the small Iraqi village under the full power of the sun. Heat waves drifted across the street.

Ten paces ahead, their interpreter Uday Abadi skittered forward. Head down, he passed by a couple of women beating rugs outside their homes. The slight man had set up this meeting with the wife of an HVT, who was willing to give them valuable intel—but only if she could speak with a woman on the Cultural Support Team that Cathal's men and an assisting team now escorted. The precarious logistics of getting the wife here had unexpectedly brought them outside the wire on the hottest day Iraq had gifted them yet.

Still, a few children played football, clearly unfazed by the heat. A wild kick shot the dirty black-and-white ball toward him. Cathal tapped it with his boot, knocking it back in their direction with a small grin. They waved, then continued with their game.

"Hey, Sarge."

Pulling up, Cathal let his men continue forward as he glanced over his shoulder. He inwardly groaned when he eyed the private from the assisting team, who couldn't have been more than eighteen. "Yeah?" This kid had been a pain in Cathal's backside ever since they left base.

"At my nine." He confidently jerked his head in that direction. The private's Kevlar'd chest rose and fell in a steady cadence as he held his weapon close. "Thought I saw movement on top of the building."

Larson strode past them. Rolled his eyes at Cathal with a shake of his head.

The kid—who Cathal had mentally dubbed "Crier," aka: the boy who cried wolf—thought he saw an IED under every *bleedin'* rock. The cocky, eager kid wanted to prove his worth but had done nothing but irritate the team with all his false alarms.

Crier lifted his chin. "I think we're being watched."

No kidding, Sherlock.

Being scrutinized was par for the course out here. While there weren't as many people outside as usual, dead streets didn't mean no one was around. It meant locals were holed up inside the clay-and-mud structures that flanked each other, likely tracking the Americans moving through their town. The team was easy pickings. Fish in a barrel.

But as sure as he didn't check, the kid would be right this time, so Cathal squinted behind his Oakleys and scanned the roof. Nothing, as suspected. He keyed his mic, turning away. "Eyes out. Possible unfriendlies taking up position to the south."

"Copy." A chorus of replies filtered through his comms as Crier stalked away.

Wouldn't hurt to check in with overwatch, too. "Echo One to base, do we have eyes in the sky?"

"Negative, Echo One," came the static-filled reply. "Overwatch is in the blind."

Cathal clenched his jaw. He didn't like this. Nothing good ever happened when base didn't have eyes on them.

"Whatcha got, Guinness?" Master Sergeant Andy Forsyth paused next to him.

Cathal looked over at his buddy. "Uncertain."

"Copy." Forsyth proceeded down the street, and Cathal knew his second was watching for anything that looked off.

Should we RTB?

Cathal again checked the rooflines. Nothing. But an eerie feeling hung in the air.

"*Salam alaikum. Salam alaikum.*" A soft voice filtered into his awareness as CST member Stella Abbot passed by, murmuring to herself. "Come on, Stell. Get this right."

Ahead, Uday entered into a two-story mud-and-plaster building.

Staying eyes out, Cathal brought himself even with Abbot in long, quick strides. He slowed to pace her as they brought up the rear of the group. She didn't seem to notice him as she wrung her hands, reciting the Arab greeting on a loop. It was her first time outside the wire, and her nervousness was palpable. "You good there, Specialist?"

Abbot startled, purple hijab shifting with her movements and contrasting against the deep blue eyes that lifted to him. Though she'd done her best to situate the head covering correctly, a strand of her brunette hair had slipped free. She nodded. "Yes, sir."

"Don't 'sir' me; I work for a living," he teased.

The warm smile she shot him—though clearly forced— reminded him of his sister's. In fact, most things about her reminded him of Maeve. Same cheerful outlook. Same concern for others. Same dark-brown hair. If Maeve had made it, he bet she would have turned out like Abbot.

He cleared his throat. Adjusted the strap of his weapon. "You'll do fine. Just stay calm and focus on making the connection to get the intel as quickly as possible. We got your six."

She expelled a breath but still looked apprehensive.

The assisting team circled around the rear of Uday's place. Echo team took up strategic positions along the road and outside the house. Something about Abbot tugged at his gut as she caught up and disappeared inside.

Cathal joined his team waiting outside in the heat. He turned to watch the kids who'd been playing football.

They were gone.

Weapon up, he frowned, sweeping the area. They were *all* gone. Rugs lay in a heap before one of the doors, but the women had vanished. And it was quiet. Too quiet.

"Where'd everybody go?"

Hearing his thoughts come out of Edgars's mouth, Cathal edged back to the house and sought cover. "This can't be good," he muttered and keyed his comms. "Echo, what do you see?"

Larson, Ryker, and Lopez spread out but confirmed no one was around anymore. A couple yards away, Forsyth reported the same.

Uday erupted from the house. Waved wildly. "No good! No good!"

Cathal's heart hammered. "What—"

"Ambush!"

He bit back a curse. Keyed his mic to warn the teams. Before he could get a word out, he saw smoke. Too late.

BOOM! BOOM!

Punched backward, Cathal fell into darkness.

Groaning, he came to. *Get up! Get up!* Something heavy pinned his chest. Ears ringing, he forced himself to press up from the ground. Uday's body rolled off of him, thudding into the dirt. Blood poured from a wound on the interpreter's head.

Cathal dragged himself on all fours. Swayed as gravity clawed at him. He looked up through the haze, preparing for attack as warbled shouting bounced around his brain. Smoke billowed from what was left of the building. Despite the damage, the structure hadn't collapsed. Yet.

Just inside the destroyed entrance lay purple fabric. Abbot's hijab. She lay unmoving, rubble around and on top of her.

Shots rang, and like a narrow funnel that widened, sound filtered back into his world.

"Guinness!"

Cathal shoved to his feet. Staggered. As his head cleared, he tucked his weapon into his shoulder and followed his team's line of sight to where men were firing on them from the rooftops across the street.

He eased the trigger back. Once. Twice. Bodies dropped to the ground. He swung the rifle behind him and lowered to hook his arms under Uday's so he could pull the man to safety.

Which was where?

Cathal saw a stack of crates beside Edgars and Lopez. Better than nothing. He dragged the unconscious man back. The rest of his men took cover behind anything they could find. A post. A car. Not much out here.

"Three o'clock!"

"Contact rear!"

Combatants were everywhere. Wood splintered at his face as a bullet narrowly missed him. He ducked for a moment then looked out.

The interpreter slumped to the side, and Cathal reached to check for a pulse. Uday had passed to eternity. "Come on!" he growled before turning back. Adrenaline coursed through his veins. How many more would they lose? He needed to try and get to Abbot before the second story collapsed onto her. Check for other survivors.

As if on cue, a blood-curdling scream followed by a string of Arabic erupted from somewhere inside the faltering building.

Ice coursed down his spine.

Above the mud home adjacent to his position, two men were readying another RPG. One dropped but the other doubled down on his efforts.

Cathal fired. Missed. With a growl, he steadied his breath. Touched the guy with his reticle. Fired again and the second man went down.

"More at your eight!" Lopez shouted.

Ryker ducked down to reload. "It's like they're respawning!"

Cathal keyed his mic. "Echo One to Base. Troops in contact, taking heavy fire! We need backup *now*."

"Copy, Echo One."

God, we're gonna need Your help here.

"Sarge!" Forsyth shot off another two rounds at the roofline. "Larson's down!"

Cathal cursed.

"Base to Echo. Air support ten mikes out."

Ten mikes. *We'll be dead in ten!* Cathal shifted to a better vantage point. "We need to get Abbot," he bellowed. "Forsyth, Lopez, cover us. Ryker, you're on me. Let's go!"

Forsyth and the others laid down suppressive fire that allowed Cathal and Ryker to reach Abbot. Cathal slowed near her figure as Ryker took a knee behind him, firing to give him time. The floor of the second story groaned above them.

Cathal reached to grab Abbot's arm but froze. Lifeless blue eyes stared up at nothing. Crimson streaked her cheeks. It was too late.

"She's gone."

Another scream brought his attention up. He ducked into what remained of the main room, followed by Ryker. Bodies were strewn across muted-toned rugs and couches. His stomach rolled but he fought through it.

Uday's wife, Aliyah, stood, blood covering her white dress as she wailed over two bodies. One was a young woman he guessed to be the daughter Uday talked about nonstop, the other wore a full burka—the HVT's wife?—and lay unmoving. A wide wound spilled out onto her weathered hands and the black fabric covering her.

Ryker crossed to Aliyah, no time for etiquette. "We have to go!" he shouted over the war outside.

Cathal bent to double-check what he already knew. The women at Aliyah's feet were dead. "Are you injured?"

The older woman sobbed, hands flailing, and Cathal's Arabic wasn't good enough to understand the speed with which she spoke.

"Just bring her." Cathal reloaded his M4. "This place is coming down any second."

Ryker did and Cathal led them back to the front of the building.

"Gotta move, Sarge!" Forsyth roared as they exited.

Cathal fired shot after shot as Ryker ushered Aliyah to the side of the home. He backed down the alley after his team, firing to hold the enemy back, but the distance between them was shortening.

A voice crackled in his earpiece. "Air support three mikes out."

"Move it!" Cathal yelled over his shoulder.

They funneled out of the alley moments before Uday's home finally gave way, collapsing in on itself. Dust and debris engulfed them. Coughing and sputtering, Forsyth led them across the next street and into the connecting alley.

A glance over his shoulder told Cathal that the collapse had bought them time, but his gaze hitched on the pile of rubble partially hidden by dust that had yet to settle. Abbot's blue eyes flashed in his mind. He stretched his neck to skate it off. Forced himself to take a mental headcount of the remaining soldiers from the assisting team. All but one were here.

Don't think about her.

"Everyone good?" he forced himself to ask as they wove between the homes of the village.

Zing! Zing!

Something hard hit his vest and pitched him forward. Stole the breath from his chest.

"Taking fire!" Ryker yelled, moments before everything went black.

Are you as smitten with MWDs as I am? Then GIVE BACK!
For the featured charity organization for HAVOC, I chose to spotlight MWDTSA because this amazing organization does many things for MWD teams. As well, they sent me a laser-engraved stainless steel tumbler with VVolt N629's EOW date as a gift. I was so touched and love having this indestructible way to remember my "Big Handsome," AKA: VVolt. Please do consider donating and following them on IG. Another thing they do is post a link to an Amazon wish list to help them fulfill their care packages. It's a great, quick way to pick-your-donation and feel like you're giving back in some small way.

MWDTSA
MILITARY WORKING DOG TEAM SUPPORT ASSOCIATION

SUPPORTING BOTH ENDS OF THE LEASH SINCE 2006

The Military Working Dog Team Support Association, Inc. is an all-volunteer 501(c)(3) nonprofit organization. We are dedicated to supporting military working dog (MWD) teams with the Army, Navy, Air Force, Marine Corps, Coast Guard, and Space

Force. MWDTSA operates with no paid staff. Historically, more than 97% of all donated funds have gone directly to execute our missions.

MWDTSA sends quarterly care packages to MWD teams currently deployed in harm's way. We also boost morale with stateside kennel visits, honor retired MWDs for K9 Veterans Day, and educate the public about the important roles of our MWD teams.

To learn more about our organization and volunteer opportunities, please our website at mwdtsa.org. If you wish to support our MWD teams with a monetary or product donation, please visit mwdtsa.org/donations. Follow @MWDTSA on FB and IG for MWD related content!

MORE ROMANTIC SUSPENSE FROM SUNRISE

BRAINS. BEAUTY. BOLDNESS.
THE ELITE GUARDIANS WILL KEEP YOU SAFE.

Start reading the series now!

FIRE. FAMILY. FAITH.
LAST CHANCE FIRE AND RESCUE

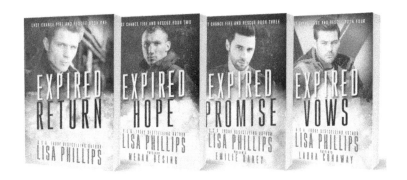

Dive into this thrilling first responder series now!

MORE ADVENTURE AWAITS...

FIND THEM ALL AT SUNRISEPUBLISHING.COM

SCAN THE QR CODE TO LEARN MORE!

CONNECT WITH SUNRISE

Thank you so much for reading *Havoc*. We hope you enjoyed the story. If you did, would you be willing to do us a favor and leave a review? It doesn't have to be long—just a few words to help other readers know what they're getting. (But no spoilers! We don't want to wreck the fun!) Thank you again for reading!

We'd love to hear from you—not only about this story, but about any characters or stories you'd like to read in the future. Contact us at www.sunrisepublishing.com/contact.

We also have a monthly update that contains sneak peeks, reviews, upcoming releases, and fun stuff for our reader friends. Sign up at www.sunrisepublishing.com or scan our QR code.

ABOUT RONIE KENDIG

Ronie Kendig is a bestselling, award-winning author of over thirty-five books. She grew up an Army brat, and now she and her Army-veteran husband have returned to their beloved Texas after a ten-year stint in the Northeast. They survive on Sonic runs, barbecue, and peach cobbler that they share—sometimes—with Benning the Stealth Golden and AAndromeda the MWD Washout. Ronie's degree in psychology has helped her pen novels of intense, raw characters.

To learn more about Ronie, visit www.roniekendig.com and follow her on social media.

facebook.com/rapidfirefiction

instagram.com/kendigronie

pinterest.com/roniek

twitter.com/roniekendig

bookbub.com/authors/ronie-kendig

goodreads.com/RonieK

amazon.com/stores/Ronie-Kendig/author/B002SFLGQ2

MORE A BREED APART NOVELS

A Breed Apart: Legacy

Havoc

Chaos

Riot

Fury

Surge

A Breed Apart by Ronie Kendig

Trinity

Talon

Beowulf

ALSO BY RONIE KENDIG

The Metcalfes

Stone

Willow

Range

Brooke

The Droseran Saga

Brand of Light

Dawn of Vengeance

Shadow of Honor

War of Torment

Lady of Basilikas (May 2024)

The Discarded Heroes

Nightshade

Digitalis

Wolfsbane

Firethorn

Lygos: A Novella

The Book of the Wars

Storm Rising

Kings Falling

Soul Raging

The Tox Files

The Warrior's Seal

Conspiracy of Silence

Crown of Souls

Thirst of Steel

The Quiet Professionals

Raptor 6

Hawk

Falcon

Titanis: A Novella

Abiassa's Fire Fantasy Series

Embers

Accelerant

Fierian

Standalone Titles

Operation Zulu: Redemption

Dead Reckoning

Havoc
A Breed Apart: Legacy, Book 1
Published by Sunrise Media Group LLC
Copyright © 2023 Ronie Kendig
Print ISBN: 978-1-953783-62-2
Large Print ISBN: 978-1-953783-64-6
Ebook ISBN: 978-1-953783-65-3

For more information about Ronie Kendig please access the author's website at roniekendig.com.

Published in the United States of America.
Cover Design: Kirk DouPonce, DogEared Design